The Arthur Machen Reader

Arthur Machen

Copyright © 2013

All rights reserved. No part of this publication may be reproduced or transmitted for commercial purposes, except for brief quotation in printed reviews, without written permission of the publisher.

This book is a work of fiction. Names, characters, places, and incidents are either products of the author's imagination or used fictitiously. Any similarity to actual people, organizations, and/or events is purely coincidental.

Printed in the United States of America

ISBN: 1481881728
ISBN-13: 978-1481881722

CONTENTS

The Great God Pan 1

The White People 50

A Fragment of Life 84

The Inmost Light 148

The Shining Pyramid 175

ABOUT THE AUTHOR 198

The Great God Pan

CHAPTER 1. THE EXPERIMENT

"I am glad you came, Clarke; very glad indeed. I was not sure you could spare the time."

"I was able to make arrangements for a few days; things are not very lively just now. But have you no misgivings, Raymond? Is it absolutely safe?"

The two men were slowly pacing the terrace in front of Dr. Raymond's house. The sun still hung above the western mountain-line, but it shone with a dull red glow that cast no shadows, and all the air was quiet; a sweet breath came from the great wood on the hillside above, and with it, at intervals, the soft murmuring call of the wild doves. Below, in the long lovely valley, the river wound in and out between the lonely hills, and, as the sun hovered and vanished into the west, a faint mist, pure white, began to rise from the hills. Dr. Raymond turned sharply to his friend.

"Safe? Of course it is. In itself the operation is a perfectly simple one; any surgeon could do it."

"And there is no danger at any other stage?"

"None; absolutely no physical danger whatsoever, I give you my word. You are always timid, Clarke, always; but you know my history. I have devoted myself to transcendental medicine for the last twenty years. I have heard myself called quack and charlatan and impostor, but all the while I knew I was on the right path. Five years ago I reached the goal, and since then every day has been a preparation for what we shall do tonight."

"I should like to believe it is all true." Clarke knit his brows, and looked doubtfully at Dr. Raymond. "Are you perfectly sure, Raymond, that your theory is not a phantasmagoria--a splendid vision, certainly, but a mere vision after all?"

Dr. Raymond stopped in his walk and turned sharply. He was a middle-aged man, gaunt and thin, of a pale yellow complexion, but as he answered Clarke and faced him, there was a flush on his cheek.

"Look about you, Clarke. You see the mountain, and hill following after hill, as wave on wave, you see the woods and orchard, the fields of ripe corn, and the meadows reaching to the reed-beds by the river. You see me standing here beside you, and hear my voice; but I tell you that all these things -- yes, from that star that has just shone out in the sky to the solid ground beneath our feet--I say that all these are but dreams and shadows; the shadows that hide the real world from our eyes. There is a real world, but it is beyond this glamour and this vision, beyond these 'chases in Arras, dreams in a career,'beyond them all as beyond a veil. I do not know whether any human being has ever lifted that veil; but I do know, Clarke, that you and I shall see it lifted this very night from before another's eyes. You may think this all strange nonsense; it may be strange, but it is true, and the ancients knew what lifting the veil means. They called it seeing the god Pan."

Clarke shivered; the white mist gathering over the river was chilly.

"It is wonderful indeed," he said. "We are standing on the brink of a strange world, Raymond, if what you say is true. I suppose the knife is absolutely necessary?"

"Yes; a slight lesion in the grey matter, that is all; a trifling rearrangement of certain cells, a microscopical alteration that would escape the attention of ninety-nine brain specialists out of a hundred. I don't want to bother you with 'shop,'Clarke; I might give you a mass of technical detail which would sound very imposing, and would leave you as enlightened as you are now. But I suppose you have read, casually, in out-of-the-way corners of your paper, that immense strides have been made recently in the physiology of the brain. I saw a paragraph the other day about Digby's theory, and Browne Faber's discoveries. Theories and discoveries! Where they are standing now, I stood fifteen years ago, and I need not tell you that I have not been standing still for the last fifteen years. It will be enough if I say that five years ago I made the discovery that I alluded to when I said that ten years ago I reached the goal. After years of labour, after years of toiling and groping in the dark, after days and nights of disappointments and sometimes of despair, in which I used now and then to tremble and grow cold with the thought that perhaps there were others seeking for what I sought, at last, after so long, a pang of sudden joy thrilled my soul, and I knew the long journey was at an end. By what seemed then and still seems a chance, the suggestion of a moment's idle thought followed up upon familiar lines and paths that I had tracked a hundred times already, the great truth burst upon me, and I saw, mapped out in lines of sight, a whole world, a sphere unknown; continents and islands, and great oceans in which no ship has sailed (to my belief) since a Man first lifted up his eyes and beheld the sun, and the stars of heaven, and the quiet earth beneath. You will think this all high-flown language, Clarke, but it is hard to be literal. And yet; I do not know whether what I am hinting at cannot be set forth in plain and lonely terms. For instance, this world of ours is pretty well girded now with the telegraph wires and cables; thought, with something less than the speed of thought, flashes from sunrise to sunset, from north to south, across the floods and the desert places. Suppose that an electrician of today were suddenly to perceive that he and his friends have merely been playing with pebbles and mistaking them for the foundations of the world; suppose that such a man saw uttermost space lie open before the current, and words of men flash forth to the sun and beyond the sun into the systems beyond, and the voice of articulate-speaking men echo in the waste void that bounds our thought. As analogies go, that is a pretty good analogy of what I have done; you can understand now a little of what I felt as I stood here one evening; it was a summer evening, and the valley looked much as it does now; I stood here, and saw before me the unutterable, the unthinkable gulf that yawns profound between two worlds, the world of matter and the world of spirit; I saw the great empty deep stretch dim before me, and in that instant a bridge of light leapt from the earth to the unknown shore, and the abyss was spanned. You may look in Browne Faber's book, if you like, and you will find that to the present day men of science are unable to account for the presence, or to specify the functions of a certain group of nerve-cells in the brain. That group is, as it were, land to let, a mere waste place for fanciful theories. I am not in the position of Browne Faber and the specialists, I am perfectly instructed as to the possible functions of those nerve-centers in the scheme of things. With a touch I can bring them into play, with a touch, I say, I can set free the current, with a touch I can complete the communication between this world of sense and--we shall be able to finish the sentence later on. Yes, the knife is necessary; but think what that knife will effect. It will level utterly the solid wall of sense, and probably, for the first time since man was made, a spirit will gaze on a spirit-world. Clarke, Mary will see the god Pan!"

"But you remember what you wrote to me? I thought it would be requisite that she--"

He whispered the rest into the doctor's ear.

"Not at all, not at all. That is nonsense. I assure you. Indeed, it is better as it is; I am quite certain of that."

"Consider the matter well, Raymond. It's a great responsibility. Something might go wrong; you would be a miserable man for the rest of your days."

"No, I think not, even if the worst happened. As you know, I rescued Mary from the gutter, and from almost certain starvation, when she was a child; I think her life is mine, to use as I see fit. Come, it's getting late; we had better go in."

Dr. Raymond led the way into the house, through the hall, and down a long dark passage. He took a key from his pocket and opened a heavy door, and motioned Clarke into his laboratory. It had once been a billiard-room, and was lighted by a glass dome in the centre of the ceiling, whence there still shone a sad grey light on the figure of the doctor as he lit a lamp with a heavy shade and placed it on a table in the middle of the room.

Clarke looked about him. Scarcely a foot of wall remained bare; there were shelves all around laden with bottles and phials of all shapes and colours, and at one end stood a little Chippendale book-case. Raymond pointed to this.

"You see that parchment Oswald Crollius? He was one of the first to show me the way, though I don't think he ever found it himself. That is a strange saying of his: 'In every grain of wheat there lies hidden the soul of a star.'"

There was not much furniture in the laboratory. The table in the centre, a stone slab with a drain in one corner, the two armchairs on which Raymond and Clarke were sitting; that was all, except an odd-looking chair at the furthest end of the room. Clarke looked at it, and raised his eyebrows.

"Yes, that is the chair," said Raymond. "We may as well place it in position." He got up and wheeled the chair to the light, and began raising and lowering it, letting down the seat, setting the back at various angles, and adjusting the foot-rest. It looked comfortable enough, and Clarke passed his hand over the soft green velvet, as the doctor manipulated the levers.

"Now, Clarke, make yourself quite comfortable. I have a couple hours' work before me; I was obliged to leave certain matters to the last."

Raymond went to the stone slab, and Clarke watched him drearily as he bent over a row of phials and lit the flame under the crucible. The doctor had a small hand-lamp, shaded as the larger one, on a ledge above his apparatus, and Clarke, who sat in the shadows, looked down at the great shadowy room, wondering at the bizarre effects of brilliant light and undefined darkness contrasting with one another. Soon he became conscious of an odd odour, at first the merest suggestion of odour, in the room, and as it grew more decided he felt surprised that he was not reminded of the chemist's shop or the surgery. Clarke found himself idly endeavouring to analyse the sensation, and half conscious, he began to think of a day, fifteen years ago, that he had spent roaming through the woods and meadows near his own home. It was a burning day at the beginning of August, the heat had dimmed the outlines of all things and all distances with a faint mist, and people who observed the thermometer spoke of an abnormal register, of a temperature that was almost tropical. Strangely that wonderful hot day of the fifties rose up again in Clarke's imagination; the sense of dazzling all-pervading sunlight seemed to blot out the shadows and the lights of the laboratory, and he felt again the heated air beating in gusts about his face, saw the shimmer rising from the turf, and heard the myriad murmur of the summer.

"I hope the smell doesn't annoy you, Clarke; there's nothing unwholesome about it. It may make you a bit sleepy, that's all."

Clarke heard the words quite distinctly, and knew that Raymond was speaking to him, but for the life of him he could not rouse himself from his lethargy. He could only think of the lonely walk he had taken fifteen years ago; it was his last look at the fields and woods he had known since he was a child, and now it all stood out in brilliant light, as a picture, before him. Above all there came to his nostrils the scent of summer, the smell of flowers mingled, and the odour of the woods, of cool shaded places, deep in the green depths, drawn forth by the sun's heat; and the scent of the good earth, lying as it were with arms stretched forth, and smiling lips, overpowered all. His fancies made him wander, as he had wandered long ago, from the fields into the wood, tracking a little path between the shining undergrowth of beech-trees; and the trickle of water dropping from the limestone rock sounded as a clear melody in the dream. Thoughts began to go astray and to mingle with other thoughts; the beech alley was transformed to a path between ilex-trees, and here and there a vine climbed from bough to bough, and sent up waving tendrils and drooped with purple grapes, and the sparse grey-green leaves of a wild olive-tree stood out against the dark shadows of the ilex. Clarke, in the deep folds of dream, was conscious that the path from his father's house had led him into an undiscovered country, and he was wondering at the strangeness of it all, when suddenly, in place of the hum and murmur of the summer, an infinite silence seemed to fall on all things, and the wood was hushed, and for a moment in time he stood face to face there with a presence, that was neither man nor beast, neither the living nor the dead, but all things mingled, the form of all things but devoid of all form. And in that moment, the sacrament of body and soul was dissolved, and a voice seemed to cry "Let us go hence," and then the darkness of darkness beyond the stars, the darkness of everlasting.

When Clarke woke up with a start he saw Raymond pouring a few drops of some oily fluid into a green phial, which he stoppered tightly.

"You have been dozing," he said; "the journey must have tired you out. It is done now. I am going to fetch Mary; I shall be back in ten minutes."

Clarke lay back in his chair and wondered. It seemed as if he had but passed from one dream into another. He half expected to see the walls of the laboratory melt and disappear, and to awake in London, shuddering at his own sleeping fancies. But at last the door opened, and the doctor returned, and behind him came a girl of about seventeen, dressed all in white. She was so beautiful that Clarke did not wonder at what the doctor had written to him. She was blushing now over face and neck and arms, but Raymond seemed unmoved.

"Mary," he said, "the time has come. You are quite free. Are you willing to trust yourself to me entirely?"

"Yes, dear."

"Do you hear that, Clarke? You are my witness. Here is the chair, Mary. It is quite easy. Just sit in it and lean back. Are you ready?"

"Yes, dear, quite ready. Give me a kiss before you begin."

The doctor stooped and kissed her mouth, kindly enough. "Now shut your eyes," he said. The girl closed her eyelids, as if she were tired, and longed for sleep, and Raymond placed the green phial to her nostrils. Her face grew white, whiter than her dress; she struggled faintly, and then with the feeling of submission strong within her, crossed her arms upon her breast as a little child about to say her prayers. The bright light of the lamp fell full upon her, and Clarke watched changes fleeting over her face as the changes of the hills when the summer clouds float across the sun. And then she lay all white and still, and the doctor turned up one of her eyelids. She was quite unconscious. Raymond pressed hard on one of the levers and the chair instantly sank back. Clarke saw him cutting away a circle, like a tonsure, from her hair, and the lamp was moved nearer. Raymond took a small glittering instrument from a little case, and Clarke turned away shudderingly. When he looked again the doctor was binding up the wound he had made.

"She will awake in five minutes." Raymond was still perfectly cool. "There is nothing more to be done; we can only wait."

The minutes passed slowly; they could hear a slow, heavy, ticking. There was an old clock in the passage. Clarke felt sick and faint; his knees shook beneath him, he could hardly stand.

Suddenly, as they watched, they heard a long-drawn sigh, and suddenly did the colour that had vanished return to the girl's cheeks, and suddenly her eyes opened. Clarke quailed before them. They shone with an awful light, looking far away, and a great wonder fell upon her face, and her hands stretched out as if to touch what was invisible; but in an instant the wonder faded, and gave place to the most awful terror. The muscles of her face were hideously convulsed, she shook from head to foot; the soul seemed struggling and shuddering within the house of flesh. It was a horrible sight, and Clarke rushed forward, as she fell shrieking to the floor.

Three days later Raymond took Clarke to Mary's bedside. She was lying wide-awake, rolling her head from side to side, and grinning vacantly.

"Yes," said the doctor, still quite cool, "it is a great pity; she is a hopeless idiot. However, it could not be helped; and, after all, she has seen the Great God Pan."

CHAPTER 2. MR. CLARKE'S MEMOIRS

Mr. Clarke, the gentleman chosen by Dr. Raymond to witness the strange experiment of the god Pan, was a person in whose character caution and curiosity were oddly mingled; in his sober moments he thought of the unusual and eccentric with undisguised aversion, and yet, deep in his heart, there was a wide-eyed inquisitiveness with respect to all the more recondite and esoteric elements in the nature of men. The latter tendency had prevailed when he accepted Raymond's invitation, for though his considered judgment had always repudiated the doctor's theories as the wildest nonsense, yet he secretly hugged a belief in fantasy, and would have rejoiced to see that belief confirmed. The horrors that he witnessed in the dreary laboratory were to a certain extent salutary; he was conscious of being involved in an affair not altogether reputable, and for many years afterwards he clung bravely to the commonplace, and rejected all occasions of occult investigation. Indeed, on some homeopathic principle, he for some time attended the seances of distinguished mediums, hoping that the clumsy tricks of these gentlemen would make him altogether disgusted with mysticism of every kind, but the remedy, though caustic, was not efficacious. Clarke knew that he still pined for the unseen, and little by little, the old passion began to reassert itself, as the face of Mary, shuddering and convulsed with an unknown terror, faded slowly from his memory. Occupied all day in pursuits both serious and lucrative, the temptation to relax in the evening was too great, especially in the winter months, when the fire cast a warm glow over his snug bachelor apartment, and a bottle of some choice claret stood ready by his elbow. His dinner digested, he would make a brief pretence of reading the evening paper, but the mere catalogue of news soon palled upon him, and Clarke would find himself casting glances of warm desire in the direction of an old Japanese bureau, which stood at a pleasant distance from the hearth. Like a boy before a jam-closet, for a few minutes he would hover indecisive, but lust always prevailed, and Clarke ended by drawing up his chair, lighting a candle, and sitting down before the bureau. Its pigeon-holes and drawers teemed with documents on the most morbid subjects, and in the well reposed a large manuscript volume, in which he had painfully entered he gems of his collection. Clarke had a fine contempt for published literature; the most ghostly story ceased to interest him if it happened to be printed; his sole pleasure was in the reading, compiling, and rearranging what he called his "Memoirs to prove the Existence of the Devil," and engaged in this pursuit the evening seemed to fly and the night appeared too short.

On one particular evening, an ugly December night, black with fog, and raw with frost, Clarke hurried over his dinner, and scarcely deigned to observe his customary ritual of taking up the paper and laying it down again. He paced two or three times up and down the room, and opened the bureau, stood still a moment, and sat down. He leant back, absorbed in one of those dreams to which he was subject, and at length drew out his book, and opened it at the last entry. There were three or four pages densely covered with Clarke's round, set penmanship, and at the beginning he had written in a somewhat larger hand:

Singular Narrative told me by my Friend, Dr. Phillips. He assures me that all the facts related therein are strictly and wholly True, but refuses to give either the Surnames of the Persons Concerned, or the Place where these Extraordinary Events occurred.

Mr. Clarke began to read over the account for the tenth time, glancing now and then at the pencil notes he had made when it was told him by his friend. It was one of his humours to pride himself on a certain literary ability; he thought well of his style, and took pains in arranging the circumstances in dramatic order. He read the following story:--

The persons concerned in this statement are Helen V., who, if she is still alive, must now be a woman of twenty-three, Rachel M., since deceased, who was a year younger than the above, and Trevor W., an imbecile, aged eighteen. These persons were at the period of the story inhabitants of a village on the borders of Wales, a place of some importance in the time of the Roman occupation, but now a scattered hamlet, of not more than five hundred souls. It is situated on rising ground, about six miles from the sea, and is sheltered by a large and picturesque forest.

Some eleven years ago, Helen V. came to the village under rather peculiar circumstances. It is understood that she, being an orphan, was adopted in her infancy by a distant relative, who brought her up in his own house until she was twelve years old. Thinking, however, that it would be better for the child to have playmates of her own age, he advertised in several local papers for a good home in a comfortable farmhouse for a girl of twelve, and this advertisement was answered by Mr. R., a well-to-do farmer in the above-mentioned village. His references proving satisfactory, the gentleman sent his adopted daughter to Mr. R., with a letter, in which he stipulated that the girl should have a room to herself, and stated that her guardians need be at no trouble in the matter of education, as she was already sufficiently educated for the position in life which she would occupy. In fact, Mr. R. was given to understand that the girl be allowed to find her own occupations and to spend her time almost as she liked. Mr. R. duly met her at the nearest station, a town seven miles away from his house, and seems to have remarked nothing extraordinary about the child except that she was reticent as to her former life and her adopted father. She was, however, of a very different type from the inhabitants of the village; her skin was a pale, clear olive, and her features were strongly marked, and of a somewhat foreign character. She appears to have settled down easily enough into farmhouse life, and became a favourite with the children, who sometimes went with her on her rambles in the forest, for this was her amusement. Mr. R. states that he has known her to go out by herself directly after their early breakfast, and not return till after dusk, and that, feeling uneasy at a young girl being out alone for so many hours, he communicated with her adopted father, who replied in a brief note that Helen must do as she chose. In the winter, when the forest paths are impassable, she spent most of her time in her bedroom, where she slept alone, according to the instructions of her relative. It was on one of these expeditions to the forest that the first of the singular incidents with which this girl is connected occurred, the date being about a year after her arrival at the village. The preceding winter had been remarkably severe, the snow drifting to a great depth, and the frost continuing for an unexampled period, and the summer following was as noteworthy for its extreme heat. On one of the very hottest days in this summer, Helen V. left the farmhouse for one of her long rambles in the forest, taking with her, as usual, some bread and meat for lunch. She was seen by some men in the fields making for the old Roman Road, a green causeway which traverses the highest part of the wood, and they were astonished to observe that the girl had taken off her hat, though the heat of the sun was already tropical. As it happened, a labourer, Joseph W. by name, was working in the forest near the Roman Road, and at twelve o'clock his little son, Trevor, brought the man his dinner of bread and cheese. After the meal, the boy, who was about seven years old at the time, left his father at work, and, as he said, went to look for flowers in the wood, and the man, who could hear him shouting with delight at his discoveries, felt no uneasiness. Suddenly, however, he was horrified at hearing the most dreadful screams, evidently the result of great terror, proceeding from the direction in which his son had gone, and he hastily threw down his tools and ran to see what had happened. Tracing his path by the sound, he met the little boy, who was running headlong, and was evidently terribly frightened, and on questioning him the man elicited that after picking a posy of flowers he felt tired, and lay down on the grass and fell asleep. He was suddenly awakened, as he stated, by a peculiar noise, a sort of singing he called it, and on peeping through the branches he saw Helen V. playing on the grass with a "strange naked man," who he seemed unable to describe more fully. He said he felt dreadfully frightened and ran away crying for his father. Joseph W. proceeded in the direction indicated by his son, and found Helen V. sitting on the grass in the middle of a glade or open space left by charcoal burners. He angrily charged her with frightening his little boy, but she entirely denied the accusation and laughed at the child's story of a "strange man," to which he himself did not attach much credence. Joseph W. came to the conclusion that the boy had woke up with a sudden fright, as children sometimes do, but Trevor persisted in his story, and continued in such evident distress that at last his father took him home, hoping that his mother would be able to soothe him. For many weeks, however, the boy gave his parents much anxiety; he became nervous and strange in his manner, refusing to leave the cottage by himself, and constantly alarming the household by waking in the night with cries of "The man in the wood! father! father!"

In course of time, however, the impression seemed to have worn off, and about three months later he accompanied his father to the home of a gentleman in the neighborhood, for whom Joseph W. occasionally did work. The man was shown into the study, and the little boy was left sitting in the hall, and a few minutes later, while the gentleman was giving W. his instructions, they were both horrified by a piercing shriek and the sound of a fall, and rushing out they found the child lying senseless on the floor, his face contorted with terror. The doctor was immediately summoned, and after some examination he pronounced the child to be suffering form a kind of fit, apparently produced by a sudden shock. The boy was taken to one of the bedrooms, and after some time recovered consciousness, but only to pass into a condition described by the medical man as one of violent hysteria. The doctor exhibited a strong sedative, and in the course of two hours pronounced him fit to walk home, but in passing through the hall the paroxysms of fright returned and with additional violence. The father perceived that the child was pointing at some object, and heard the old cry, "The man in the wood," and looking in the direction indicated saw a stone head of grotesque appearance, which had been built into the wall above one of the doors. It seems the owner of the house had recently made alterations in his premises, and on digging the foundations for some offices, the men had found a curious head, evidently of the Roman period, which had been placed in the manner described. The head is pronounced by the most experienced archaeologists of the district to be that of a faun or satyr. [Dr. Phillips tells me that he has seen the head in question, and assures me that he has never received such a vivid presentment of intense evil.]

From whatever cause arising, this second shock seemed too severe for the boy Trevor, and at the present date he suffers from a weakness of intellect, which gives but little promise of amending. The matter caused a good deal of sensation at the time, and the girl Helen was closely questioned by Mr. R., but to no purpose, she steadfastly denying that she had frightened or in any way molested Trevor.

The second event with which this girl's name is connected took place about six years ago, and is of a still more extraordinary character.

At the beginning of the summer of 1882, Helen contracted a friendship of a peculiarly intimate character with Rachel M., the daughter of a prosperous farmer in the neighbourhood. This girl, who was a year younger than Helen, was considered by most people to be the prettier of the two, though Helen's features had to a great extent softened as she became older. The two girls, who were together on every available opportunity, presented a singular contrast, the one with her clear, olive skin and almost Italian appearance, and the other of the proverbial red and white of our rural districts. It must be stated that the payments made to Mr. R. for the maintenance of Helen were known in the village for their excessive liberality, and the impression was general that she would one day inherit a large sum of money from her relative. The parents of Rachel were therefore not averse from their daughter's friendship with the girl, and even encouraged the intimacy, though they now bitterly regret having done so. Helen still retained her extraordinary fondness for the forest, and on several occasions Rachel accompanied her, the two friends setting out early in the morning, and remaining in the wood until dusk. Once or twice after these excursions Mrs. M. thought her daughter's manner rather peculiar; she seemed languid and dreamy, and as it has been expressed, "different from herself," but these peculiarities seem to have been thought too trifling for remark. One evening, however, after Rachel had come home, her mother heard a noise which sounded like suppressed weeping in the girl's room, and on going in found her lying, half undressed, upon the bed, evidently in the greatest distress. As soon as she saw her mother, she exclaimed, "Ah, mother, mother, why did you let me go to the forest with Helen?" Mrs. M. was astonished at so strange a question, and proceeded to make inquiries. Rachel told her a wild story. She said

--

Clarke closed the book with a snap, and turned his chair towards the fire. When his friend sat one evening in that very chair, and told his story, Clarke had interrupted him at a point a little subsequent to this, had cut short his words in a paroxysm of horror. "My God!" he had exclaimed, "think, think what you are saying. It is too incredible, too monstrous; such things can never be in this quiet world, where men and women live and die, and struggle, and conquer, or maybe fail, and fall down under sorrow, and grieve and suffer strange fortunes for many a year; but not this, Phillips, not such things as this. There must be some explanation, some way out of the terror. Why, man, if such a case were possible, our earth would be a nightmare."

But Phillips had told his story to the end, concluding:

"Her flight remains a mystery to this day; she vanished in broad sunlight; they saw her walking in a meadow, and a few moments later she was not there."

Clarke tried to conceive the thing again, as he sat by the fire, and again his mind shuddered and shrank back, appalled before the sight of such awful, unspeakable elements enthroned as it were, and triumphant in human flesh. Before him stretched the long dim vista of the green causeway in the forest, as his friend had described it; he saw the swaying leaves and the quivering shadows on the grass, he saw the sunlight and the flowers, and far away, far in the long distance, the two figure moved toward him. One was Rachel, but the other?

Clarke had tried his best to disbelieve it all, but at the end of the account, as he had written it in his book, he had placed the inscription:

ET DIABOLUS INCARNATE EST. ET HOMO FACTUS EST.

CHAPTER 3. THE CITY OF RESURRECTIONS

"Herbert! Good God! Is it possible?"

"Yes, my name's Herbert. I think I know your face, too, but I don't remember your name. My memory is very queer."

"Don't you recollect Villiers of Wadham?"

"So it is, so it is. I beg your pardon, Villiers, I didn't think I was begging of an old college friend. Good-night."

"My dear fellow, this haste is unnecessary. My rooms are close by, but we won't go there just yet. Suppose we walk up Shaftesbury Avenue a little way? But how in heaven's name have you come to this pass, Herbert?"

"It's a long story, Villiers, and a strange one too, but you can hear it if you like."

"Come on, then. Take my arm, you don't seem very strong."

The ill-assorted pair moved slowly up Rupert Street; the one in dirty, evil-looking rags, and the other attired in the regulation uniform of a man about town, trim, glossy, and eminently well-to-do. Villiers had emerged from his restaurant after an excellent dinner of many courses, assisted by an ingratiating little flask of Chianti, and, in that frame of mind which was with him almost chronic, had delayed a moment by the door, peering round in the dimly-lighted street in search of those mysterious incidents and persons with which the streets of London teem in every quarter and every hour. Villiers prided himself as a practised explorer of such obscure mazes and byways of London life, and in this unprofitable pursuit he displayed an assiduity which was worthy of more serious employment. Thus he stood by the lamp-post surveying the passers-by with undisguised curiosity, and with that gravity known only to the systematic diner, had just enunciated in his mind the formula: "London has been called the city of encounters; it is more than that, it is the city of Resurrections," when these reflections were suddenly interrupted by a piteous whine at his elbow, and a deplorable appeal for alms. He looked around in some irritation, and with a sudden shock found himself confronted with the embodied proof of his somewhat stilted fancies. There, close beside him, his face altered and disfigured by poverty and disgrace, his body barely covered by greasy ill-fitting rags, stood his old friend Charles Herbert, who had matriculated on the same day as himself, with whom he had been merry and wise for twelve revolving terms. Different occupations and varying interests had interrupted the friendship, and it was six years since Villiers had seen Herbert; and now he looked upon this wreck of a man with grief and dismay, mingled with a certain inquisitiveness as to what dreary chain of circumstances had dragged him down to such a doleful pass. Villiers felt together with compassion all the relish of the amateur in mysteries, and congratulated himself on his leisurely speculations outside the restaurant.

They walked on in silence for some time, and more than one passer-by stared in astonishment at the unaccustomed spectacle of a well-dressed man with an unmistakable beggar hanging on to his arm, and, observing this, Villiers led the way to an obscure street in Soho. Here he repeated his question.

"How on earth has it happened, Herbert? I always understood you would succeed to an excellent position in Dorsetshire. Did your father disinherit you? Surely not?"

"No, Villiers; I came into all the property at my poor father's death; he died a year after I left Oxford. He was a very good father to me, and I mourned his death sincerely enough. But you know what young men are; a few months later I came up to town and went a good deal into society. Of course I had excellent introductions, and I managed to enjoy myself very much in a harmless sort of way. I played a little, certainly, but never for heavy stakes, and the few bets I made on races brought me in money--only a few pounds, you know, but enough to pay for cigars and such petty pleasures. It was in my second season that the tide turned. Of course you have heard of my marriage?"

"No, I never heard anything about it."

"Yes, I married, Villiers. I met a girl, a girl of the most wonderful and most strange beauty, at the house of some people whom I knew. I cannot tell you her age; I never knew it, but, so far as I can guess, I should think she must have been about nineteen when I made her acquaintance. My friends had come to know her at Florence; she told them she was an orphan, the child of an English father and an Italian mother, and she charmed them as she charmed me. The first time I saw her was at an evening party. I was standing by the door talking to a friend, when suddenly above the hum and babble of conversation I heard a voice which seemed to thrill to my heart. She was singing an Italian song. I was introduced to her that evening, and in three months

I married Helen. Villiers, that woman, if I can call her woman, corrupted my soul. The night of the wedding I found myself sitting in her bedroom in the hotel, listening to her talk. She was sitting up in bed, and I listened to her as she spoke in her beautiful voice, spoke of things which even now I would not dare whisper in the blackest night, though I stood in the midst of a wilderness. You, Villiers, you may think you know life, and London, and what goes on day and night in this dreadful city; for all I can say you may have heard the talk of the vilest, but I tell you you can have no conception of what I know, not in your most fantastic, hideous dreams can you have imaged forth the faintest shadow of what I have heard--and seen. Yes, seen. I have seen the incredible, such horrors that even I myself sometimes stop in the middle of the street and ask whether it is possible for a man to behold such things and live. In a year, Villiers, I was a ruined man, in body and soul--in body and soul."

"But your property, Herbert? You had land in Dorset."

"I sold it all; the fields and woods, the dear old house--everything."

"And the money?"

"She took it all from me."

"And then left you?"

"Yes; she disappeared one night. I don't know where she went, but I am sure if I saw her again it would kill me. The rest of my story is of no interest; sordid misery, that is all. You may think, Villiers, that I have exaggerated and talked for effect; but I have not told you half. I could tell you certain things which would convince you, but you would never know a happy day again. You would pass the rest of your life, as I pass mine, a haunted man, a man who has seen hell."

Villiers took the unfortunate man to his rooms, and gave him a meal. Herbert could eat little, and scarcely touched the glass of wine set before him. He sat moody and silent by the fire, and seemed relieved when Villiers sent him away with a small present of money.

"By the way, Herbert," said Villiers, as they parted at the door, "what was your wife's name? You said Helen, I think? Helen what?"

"The name she passed under when I met her was Helen Vaughan, but what her real name was I can't say. I don't think she had a name. No, no, not in that sense. Only human beings have names, Villiers; I can't say anymore. Good-bye; yes, I will not fail to call if I see any way in which you can help me. Good-night."

The man went out into the bitter night, and Villiers returned to his fireside. There was something about Herbert which shocked him inexpressibly; not his poor rags nor the marks which poverty had set upon his face, but rather an indefinite terror which hung about him like a mist. He had acknowledged that he himself was not devoid of blame; the woman, he had avowed, had corrupted him body and soul, and

Villiers felt that this man, once his friend, had been an actor in scenes evil beyond the power of words. His story needed no confirmation: he himself was the embodied proof of it. Villiers mused curiously over the story he had heard, and wondered whether he had heard both the first and the last of it. "No," he thought, "certainly not the last, probably only the beginning. A case like this is like a nest of Chinese boxes; you open one after the other and find a quainter workmanship in every box. Most likely poor Herbert is merely one of the outside boxes; there are stranger ones to follow."

Villiers could not take his mind away from Herbert and his story, which seemed to grow wilder as the night wore on. The fire seemed to burn low, and the chilly air of the morning crept into the room; Villiers got up with a glance over his shoulder, and, shivering slightly, went to bed.

A few days later he saw at his club a gentleman of his acquaintance, named Austin, who was famous for his intimate knowledge of London life, both in its tenebrous and luminous phases. Villiers, still full of his encounter in Soho and its consequences, thought Austin might possibly be able to shed some light on Herbert's history, and so after some casual talk he suddenly put the question:

"Do you happen to know anything of a man named Herbert -- Charles Herbert?"

Austin turned round sharply and stared at Villiers with some astonishment.

"Charles Herbert? Weren't you in town three years ago? No; then you have not heard of the Paul Street case? It caused a good deal of sensation at the time."

"What was the case?"

"Well, a gentleman, a man of very good position, was found dead, stark dead, in the area of a certain house in Paul Street, off Tottenham Court Road. Of course the police did not make the discovery; if you happen to be sitting up all night and have a light in your window, the constable will ring the bell, but if you happen to be lying dead in somebody's area, you will be left alone. In this instance, as in many others, the alarm was raised by some kind of vagabond; I don't mean a common tramp, or a public-house loafer, but a gentleman, whose business or pleasure, or both, made him a spectator of the London streets at five o'clock in the morning. This individual was, as he said, 'going home,' it did not appear whence or whither, and had occasion to pass through Paul Street between four and five a.m. Something or other caught his eye at Number 20; he said, absurdly enough, that the house had the most unpleasant physiognomy he had ever observed, but, at any rate, he glanced down the area and was a good deal astonished to see a man lying on the stones, his limbs all huddled together, and his face turned up. Our gentleman thought his face looked peculiarly ghastly, and so set off at a run in search of the nearest policeman. The constable was at first inclined to treat the matter lightly, suspecting common drunkenness; however, he came, and after looking at the man's face, changed his tone, quickly enough. The early bird, who had picked up this fine worm, was sent off for a doctor, and the policeman rang and knocked at the door till a slatternly servant girl came down looking more than half asleep. The constable pointed out the contents of the area to the maid, who screamed loudly enough to wake up the street, but she knew nothing of the man; had never seen him at the house, and so forth. Meanwhile, the original discoverer had come back with a medical man, and the next thing was to get into the area. The gate was open, so the whole quartet stumped down the steps. The doctor hardly needed a moment's examination; he said the poor fellow had been dead for several hours, and it was then the case began to get interesting. The dead man had not been robbed, and in one of his pockets were papers identifying him as--well, as a man of good family and means, a favourite in society, and nobody's enemy, as far as could be known. I don't give his name, Villiers, because it has nothing to do with the story, and because it's no good raking up these affairs about the dead when there are no relations living. The next curious point was that the medical men couldn't agree as to how he met his death. There were some slight bruises on his shoulders, but they were so slight that it looked as if he had been pushed roughly out of the kitchen door, and not thrown over the railings from the street or even dragged down the steps. But there were positively no other marks of violence about him, certainly none that would account for his death; and when they came to the autopsy there wasn't a trace of poison of any kind. Of course the police wanted to know all about the people at Number 20, and here again, so I have heard from private sources, one or two other very curious points came out. It appears that the occupants of the house were a Mr. and Mrs. Charles Herbert; he was said to be a landed proprietor, though it struck most people that Paul Street was not exactly the place to look for country gentry. As for Mrs. Herbert, nobody seemed to know who or what she was, and, between ourselves, I fancy the divers after her history found themselves in rather strange waters. Of course they both denied knowing anything about the deceased, and in default of any evidence against them they were discharged. But some very odd things came out about them. Though it was between five and six in the morning when the dead man was removed, a large crowd had collected, and several of the neighbours ran to see what was going on. They were pretty free with their comments, by all accounts, and from these it appeared that Number 20 was in very bad odour in Paul Street. The detectives tried to trace down these rumours to some solid foundation of fact, but could not get hold of anything. People shook their heads and raised their eyebrows and thought the Herberts rather 'queer,' 'would rather not be seen going into their house,'and so on, but there was nothing tangible. The authorities were morally certain the man met his death in some way or another in the house and was thrown out by the kitchen door, but they couldn't prove it, and the absence of any indications of violence or poisoning left them helpless. An odd case, wasn't it? But curiously enough, there's something more that I haven't told you. I happened to know one of the doctors who was consulted as to the cause of death, and some time after the inquest I met him, and asked him about it. 'Do you really mean to tell me,' I said, 'that you were baffled by the case, that you actually don't know what the man died of?' 'Pardon me,' he replied, 'I know perfectly well what caused death. Blank died of fright, of sheer, awful terror; I never saw features so hideously contorted in the entire course of my practice, and I have seen the faces of a whole host of dead.' The doctor was usually a cool customer enough, and a certain vehemence in his manner struck me, but I couldn't get anything more out of him. I suppose the Treasury didn't see their way to prosecuting the Herberts for frightening a man to death; at any rate, nothing was done, and the case dropped out of men's minds. Do you happen to know anything of Herbert?"

"Well," replied Villiers, "he was an old college friend of mine."

"You don't say so? Have you ever seen his wife?"

"No, I haven't. I have lost sight of Herbert for many years."

"It's queer, isn't it, parting with a man at the college gate or at Paddington, seeing nothing of him for years, and then finding him pop up his head in such an odd place. But I should like to have seen Mrs. Herbert; people said extraordinary things about her."

"What sort of things?"

"Well, I hardly know how to tell you. Everyone who saw her at the police court said she was at once the most beautiful woman and the most repulsive they had ever set eyes on. I have spoken to a man who saw her, and I assure you he positively shuddered as he tried to describe the woman, but he couldn't tell why. She seems to have been a sort of enigma; and I expect if that one dead man could have told tales, he would have told some uncommonly queer ones. And there you are again in another puzzle; what could a respectable country gentleman like Mr. Blank (we'll call him that if you don't mind) want in such a very queer house as Number 20? It's altogether a very odd case, isn't it?"

"It is indeed, Austin; an extraordinary case. I didn't think, when I asked you about my old friend, I should strike on such strange metal. Well, I must be off; good-day."

Villiers went away, thinking of his own conceit of the Chinese boxes; here was quaint workmanship indeed.

CHAPTER 4. THE DISCOVERY IN PAUL STREET

A few months after Villers'meeting with Herbert, Mr. Clarke was sitting, as usual, by his after-dinner hearth, resolutely guarding his fancies from wandering in the direction of the bureau. For more than a week he had succeeded in keeping away from the "Memoirs," and he cherished hopes of a complete self-reformation; but, in spite of his endeavours, he could not hush the wonder and the strange curiosity that the last case he had written down had excited within him. He had put the case, or rather the outline of it, conjecturally to a scientific friend, who shook his head, and thought Clarke getting queer, and on this particular evening Clarke was making an effort to rationalize the story, when a sudden knock at the door roused him from his meditations.

"Mr. Villiers to see you sir."

"Dear me, Villiers, it is very kind of you to look me up; I have not seen you for many months; I should think nearly a year. Come in, come in. And how are you, Villiers? Want any advice about investments?"

"No, thanks, I fancy everything I have in that way is pretty safe. No, Clarke, I have really come to consult you about a rather curious matter that has been brought under my notice of late. I am afraid you will think it all rather absurd when I tell my tale. I sometimes think so myself, and that's just what I made up my mind to come to you, as I know you're a practical man."

Mr. Villiers was ignorant of the "Memoirs to prove the Existence of the Devil."

"Well, Villiers, I shall be happy to give you my advice, to the best of my ability. What is the nature of the case?"

"It's an extraordinary thing altogether. You know my ways; I always keep my eyes open in the streets, and in my time I have chanced upon some queer customers, and queer cases too, but this, I think, beats all. I was coming out of a restaurant one nasty winter night about three months ago; I had had a capital dinner and a good bottle of Chianti, and I stood for a moment on the pavement, thinking what a mystery there is about London streets and the companies that pass along them. A bottle of red wine encourages these fancies, Clarke, and I dare say I should have thought a page of small type, but I was cut short by a beggar who had come behind me, and was making the usual appeals. Of course I looked round, and this beggar turned out to be what was left of an old friend of mine, a man named Herbert. I asked him how he had come to such a wretched pass, and he told me. We walked up and down one of those long and dark Soho streets, and there I listened to his story. He said he had married a beautiful girl, some years younger than himself, and, as he put it, she had corrupted him body and soul. He wouldn't go into details; he said he dare not, that what he had seen and heard haunted him by night and day, and when I looked in his face I knew he was speaking the truth. There was something about the man that made me shiver. I don't know why, but it was there. I gave him a little money and sent him away, and I assure you that when he was gone I gasped for breath. His presence seemed to chill one's blood."

"Isn't this all just a little fanciful, Villiers? I suppose the poor fellow had made an imprudent marriage, and, in plain English, gone to the bad."

"Well, listen to this." Villiers told Clarke the story he had heard from Austin.

"You see," he concluded, "there can be but little doubt that this Mr. Blank, whoever he was, died of sheer terror; he saw something so awful, so terrible, that it cut short his life. And what he saw, he most certainly saw in that house, which, somehow or other, had got a bad name in the neighbourhood. I had the curiosity to go and look at the place for myself. It's a saddening kind of street; the houses are old enough to be mean and dreary, but not old enough to be quaint. As far as I could see most of them are let in lodgings, furnished and unfurnished, and almost every door has three bells to it. Here and there the ground floors have been made into shops of the commonest kind; it's a dismal street in every way. I found Number 20 was to let, and I went to the agent's and got the key. Of course I should have heard nothing of the Herberts in that quarter, but I asked the man, fair and square, how long they had left the house and whether there had been other tenants in the meanwhile. He looked at me queerly for a minute, and told me the Herberts had left immediately after the unpleasantness, as he called it, and since then the house had been empty."

Mr. Villiers paused for a moment.

"I have always been rather fond of going over empty houses; there's a sort of fascination about the desolate empty rooms, with the nails sticking in the walls, and the dust thick upon the window-sills. But I didn't enjoy going over Number 20, Paul Street. I had hardly put my foot inside the passage when I noticed a queer, heavy feeling about the air of the house. Of course all empty houses are stuffy, and so forth, but this was something quite different; I can't describe it to you, but it seemed to stop the breath. I went into the front room and the back room, and the kitchens downstairs; they were all dirty and dusty enough, as you would expect, but there was something strange about them all. I couldn't define it to you, I only know I felt queer. It was one of the rooms on the first floor, though, that was the worst. It was a largish room, and once on a time the paper must have been cheerful enough, but when I saw it, paint, paper, and everything were most doleful. But the room was full of horror; I felt my teeth grinding as I put my hand on the door, and when I went in, I thought I should have fallen fainting to the floor. However, I pulled myself together, and stood against the end wall, wondering what on earth there could be about the room to make my limbs tremble, and my heart beat as if I were at the hour of death. In one corner there was a pile of newspapers littered on the floor, and I began looking at them; they were papers of three or four years ago, some of them half torn, and some crumpled as if they had been used for packing. I turned the whole pile over, and amongst them I found a curious drawing; I will show it to you presently. But I couldn't stay in the room; I felt it was overpowering me. I was thankful to come out, safe and sound, into the open air. People stared at me as I walked along the street, and one man said I was drunk. I was staggering about from one side of the pavement to the other, and it was as much as I could do to take the key back to the agent and get home. I was in bed for a week, suffering from what my doctor called nervous shock and exhaustion. One of those days I was reading the evening paper, and happened to notice a paragraph headed: 'Starved to Death.' It was the usual style of thing; a model lodging-house in Marlyebone, a door locked for several days, and a dead man in his chair when they broke in. 'The deceased,' said the paragraph, 'was known as Charles Herbert, and is believed to have been once a prosperous country gentleman. His name was familiar to the public three years ago in connection with the mysterious death in Paul Street, Tottenham Court Road, the deceased being the tenant of the house Number 20, in the area of which a gentleman of good position was found dead under circumstances not devoid of suspicion.' A tragic ending, wasn't it? But after all, if what he told me were true, which I am sure it was, the man's life was all a tragedy, and a tragedy of a stranger sort than they put on the boards."

"And that is the story, is it?" said Clarke musingly.

"Yes, that is the story."

"Well, really, Villiers, I scarcely know what to say about it. There are, no doubt, circumstances in the case which seem peculiar, the finding of the dead man in the area of Herbert's house, for instance, and the extraordinary opinion of the physician as to the cause of death; but, after all, it is conceivable that the facts may be explained in a straightforward manner. As to your own sensations, when you went to see the house, I would suggest that they were due to a vivid imagination; you must have been brooding, in a semi-conscious way, over what you had heard. I don't exactly see what more can be said or done in the matter; you evidently think there is a mystery of some kind, but Herbert is dead; where then do you propose to look?"

"I propose to look for the woman; the woman whom he married. She is the mystery."

The two men sat silent by the fireside; Clarke secretly congratulating himself on having successfully kept up the character of advocate of the commonplace, and Villiers wrapped in his gloomy fancies.

"I think I will have a cigarette," he said at last, and put his hand in his pocket to feel for the cigarette-case.

"Ah!" he said, starting slightly, "I forgot I had something to show you. You remember my saying that I had found a rather curious sketch amongst the pile of old newspapers at the house in Paul Street? Here it is."

Villiers drew out a small thin parcel from his pocket. It was covered with brown paper, and secured with string, and the knots were troublesome. In spite of himself Clarke felt inquisitive; he bent forward on his chair as Villiers painfully undid the string, and unfolded the outer covering. Inside was a second wrapping of tissue, and Villiers took it off and handed the small piece of paper to Clarke without a word.

There was dead silence in the room for five minutes or more; the two man sat so still that they could hear the ticking of the tall old-fashioned clock that stood outside in the hall, and in the mind of one of them the slow monotony of sound woke up a far, far memory. He was looking intently at the small pen-and-ink sketch of the woman's head; it had evidently been drawn with great care, and by a true artist, for the woman's soul looked out of the eyes, and the lips were parted with a strange smile. Clarke gazed still at the face; it brought to his memory one summer evening, long ago; he saw again the long lovely valley, the river winding between the hills, the meadows and the cornfields, the dull red sun, and the cold white mist rising from the water. He heard a voice speaking to him across the waves of many years, and saying "Clarke, Mary will see the god Pan!" and then he was standing in the grim room beside the doctor, listening to the heavy ticking of the clock, waiting and watching, watching the figure lying on the green char beneath the lamplight. Mary rose up, and he looked into her eyes, and his heart grew cold within him.

"Who is this woman?" he said at last. His voice was dry and hoarse.

"That is the woman who Herbert married."

Clarke looked again at the sketch; it was not Mary after all. There certainly was Mary's face, but there was something else, something he had not seen on Mary's features when the white-clad girl entered the laboratory with the doctor, nor at her terrible awakening, nor when she lay grinning on the bed. Whatever it was, the glance that came from those eyes, the smile on the full lips, or the expression of the whole face, Clarke shuddered before it at his inmost soul, and thought, unconsciously, of Dr. Phillip's words, "the most vivid presentment of evil I have ever seen." He turned the paper over mechanically in his hand and glanced at the back.

"Good God! Clarke, what is the matter? You are as white as death."

Villiers had started wildly from his chair, as Clarke fell back with a groan, and let the paper drop from his hands.

"I don't feel very well, Villiers, I am subject to these attacks. Pour me out a little wine; thanks, that will do. I shall feel better in a few minutes."

Villiers picked up the fallen sketch and turned it over as Clarke had done.

"You saw that?" he said. "That's how I identified it as being a portrait of Herbert's wife, or I should say his widow. How do you feel now?"

"Better, thanks, it was only a passing faintness. I don't think I quite catch your meaning. What did you say enabled you to identify the picture?"

"This word--'Helen'--was written on the back. Didn't I tell you her name was Helen? Yes; Helen Vaughan."

Clarke groaned; there could be no shadow of doubt.

"Now, don't you agree with me," said Villiers, "that in the story I have told you to-night, and in the part this woman plays in it, there are some very strange points?"

"Yes, Villiers," Clarke muttered, "it is a strange story indeed; a strange story indeed. You must give me time to think it over; I may be able to help you or I may not. Must you be going now? Well, good-night, Villiers, good-night. Come and see me in the course of a week."

CHAPTER 5. THE LETTER OF ADVICE

"Do you know, Austin," said Villiers, as the two friends were pacing sedately along Piccadilly one pleasant morning in May, "do you know I am convinced that what you told me about Paul Street and the Herberts is a mere episode in an extraordinary history? I may as well confess to you that when I asked you about Herbert a few months ago I had just seen him."

"You had seen him? Where?"

"He begged of me in the street one night. He was in the most pitiable plight, but I recognized the man, and I got him to tell me his history, or at least the outline of it. In brief, it amounted to this--he had been ruined by his wife."

"In what manner?"

"He would not tell me; he would only say that she had destroyed him, body and soul. The man is dead now."

"And what has become of his wife?"

"Ah, that's what I should like to know, and I mean to find her sooner or later. I know a man named Clarke, a dry fellow, in fact a man of business, but shrewd enough. You understand my meaning; not shrewd in the mere business sense of the word, but a man who really knows something about men and life. Well, I laid the case before him, and he was evidently impressed. He said it needed consideration, and asked me to come again in the course of a week. A few days later I received this extraordinary letter."

Austin took the envelope, drew out the letter, and read it curiously. It ran as follows:--

"MY DEAR VILLIERS,--I have thought over the matter on which you consulted me the other night, and my advice to you is this. Throw the portrait into the fire, blot out the story from your mind. Never give it another thought, Villiers, or you will be sorry. You will think, no doubt, that I am in possession of some secret information, and to a certain extent that is the case. But I only know a little; I am like a traveller who has peered over an abyss, and has drawn back in terror. What I know is strange enough and horrible enough, but beyond my knowledge there are depths and horrors more frightful still, more incredible than any tale told of winter nights about the fire. I have resolved, and nothing shall shake that resolve, to explore no whit farther, and if you value your happiness you will make the same determination.

"Come and see me by all means; but we will talk on more cheerful topics than this."

Austin folded the letter methodically, and returned it to Villiers.

"It is certainly an extraordinary letter," he said, "what does he mean by the portrait?"

"Ah! I forgot to tell you I have been to Paul Street and have made a discovery."

Villiers told his story as he had told it to Clarke, and Austin listened in silence. He seemed puzzled.

"How very curious that you should experience such an unpleasant sensation in that room!" he said at length. "I hardly gather that it was a mere matter of the imagination; a feeling of repulsion, in short."

"No, it was more physical than mental. It was as if I were inhaling at every breath some deadly fume, which seemed to penetrate to every nerve and bone and sinew of my body. I felt racked from head to foot, my eyes began to grow dim; it was like the entrance of death."

"Yes, yes, very strange certainly. You see, your friend confesses that there is some very black story connected with this woman. Did you notice any particular emotion in him when you were telling your tale?"

"Yes, I did. He became very faint, but he assured me that it was a mere passing attack to which he was subject."

"Did you believe him?"

"I did at the time, but I don't now. He heard what I had to say with a good deal of indifference, till I showed him the portrait. It was then that he was seized with the attack of which I spoke. He looked ghastly, I assure you."

"Then he must have seen the woman before. But there might be another explanation; it might have been the name, and not the face, which was familiar to him. What do you think?"

"I couldn't say. To the best of my belief it was after turning the portrait in his hands that he nearly dropped from the chair. The name, you know, was written on the back."

"Quite so. After all, it is impossible to come to any resolution in a case like this. I hate melodrama, and nothing strikes me as more commonplace and tedious than the ordinary ghost story of commerce; but really, Villiers, it looks as if there were something very queer at the bottom of all this."

The two men had, without noticing it, turned up Ashley Street, leading northward from Piccadilly. It was a long street, and rather a gloomy one, but here and there a brighter taste had illuminated the dark houses with flowers, and gay curtains, and a cheerful paint on the doors. Villiers glanced up as Austin stopped speaking, and looked at one of these houses; geraniums, red and white, drooped from every sill, and daffodil-coloured curtains were draped back from each window.

"It looks cheerful, doesn't it?" he said.

"Yes, and the inside is still more cheery. One of the pleasantest houses of the season, so I have heard. I haven't been there myself, but I've met several men who have, and they tell me it's uncommonly jovial."

"Whose house is it?"

"A Mrs. Beaumont's."

"And who is she?"

"I couldn't tell you. I have heard she comes from South America, but after all, who she is is of little consequence. She is a very wealthy woman, there's no doubt of that, and some of the best people have taken her up. I hear she has some wonderful claret, really marvellous wine, which must have cost a fabulous sum. Lord Argentine was telling me about it; he was there last Sunday evening. He assures me he has never tasted such a wine, and Argentine, as you know, is an expert. By the way, that reminds me, she must be an oddish sort of woman, this Mrs. Beaumont. Argentine asked her how old the wine was, and what do you think she said? 'About a thousand years, I believe.' Lord Argentine thought she was chaffing him, you know, but when he laughed she said she was speaking quite seriously and offered to show him the jar. Of course, he couldn't say anything more after that; but it seems rather antiquated for a beverage, doesn't it? Why, here we are at my rooms. Come in, won't you?"

"Thanks, I think I will. I haven't seen the curiosity-shop for a while."

It was a room furnished richly, yet oddly, where every jar and bookcase and table, and every rug and jar and ornament seemed to be a thing apart, preserving each its own individuality.

"Anything fresh lately?" said Villiers after a while.

"No; I think not; you saw those queer jugs, didn't you? I thought so. I don't think I have come across anything for the last few weeks."

Austin glanced around the room from cupboard to cupboard, from shelf to shelf, in search of some new oddity. His eyes fell at last on an odd chest, pleasantly and quaintly carved, which stood in a dark corner of the room.

"Ah," he said, "I was forgetting, I have got something to show you."

Austin unlocked the chest, drew out a thick quarto volume, laid it on the table, and resumed the cigar he had put down.

"Did you know Arthur Meyrick the painter, Villiers?"

"A little; I met him two or three times at the house of a friend of mine. What has become of him? I haven't heard his name mentioned for some time."

"He's dead."

"You don't say so! Quite young, wasn't he?"

"Yes; only thirty when he died."

"What did he die of?"

"I don't know. He was an intimate friend of mine, and a thoroughly good fellow. He used to come here and talk to me for hours, and he was one of the best talkers I have met. He could even talk about painting, and that's more than can be said of most painters. About eighteen months ago he was feeling rather overworked, and partly at my suggestion he went off on a sort of roving expedition, with no very definite end or aim about it. I believe New York was to be his first port, but I never heard from him. Three months ago I got this book, with a very civil letter from an English doctor practising at Buenos Ayres, stating that he had attended the late Mr. Meyrick during his illness, and that the deceased had expressed an earnest wish that the enclosed packet should be sent to me after his death. That was all."

"And haven't you written for further particulars?"

"I have been thinking of doing so. You would advise me to write to the doctor?"

"Certainly. And what about the book?"

"It was sealed up when I got it. I don't think the doctor had seen it."

"It is something very rare? Meyrick was a collector, perhaps?"

"No, I think not, hardly a collector. Now, what do you think of these Ainu jugs?"

"They are peculiar, but I like them. But aren't you going to show me poor Meyrick's legacy?"

"Yes, yes, to be sure. The fact is, it's rather a peculiar sort of thing, and I haven't shown it to any one. I wouldn't say anything about it if I were you. There it is."

Villiers took the book, and opened it at haphazard.

"It isn't a printed volume, then?" he said.

"No. It is a collection of drawings in black and white by my poor friend Meyrick."

Villiers turned to the first page, it was blank; the second bore a brief inscription, which he read:

Silet per diem universus, nec sine horrore secretus est; lucet nocturnis ignibus, chorus Aegipanum undique personatur: audiuntur et cantus tibiarum, et tinnitus cymbalorum per oram maritimam.

"I never experienced such a feeling of horror as when I read the account of Argentine's death. I didn't understand it at the time, and I don't now. I knew him well, and it completely passes my understanding for what possible cause he -- or any of the others for the matter of that --could have resolved in cold blood to die in such an awful manner. You know how men babble away each other's characters in London, you may be sure any buried scandal or hidden skeleton would have been brought to light in such a case as this; but nothing of the sort has taken place. As for the theory of mania, that is very well, of course, for the coroner's jury, but everybody knows that it's all nonsense. Suicidal mania is not small-pox."

Austin relapsed into gloomy silence. Villiers sat silent, also, watching his friend. The expression of indecision still fleeted across his face; he seemed as if weighing his thoughts in the balance, and the considerations he was resolving left him still silent. Austin tried to shake off the remembrance of tragedies as hopeless and perplexed as the labyrinth of Daedalus, and began to talk in an indifferent voice of the more pleasant incidents and adventures of the season.

"That Mrs. Beaumont," he said, "of whom we were speaking, is a great success; she has taken London almost by storm. I met her the other night at Fulham's; she is really a remarkable woman."

"You have met Mrs. Beaumont?"

"Yes; she had quite a court around her. She would be called very handsome, I suppose, and yet there is something about her face which I didn't like. The features are exquisite, but the expression is strange. And all the time I was looking at her, and afterwards, when I was going home, I had a curious feeling that very expression was in some way or another familiar to me."

"You must have seen her in the Row."

"No, I am sure I never set eyes on the woman before; it is that which makes it puzzling. And to the best of my belief I have never seen anyone like her; what I felt was a kind of dim far-off memory, vague but persistent. The only sensation I can compare it to, is that odd feeling one sometimes has in a dream, when fantastic cities and wondrous lands and phantom personages appear familiar and accustomed."

Villiers nodded and glanced aimlessly round the room, possibly in search of something on which to turn the conversation. His eyes fell on an old chest somewhat like that in which the artist's strange legacy lay hid beneath a Gothic scutcheon.

"Have you written to the doctor about poor Meyrick?" he asked.

"Yes; I wrote asking for full particulars as to his illness and death. I don't expect to have an answer for another three weeks or a month. I thought I might as well inquire whether Meyrick knew an

Englishwoman named Herbert, and if so, whether the doctor could give me any information about her. But it's very possible that Meyrick fell in with her at New York, or Mexico, or San Francisco; I have no idea as to the extent or direction of his travels."

"Yes, and it's very possible that the woman may have more than one name."

"Exactly. I wish I had thought of asking you to lend me the portrait of her which you possess. I might have enclosed it in my letter to Dr. Matthews."

"So you might; that never occurred to me. We might send it now. Hark! what are those boys calling?"

While the two men had been talking together a confused noise of shouting had been gradually growing louder. The noise rose from the eastward and swelled down Piccadilly, drawing nearer and nearer, a very torrent of sound; surging up streets usually quiet, and making every window a frame for a face, curious or excited. The cries and voices came echoing up the silent street where Villiers lived, growing more distinct as they advanced, and, as Villiers spoke, an answer rang up from the pavement:

"The West End Horrors; Another Awful Suicide; Full Details!"

Austin rushed down the stairs and bought a paper and read out the paragraph to Villiers as the uproar in the street rose and fell. The window was open and the air seemed full of noise and terror.

"Another gentleman has fallen a victim to the terrible epidemic of suicide which for the last month has prevailed in the West End. Mr. Sidney Crashaw, of Stoke House, Fulham, and King's Pomeroy, Devon, was found, after a prolonged search, hanging dead from the branch of a tree in his garden at one o'clock today. The deceased gentleman dined last night at the Carlton Club and seemed in his usual health and spirits. He left the club at about ten o'clock, and was seen walking leisurely up St. James's Street a little later. Subsequent to this his movements cannot be traced. On the discovery of the body medical aid was at once summoned, but life had evidently been long extinct. So far as is known, Mr. Crashaw had no trouble or anxiety of any kind. This painful suicide, it will be remembered, is the fifth of the kind in the last month. The authorities at Scotland Yard are unable to suggest any explanation of these terrible occurrences."

Austin put down the paper in mute horror.

"I shall leave London to-morrow," he said, "it is a city of nightmares. How awful this is, Villiers!"

Mr. Villiers was sitting by the window quietly looking out into the street. He had listened to the newspaper report attentively, and the hint of indecision was no longer on his face.

"Wait a moment, Austin," he replied, "I have made up my mind to mention a little matter that occurred last night. It stated, I think, that Crashaw was last seen alive in St. James's Street shortly after ten?"

"Yes, I think so. I will look again. Yes, you are quite right."

"Quite so. Well, I am in a position to contradict that statement at all events. Crashaw was seen after that; considerably later indeed."

"How do you know?"

"Because I happened to see Crashaw myself at about two o'clock this morning."

"You saw Crashaw? You, Villiers?"

"Yes, I saw him quite distinctly; indeed, there were but a few feet between us."

"Where, in Heaven's name, did you see him?"

"Not far from here. I saw him in Ashley Street. He was just leaving a house."

"Did you notice what house it was?"

"Yes. It was Mrs. Beaumont's."

"Villiers! Think what you are saying; there must be some mistake. How could Crashaw be in Mrs. Beaumont's house at two o'clock in the morning? Surely, surely, you must have been dreaming, Villiers; you were always rather fanciful."

"No; I was wide awake enough. Even if I had been dreaming as you say, what I saw would have roused me effectually."

"What you saw? What did you see? Was there anything strange about Crashaw? But I can't believe it; it is impossible."

"Well, if you like I will tell you what I saw, or if you please, what I think I saw, and you can judge for yourself."

"Very good, Villiers."

The noise and clamour of the street had died away, though now and then the sound of shouting still came from the distance, and the dull, leaden silence seemed like the quiet after an earthquake or a storm. Villiers turned from the window and began speaking.

"I was at a house near Regent's Park last night, and when I came away the fancy took me to walk home instead of taking a hansom. It was a clear pleasant night enough, and after a few minutes I had the streets pretty much to myself. It's a curious thing, Austin, to be alone in London at night, the gas-lamps stretching away in perspective, and the dead silence, and then perhaps the rush and clatter of a hansom on the stones, and the fire starting up under the horse's hoofs. I walked along pretty briskly, for I was feeling a little tired of being out in the night, and as the clocks were striking two I turned down Ashley Street, which, you know, is on my way. It was quieter than ever there, and the lamps were fewer; altogether, it looked as dark and gloomy as a forest in winter. I had done about half the length of the street when I heard a door closed very softly, and naturally I looked up to see who was abroad like myself at such an hour. As it happens, there is a street lamp close to the house in question, and I saw a man standing on the step. He had just shut the door and his face was towards me, and I recognized Crashaw directly. I never knew him to speak to, but I had often seen him, and I am positive that I was not mistaken in my man. I looked into his face for a moment, and then--I will confess the truth--I set off at a good run, and kept it up till I was within my own door."

"Why?"

"Why? Because it made my blood run cold to see that man's face. I could never have supposed that such an infernal medley of passions could have glared out of any human eyes; I almost fainted as I looked. I knew I had looked into the eyes of a lost soul, Austin, the man's outward form remained, but all hell was within it. Furious lust, and hate that was like fire, and the loss of all hope and horror that seemed to shriek aloud to the night, though his teeth were shut; and the utter blackness of despair. I am sure that he did not see me; he saw nothing that you or I can see, but what he saw I hope we never shall. I do not know when he died; I suppose in an hour, or perhaps two, but when I passed down Ashley Street and heard the closing door, that man no longer belonged to this world; it was a devil's face I looked upon."

There was an interval of silence in the room when Villiers ceased speaking. The light was failing, and all the tumult of an hour ago was quite hushed. Austin had bent his head at the close of the story, and his hand covered his eyes.

"What can it mean?" he said at length.

"Who knows, Austin, who knows? It's a black business, but I think we had better keep it to ourselves, for the present at any rate. I will see if I cannot learn anything about that house through private channels of information, and if I do light upon anything I will let you know."

CHAPTER 7. THE ENCOUNTER IN SOHO

Three weeks later Austin received a note from Villiers, asking him to call either that afternoon or the next. He chose the nearer date, and found Villiers sitting as usual by the window, apparently lost in meditation on the drowsy traffic of the street. There was a bamboo table by his side, a fantastic thing, enriched with gilding and queer painted scenes, and on it lay a little pile of papers arranged and docketed as neatly as anything in Mr. Clarke's office.

"Well, Villiers, have you made any discoveries in the last three weeks?"

"I think so; I have here one or two memoranda which struck me as singular, and there is a statement to which I shall call your attention."

"And these documents relate to Mrs. Beaumont? It was really Crashaw whom you saw that night standing on the doorstep of the house in Ashley Street?"

"As to that matter my belief remains unchanged, but neither my inquiries nor their results have any special relation to Crashaw. But my investigations have had a strange issue. I have found out who Mrs. Beaumont is!"

"Who is she? In what way do you mean?"

"I mean that you and I know her better under another name."

"What name is that?"

"Herbert."

"Herbert!" Austin repeated the word, dazed with astonishment.

"Yes, Mrs. Herbert of Paul Street, Helen Vaughan of earlier adventures unknown to me. You had reason to recognize the expression of her face; when you go home look at the face in Meyrick's book of horrors, and you will know the sources of your recollection."

"And you have proof of this?"

"Yes, the best of proof; I have seen Mrs. Beaumont, or shall we say Mrs. Herbert?"

"Where did you see her?"

"Hardly in a place where you would expect to see a lady who lives in Ashley Street, Piccadilly. I saw her entering a house in one of the meanest and most disreputable streets in Soho. In fact, I had made an appointment, though not with her, and she was precise to both time and place."

"All this seems very wonderful, but I cannot call it incredible. You must remember, Villiers, that I have seen this woman, in the ordinary adventure of London society, talking and laughing, and sipping her coffee in a commonplace drawing-room with commonplace people. But you know what you are saying."

"I do; I have not allowed myself to be led by surmises or fancies. It was with no thought of finding Helen Vaughan that I searched for Mrs. Beaumont in the dark waters of the life of London, but such has been the issue."

"You must have been in strange places, Villiers."

"Yes, I have been in very strange places. It would have been useless, you know, to go to Ashley Street, and ask Mrs. Beaumont to give me a short sketch of her previous history. No; assuming, as I had to assume, that her record was not of the cleanest, it would be pretty certain that at some previous time she must have moved in circles not quite so refined as her present ones. If you see mud at the top of a stream, you may be sure that it was once at the bottom. I went to the bottom. I have always been fond of diving into Queer Street for my amusement, and I found my knowledge of that locality and its inhabitants very useful. It is, perhaps, needless to say that my friends had never heard the name of Beaumont, and as I had never seen the lady, and was quite unable to describe her, I had to set to work in an indirect way. The people there know me; I have been able to do some of them a service now and again, so they made no difficulty about giving their information; they were aware I had no communication direct or indirect with Scotland Yard. I had to cast out a good many lines, though, before I got what I wanted, and when I landed the fish I did not for a moment suppose it was my fish. But I listened to what I was told out of a constitutional liking for useless information, and I found myself in possession of a very curious story, though, as I imagined, not the story I was looking for. It was to this effect. Some five or six years ago, a woman named Raymond suddenly made her appearance in the neighbourhood to which I am referring. She was described to me as being quite young, probably not more than seventeen or eighteen, very handsome, and looking as if she came from the country. I should be wrong in saying that she found her level in going to this particular quarter, or associating with these people, for from what I was told, I should think the worst den in London far too good for her. The person from whom

I got my information, as you may suppose, no great Puritan, shuddered and grew sick in telling me of the nameless infamies which were laid to her charge. After living there for a year, or perhaps a little more, she disappeared as suddenly as she came, and they saw nothing of her till about the time of the Paul Street case. At first she came to her old haunts only occasionally, then more frequently, and finally took up her abode there as before, and remained for six or eight months. It's of no use my going into details as to the life that woman led; if you want particulars you can look at Meyrick's legacy. Those designs were not drawn from his imagination. She again disappeared, and the people of the place saw nothing of her till a few months ago. My informant told me that she had taken some rooms in a house which he pointed out, and these rooms she was in the habit of visiting two or three times a week and always at ten in the morning. I was led to expect that one of these visits would be paid on a certain day about a week ago, and I accordingly managed to be on the look-out in company with my cicerone at a quarter to ten, and the hour and the lady came with equal punctuality. My friend and I were standing under an archway, a little way back from the street, but she saw us, and gave me a glance that I shall be long in forgetting. That look was quite enough for me; I knew Miss Raymond to be Mrs. Herbert; as for Mrs. Beaumont she had quite gone out of my head. She went into the house, and I watched it till four o'clock, when she came out, and then I followed her. It was a long chase, and I had to be very careful to keep a long way in the background, and yet not lose sight of the woman. She took me down to the Strand, and then to Westminster, and then up St. James's Street, and along Piccadilly. I felt queerish when I saw her turn up Ashley Street; the thought that Mrs. Herbert was Mrs. Beaumont came into my mind, but it seemed too impossible to be true. I waited at the corner, keeping my eye on her all the time, and I took particular care to note the house at which she stopped. It was the house with the gay curtains, the home of flowers, the house out of which Crashaw came the night he hanged himself in his garden. I was just going away with my discovery, when I saw an empty carriage come round and draw up in front of the house, and I came to the conclusion that Mrs. Herbert was going out for a drive, and I was right. There, as it happened, I met a man I know, and we stood talking together a little distance from the carriage-way, to which I had my back. We had not been there for ten minutes when my friend took off his hat, and I glanced round and saw the lady I had been following all day. 'Who is that?' I said, and his answer was 'Mrs. Beaumont; lives in Ashley Street.' Of course there could be no doubt after that. I don't know whether she saw me, but I don't think she did. I went home at once, and, on consideration, I thought that I had a sufficiently good case with which to go to Clarke."

"Why to Clarke?"

"Because I am sure that Clarke is in possession of facts about this woman, facts of which I know nothing."

"Well, what then?"

Mr. Villiers leaned back in his chair and looked reflectively at Austin for a moment before he answered:

"My idea was that Clarke and I should call on Mrs. Beaumont."

"You would never go into such a house as that? No, no, Villiers, you cannot do it. Besides, consider; what result..."

"I will tell you soon. But I was going to say that my information does not end here; it has been completed in an extraordinary manner.

"Look at this neat little packet of manuscript; it is paginated, you see, and I have indulged in the civil coquetry of a ribbon of red tape. It has almost a legal air, hasn't it? Run your eye over it, Austin. It is an account of the entertainment Mrs. Beaumont provided for her choicer guests. The man who wrote this escaped with his life, but I do not think he will live many years. The doctors tell him he must have sustained some severe shock to the nerves."

Austin took the manuscript, but never read it. Opening the neat pages at haphazard his eye was caught by a word and a phrase that followed it; and, sick at heart, with white lips and a cold sweat pouring like water from his temples, he flung the paper down.

"Take it away, Villiers, never speak of this again. Are you made of stone, man? Why, the dread and horror of death itself, the thoughts of the man who stands in the keen morning air on the black platform, bound, the bell tolling in his ears, and waits for the harsh rattle of the bolt, are as nothing compared to this. I will not read it; I should never sleep again."

"Very good. I can fancy what you saw. Yes; it is horrible enough; but after all, it is an old story, an old mystery played in our day, and in dim London streets instead of amidst the vineyards and the olive gardens. We know what happened to those who chanced to meet the Great God Pan, and those who are wise know that all symbols are symbols of something, not of nothing. It was, indeed, an exquisite symbol beneath which men long ago veiled their knowledge of the most awful, most secret forces which lie at the heart of all things; forces before which the souls of men must wither and die and blacken, as their bodies blacken under the electric current. Such forces cannot be named, cannot be spoken, cannot be imagined except under a veil and a symbol, a symbol to the most of us appearing a quaint, poetic fancy, to some a foolish tale. But you and I, at all events, have known something of the terror that may dwell in the secret place of life, manifested under human flesh; that which is without form taking to itself a form. Oh, Austin, how can it be? How is it that the very sunlight does not turn to blackness before this thing, the hard earth melt and boil beneath such a burden?"

Villiers was pacing up and down the room, and the beads of sweat stood out on his forehead. Austin sat silent for a while, but Villiers saw him make a sign upon his breast.

"I say again, Villiers, you will surely never enter such a house as that? You would never pass out alive."

"Yes, Austin, I shall go out alive--I, and Clarke with me."

What do you mean? You cannot, you would not dare..."

"Wait a moment. The air was very pleasant and fresh this morning; there was a breeze blowing, even through this dull street, and I thought I would take a walk. Piccadilly stretched before me a clear, bright vista, and the sun flashed on the carriages and on the quivering leaves in the park. It was a joyous morning, and men and women looked at the sky and smiled as they went about their work or their pleasure, and the wind blew as blithely as upon the meadows and the scented gorse. But somehow or other I got out of the bustle and the gaiety, and found myself walking slowly along a quiet, dull street, where there seemed to be no sunshine and no air, and where the few foot-passengers loitered as they walked, and hung indecisively about corners and archways. I walked along, hardly knowing where I was going or what I did there, but feeling impelled, as one sometimes is, to explore still further, with a vague idea of reaching some unknown goal. Thus I forged up the street, noting the small traffic of the milk-shop, and wondering at the incongruous medley of penny pipes, black tobacco, sweets, newspapers, and comic songs which here and there jostled one another in the short compass of a single window. I think it was a cold shudder that suddenly passed through me that first told me that I had found what I wanted. I looked up from the pavement and stopped before a dusty shop, above which the lettering had faded, where the red bricks of two hundred years ago had grimed to black; where the windows had gathered to themselves the dust of winters innumerable. I saw what I required; but I think it was five minutes before I had steadied myself and could walk in and ask for it in a cool voice and with a calm face. I think there must even then have been a tremor in my words, for the old man who came out of the back parlour, and fumbled slowly amongst his goods, looked oddly at me as he tied the parcel. I paid what he asked, and stood leaning by the counter, with a strange reluctance to take up my goods and go. I asked about the business, and learnt that trade was bad and the profits cut down sadly; but then the street was not what it was before traffic had been diverted, but that was done forty years ago, 'just before my father died,' he said. I got away at last, and walked along sharply; it was a dismal street indeed, and I was glad to return to the bustle and the noise. Would you like to see my purchase?"

Austin said nothing, but nodded his head slightly; he still looked white and sick. Villiers pulled out a drawer in the bamboo table, and showed Austin a long coil of cord, hard and new; and at one end was a running noose.

"It is the best hempen cord," said Villiers, "just as it used to be made for the old trade, the man told me. Not an inch of jute from end to end."

Austin set his teeth hard, and stared at Villiers, growing whiter as he looked.

"You would not do it," he murmured at last. "You would not have blood on your hands. My God!" he exclaimed, with sudden vehemence, "you cannot mean this, Villiers, that you will make yourself a hangman?"

"No. I shall offer a choice, and leave Helen Vaughan alone with this cord in a locked room for fifteen minutes. If when we go in it is not done, I shall call the nearest policeman. That is all."

"I must go now. I cannot stay here any longer; I cannot bear this. Good-night."

"Good-night, Austin."

The door shut, but in a moment it was open again, and Austin stood, white and ghastly, in the entrance.

"I was forgetting," he said, "that I too have something to tell. I have received a letter from Dr. Harding of Buenos Ayres. He says that he attended Meyrick for three weeks before his death."

"And does he say what carried him off in the prime of life? It was not fever?"

"No, it was not fever. According to the doctor, it was an utter collapse of the whole system, probably caused by some severe shock. But he states that the patient would tell him nothing, and that he was consequently at some disadvantage in treating the case."

"Is there anything more?"

"Yes. Dr. Harding ends his letter by saying: 'I think this is all the information I can give you about your poor friend. He had not been long in Buenos Ayres, and knew scarcely any one, with the exception of a person who did not bear the best of characters, and has since left--a Mrs. Vaughan.'"

CHAPTER 8. THE FRAGMENTS

[Amongst the papers of the well-known physician, Dr. Robert Matheson, of Ashley Street, Piccadilly, who died suddenly, of apoplectic seizure, at the beginning of 1892, a leaf of manuscript paper was found, covered with pencil jottings. These notes were in Latin, much abbreviated, and had evidently been made in great haste. The MS. was only deciphered with difficulty, and some words have up to the present time evaded all the efforts of the expert employed. The date, "XXV Jul. 1888," is written on the right-hand corner of the MS. The following is a translation of Dr. Matheson's manuscript.]

"Whether science would benefit by these brief notes if they could be published, I do not know, but rather doubt. But certainly I shall never take the responsibility of publishing or divulging one word of what is here written, not only on account of my oath given freely to those two persons who were present, but also because the details are too abominable. It is probably that, upon mature consideration, and after weighting the good and evil, I shall one day destroy this paper, or at least leave it under seal to my friend D., trusting in his discretion, to use it or to burn it, as he may think fit.

"As was befitting, I did all that my knowledge suggested to make sure that I was suffering under no delusion. At first astounded, I could hardly think, but in a minute's time I was sure that my pulse was steady and regular, and that I was in my real and true senses. I then fixed my eyes quietly on what was before me.

"Though horror and revolting nausea rose up within me, and an odour of corruption choked my breath, I remained firm. I was then privileged or accursed, I dare not say which, to see that which was on the bed, lying there black like ink, transformed before my eyes. The skin, and the flesh, and the muscles, and the bones, and the firm structure of the human body that I had thought to be unchangeable, and permanent as adamant, began to melt and dissolve.

"I know that the body may be separated into its elements by external agencies, but I should have refused to believe what I saw. For here there was some internal force, of which I knew nothing, that caused dissolution and change.

"Here too was all the work by which man had been made repeated before my eyes. I saw the form waver from sex to sex, dividing itself from itself, and then again reunited. Then I saw the body descend to the beasts whence it ascended, and that which was on the heights go down to the depths, even to the abyss of all being. The principle of life, which makes organism, always remained, while the outward form changed.

"The light within the room had turned to blackness, not the darkness of night, in which objects are seen dimly, for I could see clearly and without difficulty. But it was the negation of light; objects were presented to my eyes, if I may say so, without any medium, in such a manner that if there had been a prism in the room I should have seen no colours represented in it.

"I watched, and at last I saw nothing but a substance as jelly. Then the ladder was ascended again... [here the MS. is illegible] ...for one instance I saw a Form, shaped in dimness before me, which I will not farther describe. But the symbol of this form may be seen in ancient sculptures, and in paintings which survived beneath the lava, too foul to be spoken of... as a horrible and unspeakable shape, neither man nor beast, was changed into human form, there came finally death.

"I who saw all this, not without great horror and loathing of soul, here write my name, declaring all that I have set on this paper to be true.

"ROBERT MATHESON, Med. Dr."

* * *

...Such, Raymond, is the story of what I know and what I have seen. The burden of it was too heavy for me to bear alone, and yet I could tell it to none but you. Villiers, who was with me at the last, knows nothing of that awful secret of the wood, of how what we both saw die, lay upon the smooth, sweet turf amidst the summer flowers, half in sun and half in shadow, and holding the girl Rachel's hand, called and summoned those companions, and shaped in solid form, upon the earth we tread upon, the horror which we can but hint at, which we can only name under a figure. I would not tell Villiers of this, nor of that resemblance, which struck me as with a blow upon my heart, when I saw the portrait, which filled the cup of terror at the end. What this can mean I dare not guess. I know that what I saw perish was not Mary, and yet in the last agony Mary's eyes looked into mine. Whether there can be any one who can show the last link in this chain of awful mystery, I do not know, but if there be any one who can do this, you,

Raymond, are the man. And if you know the secret, it rests with you to tell it or not, as you please.

I am writing this letter to you immediately on my getting back to town. I have been in the country for the last few days; perhaps you may be able to guess in which part. While the horror and wonder of London was at its height--for "Mrs. Beaumont," as I have told you, was well known in society--I wrote to my friend Dr. Phillips, giving some brief outline, or rather hint, of what happened, and asking him to tell me the name of the village where the events he had related to me occurred. He gave me the name, as he said with the less hesitation, because Rachel's father and mother were dead, and the rest of the family had gone to a relative in the State of Washington six months before. The parents, he said, had undoubtedly died of grief and horror caused by the terrible death of their daughter, and by what had gone before that death. On the evening of the day which I received Phillips'letter I was at Caermaen, and standing beneath the mouldering Roman walls, white with the winters of seventeen hundred years, I looked over the meadow where once had stood the older temple of the "God of the Deeps," and saw a house gleaming in the sunlight. It was the house where Helen had lived. I stayed at Caermaen for several days. The people of the place, I found, knew little and had guessed less. Those whom I spoke to on the matter seemed surprised that an antiquarian (as I professed myself to be) should trouble about a village tragedy, of which they gave a very commonplace version, and, as you may imagine, I told nothing of what I knew. Most of my time was spent in the great wood that rises just above the village and climbs the hillside, and goes down to the river in the valley; such another long lovely valley, Raymond, as that on which we looked one summer night, walking to and fro before your house. For many an hour I strayed through the maze of the forest, turning now to right and now to left, pacing slowly down long alleys of undergrowth, shadowy and chill, even under the midday sun, and halting beneath great oaks; lying on the short turf of a clearing where the faint sweet scent of wild roses came to me on the wind and mixed with the heavy perfume of the elder, whose mingled odour is like the odour of the room of the dead, a vapour of incense and corruption. I stood at the edges of the wood, gazing at all the pomp and procession of the foxgloves towering amidst the bracken and shining red in the broad sunshine, and beyond them into deep thickets of close undergrowth where springs boil up from the rock and nourish the water-weeds, dank and evil. But in all my wanderings I avoided one part of the wood; it was not till yesterday that I climbed to the summit of the hill, and stood upon the ancient Roman road that threads the highest ridge of the wood. Here they had walked, Helen and Rachel, along this quiet causeway, upon the pavement of green turf, shut in on either side by high banks of red earth, and tall hedges of shining beech, and here I followed in their steps, looking out, now and again, through partings in the boughs, and seeing on one side the sweep of the wood stretching far to right and left, and sinking into the broad level, and beyond, the yellow sea, and the land over the sea. On the other side was the valley and the river and hill following hill as wave on wave, and wood and meadow, and cornfield, and white houses gleaming, and a great wall of mountain, and far blue peaks in the north. And so at least I came to the place. The track went up a gentle slope, and widened out into an open space with a wall of thick undergrowth around it, and then, narrowing again, passed on into the distance and the faint blue mist of summer heat. And into this pleasant summer glade Rachel passed a girl, and left it, who shall say what? I did not stay long there.

In a small town near Caermaen there is a museum, containing for the most part Roman remains which have been found in the neighbourhood at various times. On the day after my arrival in Caermaen I walked over to the town in question, and took the opportunity of inspecting the museum. After I had seen most of the sculptured stones, the coffins, rings, coins, and fragments of tessellated pavement which the place contains, I was shown a small square pillar of white stone, which had been recently discovered in the wood of which I have been speaking, and, as I found on inquiry, in that open space where the Roman road broadens out. On one side of the pillar was an inscription, of which I took a note. Some of the letters have been defaced, but I do not think there can be any doubt as to those which I supply. The inscription is as follows:

DEVOMNODENTi FLAvIVSSENILISPOSSvit PROPTERNVPtias quaSVIDITSVBVMra

"To the great god Nodens (the god of the Great Deep or Abyss) Flavius Senilis has erected this pillar on account of the marriage which he saw beneath the shade."

The custodian of the museum informed me that local antiquaries were much puzzled, not by the inscription, or by any difficulty in translating it, but as to the circumstance or rite to which allusion is made.

* * *

...And now, my dear Clarke, as to what you tell me about Helen Vaughan, whom you say you saw die under circumstances of the utmost and almost incredible horror. I was interested in your account, but a good deal, nay all, of what you told me I knew already. I can understand the strange likeness you remarked in both the portrait and in the actual face; you have seen Helen's mother. You remember that still summer night so many years ago, when I talked to you of the world beyond the shadows, and of the god Pan. You remember Mary. She was the mother of Helen Vaughan, who was born nine months after that night.

Mary never recovered her reason. She lay, as you saw her, all the while upon her bed, and a few days after the child was born she died. I fancy that just at the last she knew me; I was standing by the bed, and the old look came into her eyes for a second, and then she shuddered and groaned and died. It was an ill work I did that night when you were present; I broke open the door of the house of life, without knowing or caring what might pass forth or enter in. I recollect your telling me at the time, sharply enough, and rightly too, in one sense, that I had ruined the reason of a human being by a foolish experiment, based on an absurd theory. You did well to blame me, but my theory was not all absurdity. What I said Mary would see she saw, but I forgot that no human eyes can look on such a sight with impunity. And I forgot, as I have just said, that when the house of life is thus thrown open, there may enter in that for which we have no name, and human flesh may become the veil of a horror one dare not express. I played with energies which I did not understand, you have seen the ending of it. Helen Vaughan did well to bind the cord about her neck and die, though the death was horrible. The blackened face, the hideous form upon the bed, changing and melting before your eyes from woman to man, from man to beast, and from beast to worse than beast, all the strange horror that you witness, surprises me but little. What you say the doctor whom you sent for saw and shuddered at I noticed long ago; I knew what I had done the moment the child was born, and when it was scarcely five years old I surprised it, not once or twice but several times with a playmate, you may guess of what kind. It was for me a constant, an incarnate horror, and after a few years I felt I could bear it no more, and I sent Helen Vaughan away. You know now what frightened the boy in the wood. The rest of the strange story, and all else that you tell me, as discovered by your friend, I have contrived to learn from time to time, almost to the last chapter. And now Helen is with her companions...

The White People

PROLOGUE

"SORCERY and sanctity," said Ambrose, "these are the only realities. Each is an ecstasy, a withdrawal from the common life."

Cotgrave listened, interested. He had been brought by a friend to this mouldering house in a northern suburb, through an old garden to the room where Ambrose the recluse dozed and dreamed over his books.

"Yes," he went on, "magic is justified of her children. I There are many, I think, who eat dry crusts and drink water, with a joy infinitely sharper than anything within the experience of the 'practical' epicure."

"You are speaking of the saints?"

"Yes, and of the sinners, too. I think you are falling into the very general error of confining the spiritual world to the supremely good; but the supremely wicked, necessarily, have their portion in it. The merely carnal, sensual man can no more be a great sinner than he can be a great saint. Most of us are just indifferent, mixed-up creatures; we muddle through the world without realizing the meaning and the inner sense of things, and, consequently, our wickedness and our goodness are alike second-rate, unimportant."

"And you think the great sinner, then, will be an ascetic, as well as the great saint?"

"Great people of all kinds forsake the imperfect copies and go to the perfect originals. I have no doubt but that many of the very highest among the saints have never done a 'good action' (using the words in their ordinary sense). And, on the other hand, there have been those who have sounded the very depths of sin, who all their lives have never done an 'ill deed.'"

He went out of the room for a moment, and Cotgrave, in high delight, turned to his friend and thanked him for the introduction.

"He's grand," he said. "I never saw that kind of lunatic before."

Ambrose returned with more whisky and helped the two men in a liberal manner. He abused the teetotal sect with ferocity, as he handed the seltzer, and pouring out a glass of water for himself, was about to resume his monologue, when Cotgrave broke in--

"I can't stand it, you know," he said, "your paradoxes are too monstrous. A man may be a great sinner and yet never do anything sinful! Come!"

"You're quite wrong," said Ambrose. "I never make paradoxes; I wish I could. I merely said that a man may have an exquisite taste in RomanŽe Conti, and yet never have even smelt four ale. That's all, and it's more like a truism than a paradox, isn't it? Your surprise at my remark is due to the fact that you haven't realized what sin is. Oh, yes, there is a sort of connexion between Sin with the capital letter, and actions which are commonly called sinful: with murder, theft, adultery, and so forth. Much the same connexion that there is between the A, B, C and fine literature. But I believe that the misconception--it is all but universal--arises in great measure from our looking at the matter through social spectacles. We think that a man who does evil to us and to his neighbours must be very evil. So he is, from a social standpoint; but can't you realize that Evil in its essence is a lonely thing, a passion of the solitary, individual soul? Really, the average murderer, qu‰ murderer, is not by any means a sinner in the true sense of the word. He is simply a wild beast that we have to get rid of to save our own necks from his knife. I should class him rather with tigers than with sinners."

"It seems a little strange."

"I think not. The murderer murders not from positive qualities, but from negative ones; he lacks something which non-murderers possess. Evil, of course, is wholly positive--only it is on the wrong side. You may believe me that sin in its proper sense is very rare; it is probable that there have been far fewer sinners than saints. Yes, your standpoint is all very well for practical, social purposes; we are naturally inclined to think that a person who is very disagreeable to us must be a very great sinner! It is very disagreeable to have one's pocket picked, and we pronounce the thief to be a very great sinner. In truth, he is merely an undeveloped man. He cannot be a saint, of course; but he may be, and often is, an infinitely better creature than thousands who have never broken a single commandment. He is a great nuisance to us, I admit, and we very properly lock him up if we catch him; but between his troublesome and unsocial action and evil--Oh, the connexion is of the weakest."

It was getting very late. The man who had brought Cotgrave had probably heard all this before, since he assisted with a bland and judicious smile, but Cotgrave began to think that his "lunatic" was turning into a sage.

"Do you know," he said, "you interest me immensely? You think, then, that we do not understand the real nature of evil?"

"No, I don't think we do. We over-estimate it and we under-estimate it. We take the very numerous infractions of our social 'bye-laws'--the very necessary and very proper regulations which keep the human company together--and we get frightened at the prevalence of 'sin' and 'evil.' But this is really nonsense. Take theft, for example. Have you any horror at the thought of Robin Hood, of the Highland caterans of the seventeenth century, of the moss-troopers, of the company promoters of our day?

"Then, on the other hand, we underrate evil. We attach such an enormous importance to the 'sin' of meddling with our pockets (and our wives) that we have quite forgotten the awfulness of real sin."

"And what is sin?" said Cotgrave.

"I think I must reply to your question by another. What would your feelings be, seriously, if your cat or your dog began to talk to you, and to dispute with you in human accents? You would be overwhelmed with horror. I am sure of it. And if the roses in your garden sang a weird song, you would go mad. And suppose the stones in the road began to swell and grow before your eyes, and if the pebble that you noticed at night had shot out stony blossoms in the morning?

"Well, these examples may give you some notion of what sin really is."

"Look here," said the third man, hitherto placid, "you two seem pretty well wound up. But I'm going home. I've missed my tram, and I shall have to walk."

Ambrose and Cotgrave seemed to settle down more profoundly when the other had gone out into the early misty morning and the pale light of the lamps.

"You astonish me," said Cotgrave. "I had never thought of that. If that is really so, one must turn everything upside down. Then the essence of sin really is----"

"In the taking of heaven by storm, it seems to me," said Ambrose. "It appears to me that it is simply an attempt to penetrate into another and higher sphere in a forbidden manner. You can understand why it is so rare. There are few, indeed, who wish to penetrate into other spheres, higher or lower, in ways allowed or forbidden. Men, in the mass, are amply content with life as they find it. Therefore there are few saints, and sinners (in the proper sense) are fewer still, and men of genius, who partake sometimes of each character, are rare also. Yes; on the whole, it is, perhaps, harder to be a great sinner than a great saint."

"There is something profoundly unnatural about Sin? Is that what you mean?"

"Exactly. Holiness requires as great, or almost as great, an effort;

but holiness works on lines that were natural once; it is an effort to recover the ecstasy that was before the Fall. But sin is an effort to gain the ecstasy and the knowledge that pertain alone to angels and in making this effort man becomes a demon. I told you that the mere murderer is not therefore a sinner; that is true, but the sinner is sometimes a murderer. Gilles de Raiz is an instance. So you see that while the good and the evil are unnatural to man as he now is--to man the social, civilized being--evil is unnatural in a much deeper sense than good. The saint endeavours to recover a gift which he has lost; the sinner tries to obtain something which was never his. In brief, he repeats the Fall."

"But are you a Catholic?" said Cotgrave.

"Yes; I am a member of the persecuted Anglican Church."

"Then, how about those texts which seem to reckon as sin that which you would set down as a mere trivial dereliction?"

"Yes; but in one place the word 'sorcerers' comes in the same sentence, doesn't it? That seems to me to give the key-note. Consider: can you imagine for a moment that a false statement which saves an innocent man's life is a sin? No; very good, then, it is not the mere liar who is excluded by those words; it is, above all, the 'sorcerers' who use the material life, who use the failings incidental to material life as instruments to obtain their infinitely wicked ends. And let me tell you this: our higher senses are so blunted, we are so drenched with materialism, that we should probably fail to recognize real wickedness if we encountered it."

"But shouldn't we experience a certain horror--a terror such as you hinted we would experience if a rose tree sang--in the mere presence of an evil man?"

"We should if we were natural: children and women feel this horror you speak of, even animals experience it. But with most of us convention and civilization and education have blinded and deafened and obscured the natural reason. No, sometimes we may recognize evil by its hatred of the good--one doesn't need much penetration to guess at the influence which dictated, quite unconsciously, the 'Blackwood' review of Keats--but this is purely incidental; and, as a rule, I suspect that the Hierarchs of Tophet pass quite unnoticed, or, perhaps, in certain cases, as good but mistaken men."

"But you used the word 'unconscious' just now, of Keats' reviewers. Is wickedness ever unconscious?"

"Always. It must be so. It is like holiness and genius in this as in other points; it is a certain rapture or ecstasy of the soul; a transcendent effort to surpass the ordinary bounds. So, surpassing these, it surpasses also the understanding, the faculty that takes note of that which comes before it. No, a man may be infinitely and horribly wicked and never suspect it But I tell you, evil in this, its certain and true sense, is rare, and I think it is growing rarer."

"I am trying to get hold of it all," said Cotgrave. From what you say, I gather that the true evil differs generically from that which we call evil?"

"Quite so. There is, no doubt, an analogy between the two; a resemblance such as enables us to use, quite legitimately, such terms as the 'foot of the mountain' and the 'leg of the table.' And, sometimes, of course, the two speak, as it were, in the same language. The rough miner, or 'puddler,' the untrained, undeveloped 'tiger-man,' heated by a quart or two above his usual measure, comes home and kicks his irritating and injudicious wife to death. He is a murderer. And Gilles de Raiz was a murderer. But you see the gulf that separates the two? The 'word,' if I may so speak, is accidentally the same in each case, but the 'meaning' is utterly different. It is flagrant 'Hobson Jobson' to confuse the two, or rather, it is as if one supposed that Juggernaut and the Argonauts had something to do etymologically with one another. And no doubt the same weak likeness, or analogy, runs between all the 'social' sins and the real spiritual sins, and in some cases, perhaps, the lesser may be 'schoolmasters' to lead one on to the greater--from the shadow to the reality. If you are anything of a Theologian, you will see the importance of all this."

"I am sorry to say," remarked Cotgrave, "that I have devoted very little of my time to theology. Indeed, I have often wondered on what grounds theologians have claimed the title of Science of Sciences for their favourite study; since the 'theological' books I have looked into have always seemed to me to be concerned with feeble and obvious pieties, or with the kings of Israel and Judah. I do not care to hear about those kings."

Ambrose grinned.

"We must try to avoid theological discussion," he said. "I perceive that you would be a bitter disputant. But perhaps the 'dates of the kings' have as much to do with theology as the hobnails of the murderous puddler with evil."

"Then, to return to our main subject, you think that sin is an esoteric, occult thing?"

"Yes. It is the infernal miracle as holiness is the supernal. Now and then it is raised to such a pitch that we entirely fail to suspect its existence; it is like the note of the great pedal pipes of the organ, which is so deep that we cannot hear it. In other cases it may lead to the lunatic asylum, or to still stranger issues. But you must never confuse it with mere social misdoing. Remember how the Apostle, speaking of the 'other side,' distinguishes between 'charitable' actions and charity. And as one may give all one's goods to the poor, and yet lack charity;

so, remember, one may avoid every crime and yet be a sinner"

"Your psychology is very strange to me," said Cotgrave, "but I confess I like it, and I suppose that one might fairly deduce from your premisses the conclusion that the real sinner might very possibly strike the observer as a harmless personage enough?"

"Certainly, because the true evil has nothing to do with social life or social laws, or if it has, only incidentally and accidentally. It is a lonely passion of the soul--or a passion of the lonely soul--whichever you like. If, by chance, we understand it, and grasp its full significance, then, indeed, it will fill us with horror and with awe. But this emotion is widely distinguished from the fear and the disgust with which we regard the ordinary criminal, since this latter is largely or entirely founded on the regard which we have for our own skins or purses. We hate a murder, because we know that we should hate to be murdered, or to have any one that we like murdered. So, on the 'other side,' we venerate the saints, but we don't 'like' them as well as our friends. Can you persuade yourself that you would have 'enjoyed' St. Paul's company? Do you think that you and I would have 'got on' with Sir Galahad?

"So with the sinners, as with the saints. If you met a very evil man, and recognized his evil; he would, no doubt, fill you with horror and awe; but there is no reason why you should 'dislike' him. On the contrary, it is quite possible that if you could succeed in putting the sin out of your mind you might find the sinner capital company, and in a little while you might have to reason yourself back into horror. Still, how awful it is. If the roses and the lilies suddenly sang on this coming morning; if the furniture began to move in procession, as in De Maupassant's tale!"

"I am glad you have come back to that comparison," said Cotgrave, "because I wanted to ask you what it is that corresponds in humanity to these imaginary feats of inanimate things. In a word--what is sin? You have given me, I know, an abstract definition, but I should like a concrete example."

"I told you it was very rare," said Ambrose, who appeared willing to avoid the giving of a direct answer. "The materialism of the age, which has done a good deal to suppress sanctity, has done perhaps more to suppress evil. We find the earth so very comfortable that we have no inclination either for ascents or descents. It would seem as if the scholar who decided to 'specialize' in Tophet, would be reduced to purely antiquarian researches. No pal¾ontologist could show you a live pterodactyl."

"And yet you, I think, have 'specialized,' and I believe that your researches have descended to our modern times."

"You are really interested, I see. Well, I confess, that I have dabbled a little, and if you like I can show you something that bears on the very curious subject we have been discussing."

Ambrose took a candle and went away to a far, dim corner of the room. Cotgrave saw him open a venerable bureau that stood there, and from some secret recess he drew out a parcel, and came back to the window where they had been sitting.

Ambrose undid a wrapping of paper, and produced a green pocket-book.

"You will take care of it?" he said. "Don't leave it lying about. It is one of the choicer pieces in my collection, and I should be very sorry if it were lost."

He fondled the faded binding.

"I knew the girl who wrote this," he said. "When you read it, you will see how it illustrates the talk we have had to-night. There is a sequel, too, but I won't talk of that.

"There was an odd article in one of the reviews some months ago," he began again, with the air of a man who changes the subject. "It was written by a doctor--Dr. Coryn, I think, was the name. He says that a lady, watching her little girl playing at the drawing-room window, suddenly saw the heavy sash give way and fall on the child's fingers. The lady fainted, I think, but at any rate the doctor was summoned, and when he had dressed the child's wounded and maimed fingers he was summoned to the mother. She was groaning with pain, and it was found that three fingers of her hand, corresponding with those that had been injured on the child's hand, were swollen and inflamed, and later, in the doctor's language, purulent sloughing set in."

Ambrose still handled delicately the green volume.

"Well, here it is," he said at last, parting with difficulty, it seemed, from his treasure.

"You will bring it back as soon as you have read it," he said, as they went out into the hall, into the old garden, faint with the odour of white lilies.

There was a broad red band in the east as Cotgrave turned to go, and from the high ground where he stood he saw that awful spectacle of London in a dream.

THE GREEN BOOK

The morocco binding of the book was faded, and the colour had grown faint, but there were no stains nor bruises nor marks of usage. The book looked as if it had been bought "on a visit to London" some seventy or eighty years ago, and had somehow been forgotten and suffered to lie away out of sight. There was an old, delicate, lingering odour about it, such an odour as sometimes haunts an ancient piece of furniture for a century or more. The end-papers, inside the binding, were oddly decorated with coloured patterns and faded gold. It looked small, but the paper was fine, and there were many leaves, closely covered with minute, painfully formed characters.

I found this book (the manuscript began) in a drawer in the old bureau that stands on the landing. It was a very rainy day and I could not go out, so in the afternoon I got a candle and rummaged in the bureau. Nearly all the drawers were full of old dresses, but one of the small ones looked empty, and I found this book hidden right at the back. I wanted a book like this, so I took it to write in. It is full of secrets. I have a great many other books of secrets I have written, hidden in a safe place, and I am going to write here many of the old secrets and some new ones; but there are some I shall not put down at all. I must not write down the real names of the days and months which I found out a year ago, nor the way to make the Aklo letters, or the Chian language, or the great beautiful Circles, nor the Mao Games, nor the chief songs. I may write something about all these things but not the way to do them, for peculiar reasons. And I must not say who the Nymphs are, or the D™ls, or Jeelo, or what voolas mean. All these are most secret secrets, and I am glad when I remember what they are, and how many wonderful languages I know, but there are some things that I call the secrets of the secrets of the secrets that I dare not think of unless I am quite alone, and then I shut my eyes, and put my hands over them and whisper the word, and the Alala comes. I only do this at night in my room or in certain woods that I know, but I must not describe them, as they are secret woods. Then there are the Ceremonies, which are all of them important, but some are more delightful than others--

there are the White Ceremonies, and the Green Ceremonies, and the Scarlet Ceremonies. The Scarlet Ceremonies are the best, but there is only one place where they can be performed properly, though there is a very nice imitation which I have done in other places. Besides these, I have the dances, and the Comedy, and I have done the Comedy sometimes when the others were looking, and they didn't understand anything about it. I was very little when I first knew about these things.

When I was very small, and mother was alive, I can remember remembering things before that, only it has all got confused. But I remember when I was five or six I heard them talking about me when they thought I was not noticing. They were saying how queer I was a year or two before, and how nurse had called my mother to come and listen to me talking all to myself, and I was saying words that nobody could understand. I was speaking the Xu language, but I only remember a very few of the words, as it was about the little white faces that used to look at me when I was lying in my cradle. They used to talk to me, and I learnt their language and talked to them in it about some great white place where they lived, where the trees and the grass were all white, and there were white hills as high up as the moon, and a cold wind. I have often dreamed of it afterwards, but the faces went away when I was very little. But a wonderful thing happened when I was about five. My nurse was carrying me on her shoulder; there was a field of yellow corn, and we went through it, it was very hot. Then we came to a path through a wood, and a tall man came after us, and went with us till we came to a place where there was a deep pool, and it was very dark and shady. Nurse put me down on the soft moss under a tree, and she said: "She can't get to the pond now." So they left me there, and I sat quite still and watched, and out of the water and out of the wood came two wonderful white people, and they began to play and dance and sing. They were a kind of creamy white like the old ivory figure in the drawing-room; one was a beautiful lady with kind dark eyes, and a grave face, and long black hair, and she smiled such a strange sad smile at the other, who laughed and came to her. They played together, and danced round and round the pool, and they sang a song till I fell asleep. Nurse woke me up when she came back, and she was looking something like the lady had looked, so I told her all about it, and asked her why she looked like that. At first she cried, and then she looked very frightened, and turned quite pale. She put me down on the grass and stared at me, and I could see she was shaking all over. Then she said I had been dreaming, but I knew I hadn't. Then she made me promise not to say a word about it to anybody, and if I did I should be thrown into the black pit. I was not frightened at all, though nurse was, and I never forgot about it, because when I shut my eyes and it was quite quiet, and I was all alone, I could see them again, very faint and far away, but very splendid; and little bits of the song they sang came into my head, but I couldn't sing it.

I was thirteen, nearly fourteen, when I had a very singular adventure, so strange that the day on which it happened is always called the White Day. My mother had been dead for more than a year, and in the morning I had lessons, but they let me go out for walks in the afternoon. And this afternoon I walked a new way, and a little brook led me into a new country, but I tore my frock getting through some of the difficult places, as the way was through many bushes, and beneath the low branches of trees, and up thorny thickets on the hills, and by dark woods full of creeping thorns. And it was a long, long way. It seemed as if I was going on for ever and ever, and I had to creep by a place like a tunnel where a brook must have been, but all the water had dried up, and the floor was rocky, and the bushes had grown overhead till they met, so that it was quite dark. And I went on and on through that dark place; it was a long, long way. And I came to a hill that I never saw before. I was in a dismal thicket full of black twisted boughs that tore me as I went through them, and I cried out because I was smarting all over, and then I found that I was climbing, and I went up and up a long way, till at last the thicket stopped and I came out crying just under the top of a big bare place, where there were ugly grey stones lying all about on the grass, and here and there a little twisted, stunted tree came out from under a stone, like a snake. And I went up, right to the top, a long way. I never saw such big ugly stones before; they came out of the earth some of them, and some looked as if they had been rolled to where they were, and they went on and on as far as I could see, a long, long way. I looked out from them and saw the country, but it was strange. It was winter time, and there were black terrible woods hanging from the hills all round; it was like seeing a large room hung with black curtains, and the shape of the trees seemed quite different from any I had ever seen before. I was afraid. Then beyond the woods there were other hills round in a great ring, but I had never seen any of them; it all looked black, and everything had a voor over it. It was all so still and silent, and the sky was heavy and grey and sad, like a wicked voorish dome in Deep Dendo. I went on into the dreadful rocks. There were hundreds and hundreds of them. Some were like horrid-grinning men; I could see their faces as if they would jump at me out of the stone, and catch hold of me, and drag me with them back into the rock, so that I should always be there. And there were other rocks that were like animals, creeping, horrible animals, putting out their tongues, and others were like words that I could not say, and others like dead people lying on the grass. I went on among them, though they frightened me, and my heart was full of wicked songs that they put into it; and I wanted to make faces and twist myself about in the way they did, and I went on and on a long way till at last I liked the rocks, and they didn't frighten me any more. I sang the songs I thought of; songs full of words that must not be spoken or written down. Then I made faces like the faces on the rocks, and I twisted myself about like the twisted ones, and I lay down flat on the ground like the dead ones, and I went up to one that was grinning, and put my arms round him and hugged him. And so I went on and on through the rocks till I came to a round mound in the middle of them. It was higher than a mound, it was nearly as high as our house, and it was like a great basin turned upside down, all smooth and round and green, with one stone, like a post, sticking up at the top. I climbed up the sides, but they were so steep I had to stop or I should have rolled all the way down again, and I should have knocked against the stones at the bottom, and perhaps been killed. But I wanted to get up to the very top of the big round mound, so I lay down flat on my face, and took hold of the grass with my hands and drew myself up, bit by bit, till I was at the top Then I sat down on the stone in the middle, and looked all round about. I felt I had come such a long, long way, just as if I were a hundred miles from home, or in some other country, or in one of the strange places I had read about in the "Tales of the Genie" and the "Arabian Nights," or as if I had gone across the sea, far away, for years and I had found another world that nobody had ever seen or heard of before, or as if I had somehow flown through the sky and fallen on one of the stars I had read about where everything is dead and cold and grey, and there is no air, and the wind doesn't blow. I sat on the stone and looked all round and down and round about me. It was just as if I was sitting on a tower in the middle of a great empty town, because I could see nothing all around but the grey rocks on the ground. I couldn't make out their shapes any more, but I could see them on and on for a long way, and I looked at them, and they seemed as if they had been arranged into patterns, and shapes, and figures. I knew they couldn't be. because I had seen a lot of them coming right out of the earth, joined to the deep rocks below, so I looked again, but still I saw nothing but circles, and small circles inside big ones, and pyramids, and domes, and spires, and they seemed all to go round and round the place where I was sitting, and the more I looked, the more I saw great big rings of rocks, getting bigger and bigger, and I stared so long that it felt as if they were all moving and turning, like a great wheel, and I was turning, too, in the middle. I got quite dizzy and queer in the head, and everything began to be hazy and not clear, and I saw little sparks of blue light, and the stones looked as if they were springing and dancing and twisting as they went round and round and round. I was frightened again, and I cried out loud, and jumped up from the stone I was sitting on, and fell down. When I got up I was so glad they all looked still, and I sat down on the top and slid down the mound, and went on again. I danced as I went in the peculiar way the rocks had danced when I got giddy, and I was so glad I could do it quite well, and I danced and danced along, and sang extraordinary songs that came into my head. At last I came to the edge of that great flat hill, and there were no more rocks, and the way went again through a dark thicket in a hollow. It was just as bad as the other one I went through climbing up, but I didn't mind this one, because I was so glad I had seen those singular dances and could imitate them. I went down, creeping through the bushes, and a tall nettle stung me on my leg, and made me burn, but I didn't mind it, and I tingled with the boughs and the thorns, but I only laughed and sang. Then I got out of the thicket into a close valley, a little secret place like a dark passage that nobody ever knows of, because it was so narrow and deep and the woods were so thick round it. There is a steep bank with trees hanging over it, and there the ferns keep green all through the winter, when they are dead and brown upon the hill, and the ferns there have a sweet, rich smell like what oozes out of fir trees. There was a little stream of water running down this valley, so small that I could easily step across it. I drank the water with my hand, and it tasted like bright, yellow wine, and it sparkled and bubbled as it ran down over beautiful red and yellow and green stones, so that it seemed alive and all colours at once. I drank it, and I drank more with my hand, but I couldn't drink enough, so I lay down and bent my head and sucked the water up with my lips. It tasted much better, drinking it that way, and a ripple would come up to my mouth and give me a kiss, and I laughed, and drank again, and pretended there was a nymph, like the one in the old picture at home, who lived in the water and was kissing me. So I bent low down to the water, and put my lips softly to it, and whispered to the nymph that I would come again. I felt sure it could not be common water, I was so glad when I got up and went on; and I danced again and went up and up the valley, under hanging hills. And when I came to the top, the ground rose up in front of me, tall and steep as a wall, and there was nothing but the green wall and the sky. I thought of "for ever and for ever, world without end, Amen"; and I thought I must have really found the end of the world, because it was like the end of everything, as if there could be nothing at all beyond, except the kingdom of Voor, where the light goes when it is put out, and the water goes when the sun takes it away. I began to think of all the long, long way I had journeyed, how I had found a brook and followed it, and followed it on, and gone through bushes and thorny thickets, and dark woods full of creeping thorns. Then I had crept up a tunnel under trees, and climbed a thicket, and seen all the grey rocks, and sat in the middle of them when they turned round, and then I had gone on through the grey rocks and come down the hill through the stinging thicket and up the dark valley, all a long, long way. I wondered how I should get home again, if I could ever find the way, and if my home was there any more, or if it were turned and everybody in it into grey rocks, as in the "Arabian Nights." So I sat down on the grass and thought what I should do next. I was tired, and my feet were hot with walking, and as I looked about I saw there was a wonderful well just under the high, steep wall of grass. All the ground round it was covered with bright, green, dripping moss; there was every kind of moss there, moss like beautiful little ferns, and like palms and fir trees, and it was all green as jewellery, and drops of water hung on it like diamonds. And in the middle was the great well, deep and shining and beautiful, so clear that it looked as if I could touch the red sand at the bottom, but it was far below. I stood by it and looked in, as if I were looking in a glass. At the bottom of the well, in the middle of it, the red grains of sand were moving and stirring all the time, and I saw how the water bubbled up, but at the top it was quite smooth, and full and brimming. It was a great well, large like a bath, and with the shining, glittering green moss about it, it looked like a great white jewel, with green jewels all round. My feet were so hot and tired that I took off my boots and stockings, and let my feet down into the water, and the water was soft and cold, and when I got up I wasn't tired any more, and I felt I must go on, farther and farther, and see what was on the other side of the wall. I climbed up it very slowly, going sideways all the time, and when I got to the top and looked over, I was in the queerest country I had seen, stranger even than the hill of the grey rocks. It looked as if earth-children had been playing there with their spades, as it was all hills and hollows, and castles and walls made of earth and covered with grass. There were two mounds like big beehives, round and great and solemn, and then hollow basins, and then a steep mounting wall like the ones I saw once by the seaside where the big guns and the soldiers were. I nearly fell into one of the round hollows, it went away from under my feet so suddenly, and I ran fast down the side and stood at the bottom and looked up. It was strange and solemn to look up. There was nothing but the grey, heavy sky and the sides of the hollow; everything else had gone away, and the hollow was the whole world, and I thought that at night it must be full of ghosts and moving shadows and pale things when the moon shone down to the bottom at the dead of the night, and the wind wailed up above. It was so strange and solemn and lonely, like a hollow temple of dead heathen gods. It reminded me of a tale my nurse had told me when I was quite little; it was the same nurse that took me into the wood where I saw the beautiful white people. And I remembered how nurse had told me the story one winter night, when the wind was beating the trees against the wall, and crying and moaning in the nursery chimney. She said there was, somewhere or other, a hollow pit, just like the one I was standing in, everybody was afraid to go into it or near it, it was such a bad place. But once upon a time there was a poor girl who said she would go into the hollow pit, and everybody tried to stop her, but she would go. And she went down into the pit and came back laughing, and said there was nothing there at all, except green grass and red stones, and white stones and yellow flowers. And soon after people saw she had most beautiful emerald earrings, and they asked how she got them, as she and her mother were quite poor. But she laughed, and said her earrings were not made of emeralds at all, but only of green grass. Then, one day, she wore on her breast the reddest ruby that any one had ever seen, and it was as big as a hen's egg, and glowed and sparkled like a hot burning coal of fire. And they asked how she got it, as she and her mother were quite poor. But she laughed, and said it was not a ruby at all, but only a red stone. Then one day she wore round her neck the loveliest necklace that any one had ever seen, much finer than the queen's finest, and it was made of great bright diamonds, hundreds of them, and they shone like all the stars on a night in June. So they asked her how she got it, as she and her mother were quite poor. But she laughed, and said they were not diamonds at all, but only white stones. And one day she went to the Court, and she wore on her head a crown of pure angel-gold, so nurse said, and it shone like the sun, and it was much more splendid than the crown the king was wearing himself, and in her ears she wore the emeralds, and the big ruby was the brooch on her breast, and the great diamond necklace was sparkling on her neck. And the king and queen thought she was some great princess from a long way off, and got down from their thrones and went to meet her, but somebody told the king and queen who she was, and that she was quite poor. So the king asked why she wore a gold crown, and how she got it, as she and her mother were so poor. And she laughed, and said it wasn't a gold crown at all, but only some yellow flowers she had put in her hair. And the king thought it was very strange, and said she should stay at the Court, and they would see what would happen next. And she was so lovely that everybody said that her eyes were greener than the emeralds, that her lips were redder than the ruby, that her skin was whiter than the diamonds, and that her hair was brighter than the golden crown. So the king's son said he would marry her, and the king said he might. And the bishop married them, and there was a great supper, and after- wards the king's son went to his wife's room. But just when he had his hand on the door, he saw a tall, black man, with a dreadful face, standing in

front of the door, and a voice said--
  Venture not upon your life,
  This is mine own wedded wife.
  Then the king's son fell down on the ground in a fit. And they came and tried to get into the room, but they couldn't, and they hacked at the door with hatchets, but the wood had turned hard as iron, and at last everybody ran away, they were so frightened at the screaming and laughing and shrieking and crying that came out of the room. But next day they went in, and found there was nothing in the room but thick black smoke, because the black man had come and taken her away. And on the bed there were two knots of faded grass and a red stone, and some white stones, and some faded yellow flowers. I remembered this tale of nurse's while I was standing at the bottom of the deep hollow; it was so strange and solitary there, and I felt afraid. I could not see any stones or flowers, but I was afraid of bringing them away without knowing, and I thought I would do a charm that came into my head to keep the black man away. So I stood right in the very middle of the hollow, and I made sure that I had none of those things on me, and then I walked round the place, and touched my eyes, and my lips, and my hair in a peculiar manner, and whispered some queer words that nurse taught me to keep bad things away. Then I felt safe and climbed up out of the hollow, and went on through all those mounds and hollows and walls, till I came to the end, which was high above all the rest, and I could see that all the different shapes of the earth were arranged in patterns, something like the grey rocks, only the pattern was different. It was getting late, and the air was indistinct, but it looked from where I was standing something like two great figures of people lying on the grass. And I went on, and at last I found a certain wood, which is too secret to be described, and nobody knows of the passage into it, which I found out in a very curious manner, by seeing some little animal run into the wood through it. So I went after the animal by a very narrow dark way, under thorns and bushes, and it was almost dark when I came to a kind of open place in the middle. And there I saw the most wonderful sight I have ever seen, but it was only for a minute, as I ran away directly, and crept out of the wood by the passage I had come by, and ran and ran as fast as ever I could, because I was afraid, what I had seen was so wonderful and so strange and beautiful. But I wanted to get home and think of it, and I did not know what might not happen if I stayed by the wood. I was hot all over and trembling, and my heart was beating, and strange cries that I could not help came from me as I ran from the wood. I was glad that a great white moon came up from over a round hill and showed me the way, so I went back through the mounds and hollows and down the close valley, and up through the thicket over the place of the grey rocks, and

so at last I got home again. My father was busy in his study, and the servants had not told about my not coming home, though they were frightened, and wondered what they ought to do, so I told them I had lost my way, but I did not let them find out the real way I had been. I went to bed and lay awake all through the night, thinking of what I had seen. When I came out of the narrow way, and it looked all shining, though the air was dark, it seemed so certain, and all the way home I was quite sure that I had seen it, and I wanted to be alone in my room, and be glad over it all to myself, and shut my eyes and pretend it was there, and do all the things I would have done if I had not been so afraid. But when I shut my eyes the sight would not come, and I began to think about my adventures all over again, and I remembered how dusky and queer it was at the end, and I was afraid it must be all a mistake, because it seemed impossible it could happen. It seemed like one of nurse's tales, which I didn't really believe in, though I was frightened at the bottom of the hollow; and the stories she told me when I was little came back into my head, and I wondered whether it was really there what I thought I had seen, or whether any of her tales could have happened a long time ago. It was so queer; I lay awake there in my room at the back of the house, and the moon was shining on the other side towards the river, so the bright light did not fall upon the wall. And the house was quite still. I had heard my father come upstairs, and just after the clock struck twelve, and after the house was still and empty, as if there was nobody alive in it. And though it was all dark and indistinct in my room, a pale glimmering kind of light shone in through the white blind, and once I got up and looked out, and there was a great black shadow of the house covering the garden, looking like a prison where men are hanged; and then beyond it was all white; and the wood shone white with black gulfs between the trees. It was still and clear, and there were no clouds on the sky. I wanted to think of what I had seen but I couldn't, and I began to think of all the tales that nurse had told me so long ago that I thought I had forgotten, but they all came back, and mixed up with the thickets and the grey rocks and the hollows in the earth and the secret wood, till I hardly knew what was new and what was old, or whether it was not all dreaming. And then I remembered that hot summer afternoon, so long ago, when nurse left me by myself in the shade, and the white people came out of the water and out of the wood, and played, and danced, and sang, and I began to fancy that nurse told me about something like it before I saw them, only I couldn't recollect exactly what she told me. Then I wondered whether she had been the white lady, as I remembered she was just as white and beautiful, and had the same dark eyes and black hair; and sometimes she smiled and looked like the lady had looked, when she was telling me some of her stories, beginning with "Once on a time," or "In the time of the fairies." But I thought she couldn't be the lady, as she seemed to have gone a different way into the wood, and I didn't think the man who came after us could be the other, or I couldn't have seen that wonderful secret in the secret wood. I thought of the moon: but it was afterwards when I was in the middle of the wild land, where the earth was made into the shape of great figures, and it was all walls, and mysterious hollows, and smooth round mounds, that I saw the great white moon come up over a round hill. I was wondering about all these things, till at last I got quite frightened, because I was afraid something had happened to me, and I remembered nurse's tale of the poor girl who went into the hollow pit, and was carried away at last by the black man. I knew I had gone into a hollow pit too, and perhaps it was the same, and I had done something dreadful. So I did the charm over again, and touched my eyes and my lips and my hair in a peculiar manner, and said the old words from the fairy language, so that I might be sure I had not been carried away. I tried again to see the secret wood, and to creep up the passage and see what I had seen there, but somehow I couldn't, and I kept on thinking of nurse's stories. There was one I remembered about a young man who once upon a time went hunting, and all the day he and his hounds hunted everywhere, and they crossed the rivers and went into all the woods, and went round the marshes, but they couldn't find anything at all, and they hunted all day till the sun sank down and began to set behind the mountain. And the young man was angry because he couldn't find anything, and he was going to turn back, when just as the sun touched the mountain, he saw come out of a brake in front of him a beautiful white stag. And he cheered to his hounds, but they whined and would not follow, and he cheered to his horse, but it shivered and stood stock still, and the young man jumped off the horse and left the hounds and began to follow the white stag all alone. And soon it was quite dark, and the sky was black, without a single star shining in it, and the stag went away into the darkness. And though the man had brought his gun with him he never shot at the stag, because he wanted to catch it, and he was afraid he would lose it in the night. But he never lost it once, though the sky was so black and the air was so dark, and the stag went on and on till the young man didn't know a bit where he was. And they went through enormous woods where the air was full of whispers and a pale, dead light came out from the rotten trunks that were lying on the ground, and just as the man thought he had lost the stag, he would see it all white and shining in front of him, and he would run fast to catch it, but the stag always ran faster, so he did not catch it. And they went through the enormous woods, and they swam across rivers, and they waded through black marshes where the ground bubbled, and the air was full of will-o'-the-wisps, and the stag fled away down into rocky narrow valleys, where the air was like the smell of a vault, and the man went after it. And they went over the great mountains and the man heard the wind come down from the sky, and the stag went on and the man went after. At last the sun rose and the young man found he was in a country that he had never seen before; it was a beautiful valley with a bright stream running through it, and a great, big round hill in the middle. And the stag went down the valley, towards the hill, and it seemed to be getting tired and went slower and slower, and though the man was tired, too, he began to run faster, and he was sure he would catch the stag at last. But just as they got to the bottom of the hill, and the man stretched out his hand to catch the stag, it vanished into the earth, and the man began to cry; he was so sorry that he had lost it after all his long hunting. But as he was crying he saw there was a door in the hill, just in front of him, and he went in, and it was quite dark, but he went on, as he thought he would find the white stag. And all of a sudden it got light, and there was the sky, and the sun shining, and birds singing in the trees, and there was a beautiful fountain. And by the fountain a lovely lady was sitting, who was the queen of the fairies, and she told the man that she had changed herself into a stag to bring him there because she loved him so much. Then she brought out a great gold cup, covered with jewels, from her fairy palace, and she offered him wine in the cup to drink. And he drank, and the more he drank the more he longed to drink, because the wine was enchanted. So he kissed the lovely lady, and she became his wife, and he stayed all that day and all that night in the hill where she lived, and when he woke he found he was lying on the ground, close to where he had seen the stag first, and his horse was there and his hounds were there waiting, and he looked up, and the sun sank behind the mountain. And he went home and lived a long time, but he would never kiss any other lady because he had kissed the queen of the fairies, and he would never drink common wine any more, because he had drunk enchanted wine. And sometimes nurse told me tales that she had heard from her great-grandmother, who was very old, and lived in a cottage on the mountain all alone, and most of these tales were about a hill where people used to meet at night long ago, and they used to play all sorts of strange games and do queer things that nurse told me of, but I couldn't understand, and now, she said, everybody but her great-grandmother had forgotten all about it, and nobody knew where the hill was, not even her great-grandmother. But she told me one very strange story about the hill, and I trembled when I remembered it. She said that people always went there in summer, when it was very hot, and they had to dance a good deal. It would be all dark at first, and there were trees there, which made it much darker, and people would come, one by one, from all directions, by a secret path which nobody else knew, and two persons would keep the gate, and every one as they came up had to give a very curious sign, which nurse showed me as well as she could, but she said she couldn't show me properly. And all kinds of people would come; there would be gentle folks and village folks, and some old people and boys and girls, and quite small children, who sat and watched. And it would all be dark as they came in, except in one corner where some one was burning something that smelt strong and sweet, and made them laugh, and there one would see a glaring of coals, and the smoke mounting up red. So they would all come in, and when the last had come there was no door any more, so that no one else could get in, even if they knew there was anything beyond. And once a gentleman who was a stranger and had ridden a long way, lost his path at night, and his horse took him into the very middle of the wild country, where everything was up- side down, and there were dreadful marshes and great stones everywhere, and holes underfoot, and the trees looked like gibbet-posts, because they had great black arms that stretched out across the way. And this strange gentleman was very frightened, and his horse began to shiver all over, and at last it stopped and wouldn't go any farther, and the gentleman got down and tried to lead the horse, but it wouldn't move, and it was all covered with a sweat, like death. So the gentleman went on all alone, going farther and farther into the wild country, till at last he came to a dark place, where he heard shouting and singing and crying, like nothing he had ever heard before. It all sounded quite close to him, but he couldn't get in, and so he began to call, and while he was calling, something came behind him, and in a minute his mouth and arms and legs were all bound up, and he fell into a swoon. And when he came to himself, he was lying by the roadside, just where he had first lost his way, under a blasted oak with a black trunk, and his horse was tied beside him. So he rode on to the town and told the people there what had happened, and some of them were amazed; but others knew. So when once everybody had come, there was no door at all for anybody else to pass in by. And when they were all inside, round in a ring, touching each other, some one began to sing in the darkness, and some one else would make a noise like thunder with a thing they had on purpose, and on still nights people would hear the thundering noise far, far away beyond the wild land, and some of them, who thought they knew what it was, used to make a sign on their breasts when they woke up in their beds at dead of night and heard that terrible deep noise, like thunder on the mountains. And the noise and the singing would go on and on for a long time, and the people who were in a ring swayed a little to and fro; and the song was in an old, old language that nobody knows now, and the tune was queer. Nurse said her great-grandmother had known some one who remembered a little of it, when she was quite a little girl, and nurse tried to sing some of it to me, and it was so strange a tune that I turned all cold and my flesh crept as if I had put my hand on something dead. Sometimes it was a man that sang and some- times it was a woman, and sometimes the one who sang it did it so well that two or three of the people who were there fell to the ground shrieking and tearing with their hands. The singing went on, and the people in the ring kept swaying to and fro for a long time, and at last the moon would rise over a place they called the Tole Deol, and came up and showed them swinging and swaying from side to side, with the sweet thick smoke curling up from the burning coals, and floating in circles all around them. Then they had their supper. A boy and a girl brought it to them; the boy carried a great cup of wine, and the girl carried a cake of bread, and they passed the bread and the wine round and round, but they tasted quite different from common bread and common wine, and changed everybody that tasted them. Then they all rose up and danced, and secret things were brought out of some hiding place, and they played extraordinary games, and danced round and round and round in the moonlight, and sometimes people would suddenly disappear and never be heard of afterwards, and nobody knew what had happened to them. And they drank more of that curious wine, and they made images and worshipped them, and nurse showed me how the images were made one day when we were out for a walk, and we passed by a place where there was a lot of wet clay. So nurse asked me if I would like to know what those things were like that they made on the hill, and I said yes. Then she asked me if I would promise never to tell a living soul a word about it, and if I did I was to be thrown into the black pit with the dead people, and I said I wouldn't tell anybody, and she said the same thing again and again, and I promised. So she took my wooden spade and dug a big lump of clay and put it in my tin bucket, and told me to say if any one met us that I was going to make pies when I went home. Then we went on a little way till we came to a little brake growing right down into the road, and nurse stopped, and looked up the road and down it, and then peeped through the hedge into the field on the other side, and then she said, "Quick!" and we ran into the brake, and crept in and out among the bushes till we had gone a good way from the road. Then we sat down under a bush, and I wanted so much to know what nurse was going to make with the clay, but before she would begin she made me promise again not to say a word about it, and she went again and peeped through the bushes on every side, though the lane was so small and deep that hardly anybody ever went there. So we sat down, and nurse took the clay out of the bucket, and began to knead it with her hands, and do queer things with it, and turn it about. And she hid it under a big dock-leaf for a minute or two and then she brought it out again, and then she stood up and sat down, and walked round the clay in a peculiar manner, and all the time she was softly singing a sort of rhyme, and her face got very red. Then she sat down again, and took the clay in her hands and began to shape it into a doll, but not like the dolls I have at home, and she made the queerest doll I had ever seen, all out of the wet clay, and hid it under a bush to get dry and hard, and all the time she was making it she was singing these rhymes to herself, and her face got redder and redder. So we left the doll there, hidden away in the bushes where nobody would ever find it. And a few days later we went the same walk, and when we came to that narrow, dark part of the lane where the brake runs down to the bank, nurse made me promise all over again, and she looked about, just as she had done before, and we crept into the bushes till we got to the green place where the little clay man was hidden. I remember it all so well, though I was only eight, and it is eight years ago now as I am writing it down, but the sky was a deep violet blue, and in the middle of the brake where we were sitting there was a great elder tree covered with blossoms, and on the other side there was a clump of meadowsweet, and when I think of that day the smell of the meadowsweet and elder blossom seems to fill the room, and if I shut my eyes I can see the glaring blue sky, with little clouds very white floating across it, and nurse who went away long ago sitting opposite me and looking like the beautiful white lady in the wood. So we sat down and nurse took out the clay doll from the secret place where she had hidden it, and she said we must "pay our respects," and she would show me what to do, and I must watch her all the time. So she did all sorts of queer things with the little clay man, and I noticed she was all streaming with perspiration, though we had walked so slowly, and then she told me to "pay my respects," and I did everything she did because I liked her, and it was such an odd game. And she said that if one loved very much, the clay man was very good, if one did certain things with it, and if one hated very much, it was just as good, only one had to do different things, and we played with it a long time, and pretended all sorts of things. Nurse said her great-grandmother had told her all about these images, but what we did was no harm at all, only a game. But she told me a story about these images that frightened me very much, and that was what I remembered that night when I was lying awake in my room in the pale, empty darkness, thinking of what I had seen and the secret wood. Nurse said there was once a young lady of the high gentry, who lived in a great castle. And she was so beautiful that all the gentlemen wanted to marry her, because she was the loveliest lady that anybody had ever seen, and she was kind to everybody, and everybody thought she was very good. But though she was polite to all the gentlemen who wished to marry her, she put them off, and said she couldn't make up her mind, and she wasn't sure she wanted to marry anybody at all. And her father, who was a very great lord, was angry, though he was so fond of her, and he asked her why she wouldn't choose a bachelor out of all the handsome young men who came to the castle. But she only said she didn't love any of them very much, and she must wait, and if they pestered her, she said she would go and be a nun in a nunnery. So all the gentlemen said they would go away and wait for a year and a day, and when a year and a day were gone, they would come back again and ask her to say which one she would marry. So the day was appointed and they all went away; and the lady had promised that in a year and a day it would be her wedding day with one of them. But the truth was, that she was the queen of the people who danced on the hill on summer nights, and on the proper nights she would lock the door of her room, and she and her maid would steal out of the castle by a secret passage that only they knew of, and go away up to the hill in the wild land. And she knew more of the secret things than any one else, and more than any one knew before or after, because she would not tell anybody the most secret secrets. She knew how to do all the awful things, how to destroy young men, and how to put a curse on people, and other things that I could not understand. And her real name was the Lady Avelin, but the dancing people called her Cassap, which meant somebody very wise, in the old language. And she was whiter than any of them and taller, and her eyes shone in the dark like burning rubies; and she could sing songs that none of the others could sing, and when she sang they all fell down on their faces and worshipped her. And she could do what they called shib-show, which was a very wonderful enchantment. She would tell the great lord, her father, that she wanted to go into the woods to gather flowers, so he let her go, and she and her maid went into the woods where nobody came, and the maid would keep watch. wen the lady would lie down under the trees and begin to sing a particular song, and she stretched out her arms, and from every part of the wood great serpents would come, hissing and gliding in and out among the trees, and shooting out their forked tongues as they crawled up to the lady. And they all came to her, and twisted round her, round her body, and her arms, and her neck, till she was covered with writhing serpents, and there was only her head to be seen. And she whispered to them, and she sang to them, and they writhed round and round, faster and faster, till she told them to go. And they all went away directly, back to their holes, and on the lady's breast there would be a most curious, beautiful stone, shaped something like an egg, and coloured dark blue and yellow, and red, and green, marked like a serpent's scales. It was called a glame stone, and with it one could do all sorts of wonderful things, and nurse said her great-grandmother had seen a glame stone with her own eyes, and it was for all the world shiny and scaly like a snake. And the lady could do a lot of other things as well, but she was quite fixed that she would not be married. And there were a great many gentlemen who wanted to marry her, but there were five of them who were chief, and their names were Sir Simon, Sir John, Sir Oliver, Sir Richard, and Sir Rowland. All the others believed she spoke the truth, and that she would choose one of them to be her man when a year and a day was done; it was only Sir Simon, who was very crafty, who thought she was deceiving them all, and he vowed he would watch and try if he could find out anything. And though he was very wise he was very young, and he had a smooth, soft face like a girl's, and he pre- tended, as the rest did, that he would not come to the castle for a year and a day, and he said he was going away beyond the sea to foreign parts. But he really only went a very little way, and came back dressed like a servant girl, and so he got a place in the castle to wash the dishes. And he waited and watched, and he listened and said nothing, and he hid in dark places, and woke up at night and looked out, and he heard things and he saw things that he thought were very strange. And he was so sly that he told the girl that waited on the lady that he was really a young man, and that he had dressed up as a girl because he loved her so very much and wanted to be in the same house with her, and the girl was so pleased that she told him many things, and he was more than ever certain that the Lady Avelin was deceiving him and the others. And he was so clever, and told the servant so many lies, that one night he managed to hide in the Lady Avelin's room behind the curtains. And he stayed quite still and never moved, and at last the lady came. And she bent down under the bed, and raised up a stone, and there was a hollow place underneath, and out of it she took a waxen image, just like the clay one that I and nurse had made in the brake. And all the time her eyes were burning like rubies. And she took the little wax doll up in her arms and held it to her breast, and she whispered and she murmured, and she took it up and she laid it down again, and she held it high, and she held it low, and she laid it down again. And she said, "Happy is he that begat the bishop, that ordered the clerk, that married the man, that had the wife, that fashioned the hive, that harboured the bee, that gathered the wax that my own true love was made of." And she brought out of an aumbry a great golden bowl, and she brought out of a closet a great jar of wine, and she poured some of the wine into the bowl, and she laid her mannikin very gently in the wine, and washed it in the wine all over. Then she went to a cupboard and took a small round cake and laid it on the image's mouth, and then she bore it softly and covered it up. And Sir Simon, who was watching all the time, though he was terribly frightened, saw the lady bend down and stretch out her arms and whisper and sing, and then Sir Simon saw beside her a handsome young man, who kissed her on the lips. And they drank wine out of the golden bowl together, and they ate the cake together. But when the sun rose there was only the little wax doll, and the lady hid it again under the bed in the hollow place. So Sir Simon knew quite well what the lady was, and he waited and he watched, till the time she had said was nearly over, and in a week the year and a day would be done. And one night, when he was watching behind the curtains in her room, he saw her making more wax dolls. And she made five, and hid them away. And the next night she took one out, and held it up, and filled the golden bowl with water, and took the doll by the neck and held it under the water. Then she said--

Sir Dickon, Sir Dickon, your day is done,

You shall be drowned in the water wan.

And the next day news came to the castle that Sir Richard had been drowned at the ford. And at night she took another doll and tied a violet cord round its neck and hung it up on a nail. Then she said--

Sir Rowland, your life has ended its span,

High on a tree I see you hang.

And the next day news came to the castle that Sir Rowland had been hanged by robbers in the wood. And at night she took another doll, and drove her bodkin right into its heart. Then she said--

Sir Noll, Sir Noll, so cease your life,

Your heart piercd with the knife.

And the next day news came to the castle that Sir Oliver had fought in a tavern, and a stranger had stabbed him to the heart. And at night she took another doll, and held it to a fire of charcoal till it was melted. Then she said--

Sir John, return, and turn to clay,

In fire of fever you waste away.

And the next day news came to the castle that Sir John had died in a burning fever. So then Sir Simon went out of the castle and mounted his horse and rode away to the bishop and told him everything. And the bishop sent his men, and they took the Lady Avelin, and everything she had done was found out. So on the day after the year and a day, when she was to have been married, they carried her through the town in her smock, and they tied her to a great stake in the market-place, and burned her alive before the bishop with her wax image hung round her neck. And people said the wax man screamed in the burning of the flames. And I thought of this story again and again as I was lying awake in my bed, and I seemed to see the Lady Avelin in the market-place, with the yellow flames eating up her beautiful white body. And I thought of it so much that I seemed to get into the story myself, and I fancied I was the lady, and that they were coming to take me to be burnt with fire, with all the people in the town looking at me. And I wondered whether she cared, after all the strange things she had done, and whether it hurt very much to be burned at the stake. I tried again and again to forget nurse's stories, and to remember the secret I had seen that afternoon, and what was in the secret wood, but I could only see the dark and a glimmering in the dark, and then it went away, and I only saw myself running, and then a great moon came up white over a dark round hill. Then all the old stories came back again, and the queer rhymes that nurse used to sing to me; and there was one beginning "Halsy cumsy Helen musty," that she used to sing very softly when she wanted me to go to sleep. And I began to sing it to myself inside of my head, and I went to sleep.

The next morning I was very tired and sleepy, and could hardly do my lessons, and I was very glad when they were over and I had had my dinner, as I wanted to go out and be alone. It was a warm day, and I went to a nice turfy hill by the river, and sat down on my mother's old shawl that I had brought with me on purpose. The sky was grey, like the day before, but there was a kind of white gleam behind it, and from where I was sitting I could look down on the town, and b it was all still and quiet and white, like a picture. I remembered that it was on that hill that nurse taught me to play an old game called "Troy Town," in which one had to dance, and wind in and out on a pattern in the grass, and then when one had danced and turned long enough the other person asks you questions, and you can't help answering whether you want to or not, and whatever you are told to do you feel you have to do it. Nurse said there used to be a lot of games like that that some people knew of, and there was one by which people could be turned into anything you liked and an old man her great-grandmother had seen had known a girl who had been turned into a large snake. And there was another very ancient game of dancing and winding and turning, by which you could take a person out of himself and hide him away as long as you liked, and his body went walking about quite empty, without any sense in it. But I came to that hill because I wanted to think of what had happened the day before, and of the secret of the wood. From the place where I was sitting I could see beyond the town, into the opening I had found, where a little brook had led me into an unknown country. And I pretended I was following the brook over again, and I went all the way in my mind, and at last I found the wood, and crept into it under the bushes, and then in the dusk I saw something that made me feel as if I were filled with fire, as if I wanted to dance and sing and fly up into the air, because I was changed and wonderful. But what I saw was not changed at all, and had not grown old, and I wondered again and again how such things could happen, and whether nurse's stories were really true, because in the daytime in the open air everything seemed quite different from what it was at night, when I was frightened, and thought I was to be burned alive. I once told my father one of her little tales, which was about a ghost, and asked him if it was true, and he told me it was not true at all, and that only common, ignorant people believed in such rubbish. He was very angry with nurse for telling me the story, and scolded her, and after that I promised her I would never whisper a word of what she told me, and if I did I should be bitten by the great black snake that lived in the pool in the wood. And all alone on the hill I wondered what was true. I had seen something very amazing and very lovely, and I knew a story, and if I had really seen it, and not made it up out of the dark, and the black bough, and the bright shining that was mounting up to the sky from over the great round hill, but had really seen it in truth, then there were all kinds of wonderful and lovely and terrible things to think of, so I longed and trembled, and I burned and got cold. And I looked down on the town, so quiet and still, like a little white picture, and I thought over and over if it could be true. I was a long time before I could make up my mind to anything; there was such a strange fluttering at my heart that seemed to whisper to me all the time that I had not made it up out of my head, and yet it seemed quite impossible, and I knew my father and everybody would say it was dreadful rubbish. I never dreamed of telling him or anybody else a word about it, because I knew it would be of no use, and I should only get laughed at or scolded, so for a long time I was very quiet, and went about thinking and wondering; and at night I used to dream of amazing things, and sometimes I woke up in the early morning and held out my arms with a cry. And I was frightened, too, because there were dangers, and some awful thing would happen to me, unless I took great care, if the story were true. These old tales were always in my head, night and morning, and I went over them and told them to myself over and over again, and went for walks in the places where nurse had told them to me; and when I sat in the nursery by the fire in the evenings I used to fancy nurse was sitting in the other chair, and telling me some wonderful story in a low voice, for fear anybody should be listening. But she used to like best to tell me about things when we were right out in the country, far from the house, because she said she was telling me such secrets, and walls have ears. And if it was something more than ever secret, we had to hide in brakes or woods; and I used to think it was such fun creeping along a hedge, and going very softly, and then we would get behind the bushes or run into the wood all of a sudden, when we were sure that none was watching us; so we knew that we had our secrets quite all to ourselves, and nobody else at all knew anything about them. Now and then, when we had hidden ourselves as I have described, she used to show me all sorts of odd things. One day, I remember, we were in a hazel brake, over-looking the brook, and we were so snug and warm, as though it was April; the sun was quite hot, and the leaves were just coming out. Nurse said she would show me something funny that would make me laugh, and then she showed me, as she said, how one could turn a whole house upside down, without anybody being able to find out, and the pots and pans would jump about, and the china would be broken, and the chairs would tumble over of themselves. I tried it one day in the kitchen, and I found I could do it quite well, and a whole row of plates on the dresser fell off it, and cook's little work-table tilted up and turned right over "before her eyes," as she said, but she was so frightened and turned so white that I didn't do it again, as I liked her. And afterwards, in the hazel copse, when she had shown me how to make things tumble about, she showed me how to make rapping noises, and I learnt how to do that, too. Then she taught me rhymes to say on certain occasions, and peculiar marks to make on other occasions, and other things that her great-grandmother had taught her when she was a little girl herself. And these were all the things I was thinking about in those days after the strange walk when I thought I had seen a great secret, and I wished nurse were there for me to ask her about it, but she had gone away more than two years before, and nobody seemed to know what had become of her, or where she had gone. But I shall always remember those days if I live to be quite old, because all the time I felt so strange, wondering and doubting, and feeling quite sure at one time, and making up my mind, and then I would feel quite sure that such things couldn't happen really, and it began all over again. But I took great care not to do certain things that might be very dangerous. So I waited and wondered for a long time, and though I was not sure at all, I never dared to try to find out. But one day I became sure that all that nurse said was quite true, and I was all alone when I found it out. I trembled all over with joy and terror, and as fast as I could I ran into one of the old brakes where we used to go--it was the one by the lane, where nurse made the little clay man--and I ran into it, and I crept into it; and when I came to the place where the elder was, I covered up my face with my hands and lay down flat on the grass, and I stayed there for two hours without moving, whispering to myself delicious, terrible things, and saying some words over and over again. It was all true and wonderful and splendid, and when I remembered the story I knew and thought of what I had really seen, I got hot and I got cold, and the air seemed full of scent, and flowers, and singing. And first I wanted to make a little clay man, like the one nurse had made so long ago, and I had to invent plans and stratagems, and to look about, and to think of things beforehand, because nobody must dream of anything that I was doing or going to do, and I was too old to carry clay about in a tin bucket. At last I thought of a plan, and I brought the wet clay to the brake, and did everything that nurse had done, only I made a much finer image than the one she had made; and when it was finished I did everything that I could imagine and much more than she did, because it was the likeness of something far better. And a few days later, when I had done my lessons early, I went for the second time by the way of the little brook that had led me into a strange country. And I followed the brook, and went through the bushes, and beneath the low branches of trees, and up thorny thickets on the hill, and by dark woods full of creeping thorns, a long, long way. Then I crept through the dark tunnel where the brook had been and the ground was stony, till at last I came to the thicket that climbed up the hill, and though the leaves were coming out upon the trees, everything looked almost as black as it was on the first day that I went there. And the thicket was just the same, and I went up slowly till I came out on the big bare hill, and began to walk among the wonderful rocks. I saw the terrible voor again on everything, for though the sky was brighter, the ring of wild hills all around was still dark, and the hanging woods looked dark and dreadful, and the strange rocks were as grey as ever; and when I looked down on them from the great mound, sitting on the stone, I saw all their amazing circles and rounds within rounds, and I had to sit quite still and watch them as they began to turn about me, and each stone danced in its place, and they seemed to go round and round in a great whirl, as if one were in the middle of all the stars and heard them rushing through the air. So I went down among the rocks to dance with them and to sing extraordinary songs; and I went down through the other thicket, and drank from the bright stream in the close and secret valley, putting my lips down to the bubbling water; and then I went on till I came to the deep, brimming well among the glittering moss, and I sat down. I looked before me into the secret darkness of the valley, and behind me was the great high wall of grass, and all around me there were the hanging woods that made the valley such a secret place. I knew there was nobody here at all besides myself, and that no one could see me. So I took off my boots and stockings, and let my feet down into the water, saying the words that I knew. And it was not cold at all, as I expected, but warm and very pleasant, and when my feet were in it I felt as if they were in silk, or as if the nymph were kissing them. So when I had done, I said the other words and made the signs, and then I dried my feet with a towel I had brought on purpose, and put on my stockings and boots. Then I climbed up the steep wall, and went into the place where there are the hollows, and the two beautiful mounds, and the round ridges of land, and all the strange shapes. I did not go down into the hollow this time, but I turned at the end, and made out the figures quite plainly, as it was lighter, and I had remembered the story I had quite forgotten before, and in the story the two figures are called Adam and Eve, and only those who know the story understand what they mean. So I went on and on till I came to the secret wood which must not be described, and I crept into it by the way I had found. And when I had gone about halfway I stopped, and turned round, and got ready, and I bound the handkerchief tightly round my eyes, and made quite sure that I could not see at all, not a twig, nor the end of a leaf, nor the light of the sky, as it was an old red silk handkerchief with large yellow spots, that went round twice and covered my eyes, so that I could see nothing. Then I began to go on, step by step, very slowly. My heart beat faster and faster, and something rose in my throat that choked me and made me want to cry out, but I shut my lips, and went on. Boughs caught in my hair as I went, and great thorns tore me; but I went on to the end of the path. Then I stopped, and held out my arms and bowed, and I went round the first time, feeling with my hands, and there was nothing. I went round the second time, feeling with my hands, and there was nothing. Then I went round the third time, feeling with my hands, and the story was all true, and I wished that the years were gone by, and that I had not so long a time to wait before I was happy for ever and ever.

Nurse must have been a prophet like those we read of in the Bible. Everything that she said began to come true, and since then other things that she told me of have happened. That was how I came to know that her stories were true and that I had not made up the secret myself out of my own head. But there was another thing that happened that day. I went a second time to the secret place. It was at the deep brimming well, and when I was standing on the moss I bent over and looked in, and then I knew who the white lady was that I had seen come out of the water in the wood long ago when I was quite little. And I trembled all over, because that told me other things. Then I remembered how sometime after I had seen the white people in the wood, nurse asked me more about them, and I told her all over again, and she listened, and said nothing for a long, long time, and at last she said, "You will see her again." So I understood what had happened and what was to happen. And I understood about the nymphs; how I might meet them in all kinds of places, and they would always help me, and I must always look for them, and find them in all sorts of strange shapes and appearances. And without the nymphs I could never have found the secret, and without them none of the other things could happen. Nurse had told me all about them long ago, but she called them by another name, and I did not know what she meant, or what her tales of them were about, only that they were very queer. And there were two kinds, the bright and the dark, and both were very lovely and very wonderful, and some people saw only one kind, and some only the other, but some saw them both. But usually the dark appeared first, and the bright ones came afterwards, and there were extraordinary tales about them. It was a day or two after I had come home from the secret place that I first really knew the nymphs. Nurse had shown me how to call them, and I had tried, but I did not know what she meant, and so I thought it was all nonsense. But I made up my mind I would try again, so I went to the wood where the pool was, where I saw the white people, and I tried again. The dark nymph, Alanna, came, and she turned the pool of water into a pool of fire. . . .

EPILOGUE

"That's a very queer story," said Cotgrave, handing back the green book to the recluse, Ambrose. "I see the drift of a good deal, but there are many things that I do not grasp at all. On the last page, for example, what does she mean by 'nymphs'?"

"Well, I think there are references throughout the manuscript to certain 'processes' which have been handed down by tradition from age to age. Some of these processes are just beginning to come within the purview of science, which has arrived at them--or rather at the steps which lead to them--by quite different paths. I have interpreted the reference to 'nymphs' as a reference to one of these processes."

"And you believe that there are such things?"

"Oh, I think so. Yes, I believe I could give you convincing evidence on that point. I am afraid you have neglected the study of alchemy? It is a pity, for the symbolism, at all events, is very beautiful, and moreover if you were acquainted with certain books on the subject, I could recall to your mind phrases which might explain a good deal in the manuscript that you have been reading."

"Yes; but I want to know whether you seriously think that there is any foundation of fact beneath these fancies. Is it not all a department of poetry; a curious dream with which man has indulged himself?"

"I can only say that it is no doubt better for the great mass of people to dismiss it all as a dream. But if you ask my veritable belief--that goes quite the other way. No; I should not say belief, but rather knowledge. I may tell you that I have known cases in which men have stumbled quite by accident on certain of these 'processes,' and have been astonished by wholly unexpected results. In the cases I am thinking of there could have been no possibility of 'suggestion' or sub-conscious action of any kind. One might as well suppose a schoolboy 'suggesting' the existence of &Aelig;schylus to himself, while he plods mechanically through the declensions.

"But you have noticed the obscurity," Ambrose went on, "and in this particular case it must have been dictated by instinct, since the writer never thought that her manuscripts would fall into other hands. But the practice is universal, and for most excellent reasons. Powerful and sovereign medicines, which are, of necessity, virulent poisons also, are kept in a locked cabinet. The child may find the key by chance, and drink herself dead; but in most cases the search is educational, and the phials contain precious elixirs for him who has patiently fashioned the key for himself."

"You do not care to go into details?"

"No, frankly, I do not. No, you must remain unconvinced. But you saw how the manuscript illustrates the talk we had last week?"

"Is this girl still alive?"

"No. I was one of those who found her. I knew the father well; he was a lawyer, and had always left her very much to herself. He thought of nothing but deeds and leases, and the news came to him as an awful surprise. She was missing one morning; I suppose it was about a year after she had written what you have read. The servants were called, and they told things, and put the only natural interpretation on them--a perfectly erroneous one.

"They discovered that green book somewhere in her room, and I found her in the place that she described with so much dread, lying on the ground before the image."

"It was an image?"

"Yes, it was hidden by the thorns and the thick undergrowth that had surrounded it. It was a wild, lonely country; but you know what it was like by her description, though of course you will understand that the colours have been heightened. A child's imagination always makes the heights higher and the depths deeper than they really are; and she had, unfortunately for herself, something more than imagination. One might say, perhaps, that the picture in her mind which she succeeded in a measure in putting into words, was the scene as it would have appeared to an imaginative artist. But it is a strange, desolate land."

"And she was dead?"

"Yes. She had poisoned herself--in time. No; there was not a word to be said against her in the ordinary sense. You may recollect a story I told you the other night about a lady who saw her child's fingers crushed by a window?"

"And what was this statue?"

"Well, it was of Roman workmanship, of a stone that with the centuries had not blackened, but had become white and luminous. The thicket had grown up about it and concealed it, and in the Middle Ages the followers of a very old tradition had known how to use it for their own purposes. In fact it had been incorporated into the monstrous mythology of the Sabbath. You will have noted that those to whom a sight of that shining whiteness had been vouchsafed by chance, or rather, perhaps, by apparent chance, were required to blindfold themselves on their second approach. That is very significant."

"And is it there still?"

"I sent for tools, and we hammered it into dust and fragments."

"The persistence of tradition never surprises me," Ambrose went on after a pause. "I could name many an English parish where such traditions as that girl had listened to in her childhood are still existent in occult but unabated vigour. No, for me, it is the 'story' not the 'sequel,' which is strange and awful, for I have always believed that wonder is of the soul."

A Fragment of Life

CHAPTER 1

Edward Darnell awoke from a dream of an ancient wood, and of a clear well rising into grey film and vapour beneath a misty, glimmering heat; and as his eyes opened he saw the sunlight bright in the room, sparkling on the varnish of the new furniture. He turned and found his wife's place vacant, and with some confusion and wonder of the dream still lingering in his mind, he rose also, and began hurriedly to set about his dressing, for he had overslept a little, and the 'bus passed the corner at 9.15. He was a tall, thin man, dark-haired and dark-eyed, and in spite of the routine of the City, the counting of coupons, and all the mechanical drudgery that had lasted for ten years, there still remained about him the curious hint of a wild grace, as if he had been born a creature of the antique wood, and had seen the fountain rising from the green moss and the grey rocks.

The breakfast was laid in the room on the ground floor, the back room with the French windows looking on the garden, and before he sat down to his fried bacon he kissed his wife seriously and dutifully. She had brown hair and brown eyes, and though her lovely face was grave and quiet, one would have said that she might have awaited her husband under the old trees, and bathed in the pool hollowed out of the rocks.

They had a good deal to talk over while the coffee was poured out and the bacon eaten, and Darnell's egg brought in by the stupid, staring servant-girl of the dusty face. They had been married for a year, and they had got on excellently, rarely sitting silent for more than an hour, but for the past few weeks Aunt Marian's present had afforded a subject for conversation which seemed inexhaustible. Mrs. Darnell had been Miss Mary Reynolds, the daughter of an auctioneer and estate agent in Notting Hill, and Aunt Marian was her mother's sister, who was supposed rather to have lowered herself by marrying a coal merchant, in a small way, at Turnham Green. Marian had felt the family attitude a good deal, and the Reynoldses were sorry for many things that had been said, when the coal merchant saved money and took up land on building leases in the neighbourhood of Crouch End, greatly to his advantage, as it appeared. Nobody had thought that Nixon could ever do very much; but he and his wife had been living for years in a beautiful house at Barnet, with bow-windows, shrubs, and a paddock, and the two families saw but little of each other, for Mr. Reynolds was not very prosperous. Of course, Aunt Marian and her husband had been asked to Mary's wedding, but they had sent excuses with a nice little set of silver apostle spoons, and it was feared that nothing more was to be looked for. However, on Mary's birthday her aunt had written a most affectionate letter, enclosing a cheque for a hundred pounds from 'Robert' and herself, and ever since the receipt of the money the Darnells had discussed the question of its judicious disposal. Mrs. Darnell had wished to invest the whole sum in Government securities, but Mr. Darnell had pointed out that the rate of interest was absurdly low, and after a good deal of talk he had persuaded his wife to put ninety pounds of the money in a safe mine, which was paying five per cent. This was very well, but the remaining ten pounds, which Mrs. Darnell had insisted on reserving, gave rise to legends and discourses as interminable as the disputes of the schools.

At first Mr. Darnell had proposed that they should furnish the 'spare' room. There were four bedrooms in the house: their own room, the small one for the servant, and two others overlooking the garden, one of which had been used for storing boxes, ends of rope, and odd numbers of 'Quiet Days' and 'Sunday Evenings,' besides some worn suits belonging to Mr. Darnell which had been carefully wrapped up and laid by, as he scarcely knew what to do with them. The other room was frankly waste and vacant, and one Saturday afternoon, as he was coming home in the 'bus, and while he revolved that difficult question of the ten pounds, the unseemly emptiness of the spare room suddenly came into his mind, and he glowed with the idea that now, thanks to Aunt Marian, it could be furnished. He was busied with this delightful thought all the way home, but when he let himself in, he said nothing to his wife, since he felt that his idea must be matured. He told Mrs. Darnell that, having important business, he was obliged to go out again directly, but that he should be back without fail for tea at half-past six; and Mary, on her side, was not sorry to be alone, as she was a little behindhand with the household books. The fact was, that Darnell, full of the design of furnishing the spare bedroom, wished to consult his friend Wilson, who lived at Fulham, and had often given him judicious advice as to the laying out of money to the very best advantage. Wilson was connected with the Bordeaux wine trade, and Darnell's only anxiety was lest he should not be at home.

However, it was all right; Darnell took a tram along the Goldhawk Road, and walked the rest of the way, and was delighted to see Wilson in the front garden of his house, busy amongst his flower-beds.

'Haven't seen you for an age,' he said cheerily, when he heard Darnell's hand on the gate; 'come in. Oh, I forgot,' he added, as Darnell still fumbled with the handle, and vainly attempted to enter. 'Of course you can't get in; I haven't shown it you.'

It was a hot day in June, and Wilson appeared in a costume which he had put on in haste as soon as he arrived from the City. He wore a straw hat with a neat pugaree protecting the back of his neck, and his dress was a Norfolk jacket and knickers in heather mixture.

'See,' he said, as he let Darnell in; 'see the dodge. You don't turn the handle at all. First of all push hard, and then pull. It's a trick of my own, and I shall have it patented. You see, it keeps undesirable characters at a distance--such a great thing in the suburbs. I feel I can leave Mrs. Wilson alone now; and, formerly, you have no idea how she used to be pestered.'

'But how about visitors?' said Darnell. 'How do they get in?'

'Oh, we put them up to it. Besides,' he said vaguely, 'there is sure to be somebody looking out. Mrs. Wilson is nearly always at the window. She's out now; gone to call on some friends. The Bennetts' At Home day, I think it is. This is the first Saturday, isn't it? You know J. W. Bennett, don't you? Ah, he's in the House; doing very well, I believe. He put me on to a very good thing the other day.'

'But, I say,' said Wilson, as they turned and strolled towards the front door, 'what do you wear those black things for? You look hot. Look at me. Well, I've been gardening, you know, but I feel as cool as a cucumber. I dare say you don't know where to get these things? Very few men do. Where do you suppose I got 'em?'

'In the West End, I suppose,' said Darnell, wishing to be polite.

'Yes, that's what everybody says. And it is a good cut. Well, I'll tell you, but you needn't pass it on to everybody. I got the tip from Jameson--you know him, "Jim-Jams," in the China trade, 39 Eastbrook--and he said he didn't want everybody in the City to know about it. But just go to Jennings, in Old Wall, and mention my name, and you'll be all right. And what d'you think they cost?'

'I haven't a notion,' said Darnell, who had never bought such a suit in his life.

'Well, have a guess.'

Darnell regarded Wilson gravely.

The jacket hung about his body like a sack, the knickerbockers drooped lamentably over his calves, and in prominent positions the bloom of the heather seemed about to fade and disappear.

'Three pounds, I suppose, at least,' he said at length.

'Well, I asked Dench, in our place, the other day, and he guessed four ten, and his father's got something to do with a big business in Conduit Street. But I only gave thirty-five and six. To measure? Of course; look at the cut, man.'

Darnell was astonished at so low a price.

'And, by the way,' Wilson went on, pointing to his new brown boots, 'you know where to go for shoe-leather? Oh, I thought everybody was up to that! There's only one place. "Mr. Bill," in Gunning Street,--nine and six.'

They were walking round and round the garden, and Wilson pointed out the flowers in the beds and borders. There were hardly any blossoms, but everything was neatly arranged.

'Here are the tuberous-rooted Glasgownias,' he said, showing a rigid row of stunted plants; 'those are Squintaceæ; this is a new introduction, Moldavia Semperflorida Andersonii; and this is Prattsia.'

'When do they come out?' said Darnell.

'Most of them in the end of August or beginning of September,' said Wilson briefly. He was slightly annoyed with himself for having talked so much about his plants, since he saw that Darnell cared nothing for flowers; and, indeed, the visitor could hardly dissemble vague recollections that came to him; thoughts of an old, wild garden, full of odours, beneath grey walls, of the fragrance of the meadowsweet beside the brook.

'I wanted to consult you about some furniture,' Darnell said at last. 'You know we've got a spare room, and I'm thinking of putting a few things into it. I haven't exactly made up my mind, but I thought you might advise me.'

'Come into my den,' said Wilson. 'No; this way, by the back'; and he showed Darnell another ingenious arrangement at the side door whereby a violent high-toned bell was set pealing in the house if one did but touch the latch. Indeed, Wilson handled it so briskly that the bell rang a wild alarm, and the servant, who was trying on her mistress's things in the bedroom, jumped madly to the window and then danced a hysteric dance. There was plaster found on the drawing-room table on Sunday afternoon, and Wilson wrote a letter to the 'Fulham Chronicle,' ascribing the phenomenon 'to some disturbance of a seismic nature.'

For the moment he knew nothing of the great results of his contrivance, and solemnly led the way towards the back of the house. Here there was a patch of turf, beginning to look a little brown, with a background of shrubs. In the middle of the turf, a boy of nine or ten was standing all alone, with something of an air.

'The eldest,' said Wilson. 'Havelock. Well, Lockie, what are ye doing now? And where are your brother and sister?'

The boy was not at all shy. Indeed, he seemed eager to explain the course of events.

'I'm playing at being Gawd,' he said, with an engaging frankness. 'And I've sent Fergus and Janet to the bad place. That's in the shrubbery. And they're never to come out any more. And they're burning for ever and ever.'

'What d'you think of that?' said Wilson admiringly. 'Not bad for a youngster of nine, is it? They think a lot of him at the Sunday-school. But come into my den.'

The den was an apartment projecting from the back of the house. It had been designed as a back kitchen and washhouse, but Wilson had draped the 'copper' in art muslin and had boarded over the sink, so that it served as a workman's bench.

'Snug, isn't it?' he said, as he pushed forward one of the two wicker chairs. 'I think out things here, you know; it's quiet. And what about this furnishing? Do you want to do the thing on a grand scale?'

'Oh, not at all. Quite the reverse. In fact, I don't know whether the sum at our disposal will be sufficient. You see the spare room is ten feet by twelve, with a western exposure, and I thought if we could manage it, that it would seem more cheerful furnished. Besides, it's pleasant to be able to ask a visitor; our aunt, Mrs. Nixon, for example. But she is accustomed to have everything very nice.'

'And how much do you want to spend?'

'Well, I hardly think we should be justified in going much beyond ten pounds. That isn't enough, eh?'

Wilson got up and shut the door of the back kitchen impressively.

'Look here,' he said, 'I'm glad you came to me in the first place. Now you'll just tell me where you thought of going yourself.'

'Well, I had thought of the Hampstead Road,' said Darnell in a hesitating manner.

'I just thought you'd say that. But I'll ask you, what is the good of going to those expensive shops in the West End? You don't get a better article for your money. You're merely paying for fashion.'

'I've seen some nice things in Samuel's, though. They get a brilliant polish on their goods in those superior shops. We went there when we were married.'

'Exactly, and paid ten per cent more than you need have paid. It's throwing money away. And how much did you say you had to spend? Ten pounds. Well, I can tell you where to get a beautiful bedroom suite, in the very highest finish, for six pound ten. What d'you think of that? China included, mind you; and a square of carpet, brilliant colours, will only cost you fifteen and six. Look here, go any Saturday afternoon to Dick's, in the Seven Sisters Road, mention my name, and ask for Mr. Johnston. The suite's in ash, "Elizabethan" they call it. Six pound ten, including the china, with one of their "Orient" carpets, nine by nine, for fifteen and six. Dick's.'

Wilson spoke with some eloquence on the subject of furnishing. He pointed out that the times were changed, and that the old heavy style was quite out of date.

'You know,' he said, 'it isn't like it was in the old days, when people used to buy things to last hundreds of years. Why, just before the wife and I were married, an uncle of mine died up in the North and left me his furniture. I was thinking of furnishing at the time, and I thought the things might come in handy; but I assure you there wasn't a single article that I cared to give house-room to. All dingy, old mahogany; big bookcases and bureaus, and claw-legged chairs and tables. As I said to the wife (as she was soon afterwards), "We don't exactly want to set up a chamber of horrors, do we?" So I sold off the lot for what I could get. I must confess I like a cheerful room.'

Darnell said he had heard that artists liked the old-fashioned furniture.

'Oh, I dare say. The "unclean cult of the sunflower," eh? You saw that piece in the "Daily Post"? I hate all that rot myself. It isn't healthy, you know, and I don't believe the English people will stand it. But talking of curiosities, I've got something here that's worth a bit of money.'

He dived into some dusty receptacle in a corner of the room, and showed Darnell a small, worm-eaten Bible, wanting the first five chapters of Genesis and the last leaf of the Apocalypse. It bore the date of 1753.

'It's my belief that's worth a lot,' said Wilson. 'Look at the worm-holes. And you see it's "imperfect," as they call it. You've noticed that some of the most valuable books are "imperfect" at the sales?'

The interview came to an end soon after, and Darnell went home to his tea. He thought seriously of taking Wilson's advice, and after tea he told Mary of his idea and of what Wilson had said about Dick's.

Mary was a good deal taken by the plan when she had heard all the details. The prices struck her as very moderate. They were sitting one on each side of the grate (which was concealed by a pretty cardboard screen, painted with landscapes), and she rested her cheek on her hand, and her beautiful dark eyes seemed to dream and behold strange visions. In reality she was thinking of Darnell's plan.

'It would be very nice in some ways,' she said at last. 'But we must talk it over. What I am afraid of is that it will come to much more than ten pounds in the long run. There are so many things to be considered. There's the bed. It would look shabby if we got a common bed without brass mounts. Then the bedding, the mattress, and blankets, and sheets, and counterpane would all cost something.'

She dreamed again, calculating the cost of all the necessaries, and

Darnell stared anxiously; reckoning with her, and wondering what her conclusion would be. For a moment the delicate colouring of her face, the grace of her form, and the brown hair, drooping over her ears and clustering in little curls about her neck, seemed to hint at a language which he had not yet learned; but she spoke again.

'The bedding would come to a great deal, I am afraid. Even if Dick's are considerably cheaper than Boon's or Samuel's. And, my dear, we must have some ornaments on the mantelpiece. I saw some very nice vases at eleven-three the other day at Wilkin and Dodd's. We should want six at least, and there ought to be a centre-piece. You see how it mounts up.'

Darnell was silent. He saw that his wife was summing up against his scheme, and though he had set his heart on it, he could not resist her arguments.

'It would be nearer twelve pounds than ten,' she said.

'The floor would have to be stained round the carpet (nine by nine, you said?), and we should want a piece of linoleum to go under the washstand. And the walls would look very bare without any pictures.'

'I thought about the pictures,' said Darnell; and he spoke quite eagerly. He felt that here, at least, he was unassailable. 'You know there's the "Derby Day" and the "Railway Station," ready framed, standing in the corner of the box-room already. They're a bit old-fashioned, perhaps, but that doesn't matter in a bedroom. And couldn't we use some photographs? I saw a very neat frame in natural oak in the City, to hold half a dozen, for one and six. We might put in your father, and your brother James, and Aunt Marian, and your grandmother, in her widow's cap--and any of the others in the album. And then there's that old family picture in the hair-trunk--that might do over the mantelpiece.'

'You mean your great-grandfather in the gilt frame? But that's very old-fashioned, isn't it? He looks so queer in his wig. I don't think it would quite go with the room, somehow.'

Darnell thought a moment. The portrait was a 'kitcat' of a young gentleman, bravely dressed in the fashion of 1750, and he very faintly remembered some old tales that his father had told him about this ancestor--tales of the woods and fields, of the deep sunken lanes, and the forgotten country in the west.

'No,' he said, 'I suppose it is rather out of date. But I saw some very nice prints in the City, framed and quite cheap.'

'Yes, but everything counts. Well, we will talk it over, as you say. You know we must be careful.'

The servant came in with the supper, a tin of biscuits, a glass of milk for the mistress, and a modest pint of beer for the master, with a little cheese and butter. Afterwards Edward smoked two pipes of honeydew, and they went quietly to bed; Mary going first, and her husband following a quarter of an hour later, according to the ritual established from the first days of their marriage. Front and back doors were locked, the gas was turned off at the meter, and when Darnell got upstairs he found his wife already in bed, her face turned round on the pillow.

She spoke softly to him as he came into the room.

'It would be impossible to buy a presentable bed at anything under one pound eleven, and good sheets are dear, anywhere.'

He slipped off his clothes and slid gently into bed, putting out the candle on the table. The blinds were all evenly and duly drawn, but it was a June night, and beyond the walls, beyond that desolate world and wilderness of grey Shepherd's Bush, a great golden moon had floated up through magic films of cloud, above the hill, and the earth was filled with a wonderful light between red sunset lingering over the mountain and that marvellous glory that shone into the woods from the summit of the hill. Darnell seemed to see some reflection of that wizard brightness in the room; the pale walls and the white bed and his wife's face lying amidst brown hair upon the pillow were illuminated, and listening he could almost hear the corncrake in the fields, the fern-owl sounding his strange note from the quiet of the rugged place where the bracken grew, and, like the echo of a magic song, the melody of the nightingale that sang all night in the alder by the little brook. There was nothing that he could say, but he slowly stole his arm under his wife's neck, and played with the ringlets of brown hair. She never moved, she lay there gently breathing, looking up to the blank ceiling of the room with her beautiful eyes, thinking also, no doubt, thoughts that she could not utter, kissing her husband obediently when he asked her to do so, and he stammered and hesitated as he spoke.

They were nearly asleep, indeed Darnell was on the very eve of dreaming, when she said very softly--

'I am afraid, darling, that we could never afford it.' And he heard her words through the murmur of the water, dripping from the grey rock, and falling into the clear pool beneath.

Sunday morning was always an occasion of idleness. Indeed, they would never have got breakfast if Mrs. Darnell, who had the instincts of the housewife, had not awoke and seen the bright sunshine, and felt that the house was too still. She lay quiet for five minutes, while her husband slept beside her, and listened intently, waiting for the sound of Alice stirring down below. A golden tube of sunlight shone through some opening in the Venetian blinds, and it shone on the brown hair that lay about her head on the pillow, and she looked steadily into the room at the 'duchesse' toilet-table, the coloured ware of the washstand, and the two photogravures in oak frames, 'The Meeting' and 'The Parting,' that hung upon the wall. She was half dreaming as she listened for the servant's footsteps, and the faint shadow of a shade of a thought came over her, and she imagined dimly, for the quick moment of a dream, another world where rapture was wine, where one wandered in a deep and happy valley, and the moon was always rising red above the trees. She was thinking of Hampstead, which represented to her the vision of the world beyond the walls, and the thought of the heath led her away to Bank Holidays, and then to Alice. There was not a sound in the house; it might have been midnight for the stillness if the drawling cry of the Sunday paper had not suddenly echoed round the corner of Edna Road, and with it came the warning clank and shriek of the milkman with his pails.

Mrs. Darnell sat up, and wide awake, listened more intently. The girl was evidently fast asleep, and must be roused, or all the work of the day would be out of joint, and she remembered how Edward hated any fuss or discussion about household matters, more especially on a Sunday, after his long week's work in the City. She gave her husband an affectionate glance as he slept on, for she was very fond of him, and so she gently rose from the bed and went in her nightgown to call the maid.

The servant's room was small and stuffy, the night had been very hot, and Mrs. Darnell paused for a moment at the door, wondering whether the girl on the bed was really the dusty-faced servant who bustled day by day about the house, or even the strangely bedizened creature, dressed in purple, with a shiny face, who would appear on the Sunday afternoon, bringing in an early tea, because it was her 'evening out.' Alice's hair was black and her skin was pale, almost of the olive tinge, and she lay asleep, her head resting on one arm, reminding Mrs. Darnell of a queer print of a 'Tired Bacchante' that she had seen long ago in a shop window in Upper Street, Islington. And a cracked bell was ringing; that meant five minutes to eight, and nothing done.

She touched the girl gently on the shoulder, and only smiled when her eyes opened, and waking with a start, she got up in sudden confusion. Mrs. Darnell went back to her room and dressed slowly while her husband still slept, and it was only at the last moment, as she fastened her cherry-coloured bodice, that she roused him, telling him that the bacon would be overdone unless he hurried over his dressing.

Over the breakfast they discussed the question of the spare room all over again. Mrs. Darnell still admitted that the plan of furnishing it attracted her, but she could not see how it could be done for the ten pounds, and as they were prudent people they did not care to encroach on their savings. Edward was highly paid, having (with allowances for extra work in busy weeks) a hundred and forty pounds a year, and Mary had inherited from an old uncle, her godfather, three hundred pounds, which had been judiciously laid out in mortgage at 4-1/2 per cent.

Their total income, then, counting in Aunt Marian's present, was a hundred and fifty-eight pounds a year, and they were clear of debt, since Darnell had bought the furniture for the house out of money which he had saved for five or six years before. In the first few years of his life in the City his income had, of course, been smaller, and at first he had lived very freely, without a thought of laying by. The theatres and music-halls had attracted him, and scarcely a week passed without his going (in the pit) to one or the other; and he had occasionally bought photographs of actresses who pleased him. These he had solemnly burnt when he became engaged to Mary; he remembered the evening well; his heart had been so full of joy and wonder, and the landlady had complained bitterly of the mess in the grate when he came home from the City the next night. Still, the money was lost, as far as he could recollect, ten or twelve shillings; and it annoyed him all the more to reflect that if he had put it by, it would have gone far towards the purchase of an 'Orient' carpet in brilliant colours. Then there had been other expenses of his youth: he had purchased threepenny and even fourpenny cigars, the latter rarely, but the former frequently, sometimes singly, and sometimes in bundles of twelve for half-a-crown. Once a meerschaum pipe had haunted him for six weeks; the tobacconist had drawn it out of a drawer with some air of secrecy as he was buying a packet of 'Lone Star.' Here was another useless expense, these American-manufactured tobaccos; his 'Lone Star,' 'Long Judge,' 'Old Hank,' 'Sultry Clime,' and the rest of them cost from a shilling to one and six the two-ounce packet; whereas now he got excellent loose honeydew for threepence halfpenny an ounce. But the crafty tradesman, who had marked him down as a buyer of expensive fancy goods, nodded with his air of mystery, and, snapping open the case, displayed the meerschaum before the dazzled eyes of Darnell. The bowl was carved in the likeness of a female figure, showing the head and torso, and the mouthpiece was of the very best amber--only twelve and six, the man said, and the amber alone, he declared, was worth more than that. He explained that he felt some delicacy about showing the pipe to any but a regular customer, and was willing to take a little under cost price and 'cut the loss.' Darnell resisted for the time, but the pipe troubled him, and at last he bought it. He was pleased to show it to the younger men in the office for a while, but it never smoked very well, and he gave it away just before his marriage, as from the nature of the carving it would have been impossible to use it in his wife's presence. Once, while he was taking his holidays at Hastings, he had purchased a malacca cane--a useless thing that had cost seven shillings--and he reflected with sorrow on the innumerable evenings on which he had rejected his landlady's plain fried chop, and had gone out to flaner among the Italian restaurants in Upper Street, Islington (he lodged in

Holloway), pampering himself with expensive delicacies: cutlets and green peas, braised beef with tomato sauce, fillet steak and chipped potatoes, ending the banquet very often with a small wedge of Gruyère, which cost twopence. One night, after receiving a rise in his salary, he had actually drunk a quarter-flask of Chianti and had added the enormities of Benedictine, coffee, and cigarettes to an expenditure already disgraceful, and sixpence to the waiter made the bill amount to four shillings instead of the shilling that would have provided him with a wholesome and sufficient repast at home. Oh, there were many other items in this account of extravagance, and Darnell had often regretted his way of life, thinking that if he had been more careful, five or six pounds a year might have been added to their income.

And the question of the spare room brought back these regrets in an exaggerated degree. He persuaded himself that the extra five pounds would have given a sufficient margin for the outlay that he desired to make; though this was, no doubt, a mistake on his part. But he saw quite clearly that, under the present conditions, there must be no levies made on the very small sum of money that they had saved. The rent of the house was thirty-five, and rates and taxes added another ten pounds--nearly a quarter of their income for house-room. Mary kept down the housekeeping bills to the very best of her ability, but meat was always dear, and she suspected the maid of cutting surreptitious slices from the joint and eating them in her bedroom with bread and treacle in the dead of night, for the girl had disordered and eccentric appetites. Mr. Darnell thought no more of restaurants, cheap or dear; he took his lunch with him to the City, and joined his wife in the evening at high tea--chops, a bit of steak, or cold meat from the Sunday's dinner. Mrs. Darnell ate bread and jam and drank a little milk in the middle of the day; but, with the utmost economy, the effort to live within their means and to save for future contingencies was a very hard one. They had determined to do without change of air for at least three years, as the honeymoon at Walton-on-the-Naze had cost a good deal; and it was on this ground that they had, somewhat illogically, reserved the ten pounds, declaring that as they were not to have any holiday they would spend the money on something useful.

And it was this consideration of utility that was finally fatal to Darnell's scheme. They had calculated and recalculated the expense of the bed and bedding, the linoleum, and the ornaments, and by a great deal of exertion the total expenditure had been made to assume the shape of 'something very little over ten pounds,' when Mary said quite suddenly--

'But, after all, Edward, we don't really want to furnish the room at all. I mean it isn't necessary. And if we did so it might lead to no end of expense. People would hear of it and be sure to fish for invitations.

You know we have relatives in the country, and they would be almost certain, the Mallings, at any rate, to give hints.'

Darnell saw the force of the argument and gave way. But he was bitterly disappointed.

'It would have been very nice, wouldn't it?' he said with a sigh.

'Never mind, dear,' said Mary, who saw that he was a good deal cast down. 'We must think of some other plan that will be nice and useful too.'

She often spoke to him in that tone of a kind mother, though she was by three years the younger.

'And now,' she said, 'I must get ready for church. Are you coming?'

Darnell said that he thought not. He usually accompanied his wife to morning service, but that day he felt some bitterness in his heart, and preferred to lounge under the shade of the big mulberry tree that stood in the middle of their patch of garden--relic of the spacious lawns that had once lain smooth and green and sweet, where the dismal streets now swarmed in a hopeless labyrinth.

So Mary went quietly and alone to church. St. Paul's stood in a neighbouring street, and its Gothic design would have interested a curious inquirer into the history of a strange revival. Obviously, mechanically, there was nothing amiss. The style chosen was 'geometrical decorated,' and the tracery of the windows seemed correct. The nave, the aisles, the spacious chancel, were reasonably proportioned; and, to be quite serious, the only feature obviously wrong was the substitution of a low 'chancel wall' with iron gates for the rood screen with the loft and rood. But this, it might plausibly be contended, was merely an adaptation of the old idea to modern requirements, and it would have been quite difficult to explain why the whole building, from the mere mortar setting between the stones to the Gothic gas standards, was a mysterious and elaborate blasphemy. The canticles were sung to Joll in B flat, the chants were 'Anglican,' and the sermon was the gospel for the day, amplified and rendered into the more modern and graceful English of the preacher. And Mary came away.

After their dinner (an excellent piece of Australian mutton, bought in the 'World Wide' Stores, in Hammersmith), they sat for some time in the garden, partly sheltered by the big mulberry tree from the observation of their neighbours. Edward smoked his honeydew, and Mary looked at him with placid affection.

'You never tell me about the men in your office,' she said at length. 'Some of them are nice fellows, aren't they?'

'Oh, yes, they're very decent. I must bring some of them round, one of these days.'

He remembered with a pang that it would be necessary to provide whisky. One couldn't ask the guest to drink table beer at tenpence the gallon.

'Who are they, though?' said Mary. 'I think they might have given you a wedding present.'

'Well, I don't know. We never have gone in for that sort of thing. But they're very decent chaps. Well, there's Harvey; "Sauce" they call him behind his back. He's mad on bicycling. He went in last year for the Two Miles Amateur Record. He'd have made it, too, if he could have got into better training.

'Then there's James, a sporting man. You wouldn't care for him. I always think he smells of the stable.'

'How horrid!' said Mrs. Darnell, finding her husband a little frank, lowering her eyes as she spoke.

'Dickenson might amuse you,' Darnell went on. 'He's always got a joke. A terrible liar, though. When he tells a tale we never know how much to believe. He swore the other day he'd seen one of the governors buying cockles off a barrow near London Bridge, and Jones, who's just come, believed every word of it.'

Darnell laughed at the humorous recollection of the jest.

'And that wasn't a bad yarn about Salter's wife,' he went on. 'Salter is the manager, you know. Dickenson lives close by, in Notting Hill, and he said one morning that he had seen Mrs. Salter, in the Portobello Road, in red stockings, dancing to a piano organ.'

'He's a little coarse, isn't he?' said Mrs. Darnell. 'I don't see much fun in that.'

'Well, you know, amongst men it's different. You might like Wallis; he's a tremendous photographer. He often shows us photos he's taken of his children--one, a little girl of three, in her bath. I asked him how he thought she'd like it when she was twenty-three.'

Mrs. Darnell looked down and made no answer.

There was silence for some minutes while Darnell smoked his pipe. 'I say, Mary,' he said at length, 'what do you say to our taking a paying guest?'

'A paying guest! I never thought of it. Where should we put him?'

'Why, I was thinking of the spare room. The plan would obviate your objection, wouldn't it? Lots of men in the City take them, and make money of it too. I dare say it would add ten pounds a year to our income. Redgrave, the cashier, finds it worth his while to take a large house on purpose. They have a regular lawn for tennis and a billiard-room.'

Mary considered gravely, always with the dream in her eyes. 'I don't think we could manage it, Edward,' she said; 'it would be inconvenient in many ways.' She hesitated for a moment. 'And I don't think I should care to have a young man in the house. It is so very small, and our accommodation, as you know, is so limited.'

She blushed slightly, and Edward, a little disappointed as he was, looked at her with a singular longing, as if he were a scholar confronted with a doubtful hieroglyph, either wholly wonderful or altogether commonplace. Next door children were playing in the garden, playing shrilly, laughing, crying, quarrelling, racing to and fro. Suddenly a clear, pleasant voice sounded from an upper window.

'Enid! Charles! Come up to my room at once!'

There was an instant sudden hush. The children's voices died away.

'Mrs. Parker is supposed to keep her children in great order,' said Mary. 'Alice was telling me about it the other day. She had been talking to Mrs. Parker's servant. I listened to her without any remark, as I don't think it right to encourage servants' gossip; they always exaggerate everything. And I dare say children often require to be corrected.'

The children were struck silent as if some ghastly terror had seized them.

Darnell fancied that he heard a queer sort of cry from the house, but could not be quite sure. He turned to the other side, where an elderly, ordinary man with a grey moustache was strolling up and down on the further side of his garden. He caught Darnell's eye, and Mrs. Darnell looking towards him at the same moment, he very politely raised his tweed cap. Darnell was surprised to see his wife blushing fiercely.

'Sayce and I often go into the City by the same 'bus,' he said, 'and as it happens we've sat next to each other two or three times lately. I believe he's a traveller for a leather firm in Bermondsey. He struck me as a pleasant man. Haven't they got rather a good-looking servant?'

'Alice has spoken to me about her--and the Sayces,' said Mrs. Darnell. 'I understand that they are not very well thought of in the neighbourhood. But I must go in and see whether the tea is ready. Alice will be wanting to go out directly.'

Darnell looked after his wife as she walked quickly away. He only dimly understood, but he could see the charm of her figure, the delight of the brown curls clustering about her neck, and he again felt that sense of the scholar confronted by the hieroglyphic. He could not have expressed his emotion, but he wondered whether he would ever find the key, and something told him that before she could speak to him his own lips must be unclosed. She had gone into the house by the back kitchen door, leaving it open, and he heard her speaking to the girl about the water being 'really boiling.' He was amazed, almost indignant with himself; but the sound of the words came to his ears as strange, heart-piercing music, tones from another, wonderful sphere. And yet he was her husband, and they had been married nearly a year; and yet, whenever she spoke, he had to listen to the sense of what she said, constraining himself, lest he should believe she was a magic creature, knowing the secrets of immeasurable delight.

He looked out through the leaves of the mulberry tree. Mr. Sayce had disappeared from his view, but he saw the light-blue fume of the cigar that he was smoking floating slowly across the shadowed air. He was wondering at his wife's manner when Sayce's name was mentioned, puzzling his head as to what could be amiss in the household of a most respectable personage, when his wife appeared at the dining-room window and called him in to tea. She smiled as he looked up, and he rose hastily and walked in, wondering whether he were not a little 'queer,' so strange were the dim emotions and the dimmer impulses that rose within him.

Alice was all shining purple and strong scent, as she brought in the teapot and the jug of hot water. It seemed that a visit to the kitchen had inspired Mrs. Darnell in her turn with a novel plan for disposing of the famous ten pounds. The range had always been a trouble to her, and when sometimes she went into the kitchen, and found, as she said, the fire 'roaring halfway up the chimney,' it was in vain that she reproved the maid on the ground of extravagance and waste of coal. Alice was ready to admit the absurdity of making up such an enormous fire merely to bake (they called it 'roast') a bit of beef or mutton, and to boil the potatoes and the cabbage; but she was able to show Mrs. Darnell that the fault lay in the defective contrivance of the range, in an oven which 'would not get hot.' Even with a chop or a steak it was almost as bad; the heat seemed to escape up the chimney or into the room, and Mary had spoken several times to her husband on the shocking waste of coal, and the cheapest coal procurable was never less than eighteen shillings the ton. Mr. Darnell had written to the landlord, a builder, who had replied in an illiterate but offensive communication, maintaining the excellence of the stove and charging all the faults to the account of 'your good lady,' which really implied that the Darnells kept no servant, and that Mrs. Darnell did everything. The range, then, remained, a standing annoyance and expense. Every morning, Alice said, she had the greatest difficulty in getting the fire to light at all, and once lighted it 'seemed as if it fled right up the chimney.' Only a few nights before Mrs. Darnell had spoken seriously to her husband about it; she had got Alice to weigh the coals expended in cooking a cottage pie, the dish of the evening, and deducting what remained in the scuttle after the pie was done, it appeared that the wretched thing had consumed nearly twice the proper quantity of fuel.

'You remember what I said the other night about the range?' said Mrs. Darnell, as she poured out the tea and watered the leaves. She thought the introduction a good one, for though her husband was a most amiable man, she guessed that he had been just a little hurt by her decision against his furnishing scheme.

'The range?' said Darnell. He paused as he helped himself to the marmalade and considered for a moment. 'No, I don't recollect. What night was it?'

'Tuesday. Don't you remember? You had "overtime," and didn't get home till quite late.'

She paused for a moment, blushing slightly; and then began to recapitulate the misdeeds of the range, and the outrageous outlay of coal in the preparation of the cottage pie.

'Oh, I recollect now. That was the night I thought I heard the nightingale (people say there are nightingales in Bedford Park), and the sky was such a wonderful deep blue.'

He remembered how he had walked from Uxbridge Road Station, where the green 'bus stopped, and in spite of the fuming kilns under Acton, a delicate odour of the woods and summer fields was mysteriously in the air, and he had fancied that he smelt the red wild roses, drooping from the hedge. As he came to his gate he saw his wife standing in the doorway, with a light in her hand, and he threw his arms violently about her as she welcomed him, and whispered something in her ear, kissing her scented hair. He had felt quite abashed a moment afterwards, and he was afraid that he had frightened her by his nonsense; she seemed trembling and confused. And then she had told him how they had weighed the coal.

'Yes, I remember now,' he said. 'It is a great nuisance, isn't it? I hate to throw away money like that.'

'Well, what do you think? Suppose we bought a really good range with aunt's money? It would save us a lot, and I expect the things would taste much nicer.'

Darnell passed the marmalade, and confessed that the idea was brilliant.

'It's much better than mine, Mary,' he said quite frankly. 'I am so glad you thought of it. But we must talk it over; it doesn't do to buy in a hurry. There are so many makes.'

Each had seen ranges which looked miraculous inventions; he in the neighbourhood of the City; she in Oxford Street and Regent Street, on visits to the dentist. They discussed the matter at tea, and afterwards they discussed it walking round and round the garden, in the sweet cool of the evening.

'They say the "Newcastle" will burn anything, coke even,' said Mary.

'But the "Glow" got the gold medal at the Paris Exhibition,' said Edward.

'But what about the "Eutopia" Kitchener? Have you seen it at work in Oxford Street?' said Mary. 'They say their plan of ventilating the oven is quite unique.'

'I was in Fleet Street the other day,' answered Edward, 'and I was looking at the "Bliss" Patent Stoves. They burn less fuel than any in the market--so the makers declare.'

He put his arm gently round her waist. She did not repel him; she whispered quite softly--

'I think Mrs. Parker is at her window,' and he drew his arm back slowly.

'But we will talk it over,' he said. 'There is no hurry. I might call at some of the places near the City, and you might do the same thing in Oxford Street and Regent Street and Piccadilly, and we could compare notes.'

Mary was quite pleased with her husband's good temper. It was so nice of him not to find fault with her plan; 'He's so good to me,' she thought, and that was what she often said to her brother, who did not care much for Darnell. They sat down on the seat under the mulberry, close together, and she let Darnell take her hand, and as she felt his shy, hesitating fingers touch her in the shadow, she pressed them ever so softly, and as he fondled her hand, his breath was on her neck, and she heard his passionate, hesitating voice whisper, 'My dear, my dear,' as his lips touched her cheek. She trembled a little, and waited. Darnell kissed her gently on the cheek and drew away his hand, and when he spoke he was almost breathless.

'We had better go in now,' he said. 'There is a heavy dew, and you might catch cold.'

A warm, scented gale came to them from beyond the walls. He longed to ask her to stay out with him all night beneath the tree, that they might whisper to one another, that the scent of her hair might inebriate him, that he might feel her dress still brushing against his ankles. But he could not find the words, and it was absurd, and she was so gentle that she would do whatever he asked, however foolish it might be, just because he asked her. He was not worthy to kiss her lips; he bent down and kissed her silk bodice, and again he felt that she trembled, and he was ashamed, fearing that he had frightened her.

They went slowly into the house, side by side, and Darnell lit the gas in the drawing-room, where they always sat on Sunday evenings. Mrs. Darnell felt a little tired and lay down on the sofa, and Darnell took the arm-chair opposite. For a while they were silent, and then Darnell said suddenly--

'What's wrong with the Sayces? You seemed to think there was something a little strange about them. Their maid looks quite quiet.'

'Oh, I don't know that one ought to pay any attention to servants' gossip. They're not always very truthful.'

'It was Alice told you, wasn't it?'

'Yes. She was speaking to me the other day, when I was in the kitchen in the afternoon.'

'But what was it?'

'Oh, I'd rather not tell you, Edward. It's not pleasant. I scolded Alice for repeating it to me.'

Darnell got up and took a small, frail chair near the sofa.

'Tell me,' he said again, with an odd perversity. He did not really care to hear about the household next door, but he remembered how his wife's cheeks flushed in the afternoon, and now he was looking at her eyes.

'Oh, I really couldn't tell you, dear. I should feel ashamed.'

'But you're my wife.'

'Yes, but it doesn't make any difference. A woman doesn't like to talk about such things.'

Darnell bent his head down. His heart was beating; he put his ear to her mouth and said, 'Whisper.'

Mary drew his head down still lower with her gentle hand, and her cheeks burned as she whispered--

'Alice says that--upstairs--they have only--one room furnished. The maid told her--herself.'

With an unconscious gesture she pressed his head to her breast, and he in turn was bending her red lips to his own, when a violent jangle clamoured through the silent house. They sat up, and Mrs. Darnell went hurriedly to the door.

'That's Alice,' she said. 'She is always in in time. It has only just struck ten.'

Darnell shivered with annoyance. His lips, he knew, had almost been opened. Mary's pretty handkerchief, delicately scented from a little flagon that a school friend had given her, lay on the floor, and he picked it up, and kissed it, and hid it away.

The question of the range occupied them all through June and far into July. Mrs. Darnell took every opportunity of going to the West End and investigating the capacity of the latest makes, gravely viewing the new improvements and hearing what the shopmen had to say; while Darnell, as he said, 'kept his eyes open' about the City. They accumulated quite a literature of the subject, bringing away illustrated pamphlets, and in the evenings it was an amusement to look at the pictures. They viewed with reverence and interest the drawings of great ranges for hotels and public institutions, mighty contrivances furnished with a series of ovens each for a different use, with wonderful apparatus for grilling, with batteries of accessories which seemed to invest the cook almost with the dignity of a chief engineer. But when, in one of the lists, they encountered the images of little toy 'cottage' ranges, for four pounds, and even for three pounds ten, they grew scornful, on the strength of the eight or ten pound article which they meant to purchase--when the merits of the divers patents had been thoroughly thrashed out.

The 'Raven' was for a long time Mary's favourite. It promised the utmost economy with the highest efficiency, and many times they were on the point of giving the order. But the 'Glow' seemed equally seductive, and it was only £8. 5s. as compared with £9. 7s. 6d., and though the 'Raven' was supplied to the Royal Kitchen, the 'Glow' could show more fervent testimonials from continental potentates.

It seemed a debate without end, and it endured day after day till that morning, when Darnell woke from the dream of the ancient wood, of the fountains rising into grey vapour beneath the heat of the sun. As he dressed, an idea struck him, and he brought it as a shock to the hurried breakfast, disturbed by the thought of the City 'bus which passed the corner of the street at 9.15.

'I've got an improvement on your plan, Mary,' he said, with triumph. 'Look at that,' and he flung a little book on the table.

He laughed. 'It beats your notion all to fits. After all, the great expense is the coal. It's not the stove--at least that's not the real mischief. It's the coal is so dear. And here you are. Look at those oil stoves. They don't burn any coal, but the cheapest fuel in the world-- oil; and for two pounds ten you can get a range that will do everything you want.'

'Give me the book,' said Mary, 'and we will talk it over in the evening, when you come home. Must you be going?'

Darnell cast an anxious glance at the clock.

'Good-bye,' and they kissed each other seriously and dutifully, and Mary's eyes made Darnell think of those lonely water-pools, hidden in the shadow of the ancient woods.

So, day after day, he lived in the grey phantasmal world, akin to death, that has, somehow, with most of us, made good its claim to be called life. To Darnell the true life would have seemed madness, and when, now and again, the shadows and vague images reflected from its splendour fell across his path, he was afraid, and took refuge in what he would have called the sane 'reality' of common and usual incidents and interests. His absurdity was, perhaps, the more evident, inasmuch as 'reality' for him was a matter of kitchen ranges, of saving a few shillings; but in truth the folly would have been greater if it had been concerned with racing stables, steam yachts, and the spending of many thousand pounds.

But so went forth Darnell, day by day, strangely mistaking death for life, madness for sanity, and purposeless and wandering phantoms for true beings. He was sincerely of opinion that he was a City clerk, living in Shepherd's Bush--having forgotten the mysteries and the far-shining glories of the kingdom which was his by legitimate inheritance.

CHAPTER 2

All day long a fierce and heavy heat had brooded over the City, and as Darnell neared home he saw the mist lying on all the damp lowlands, wreathed in coils about Bedford Park to the south, and mounting to the west, so that the tower of Acton Church loomed out of a grey lake. The grass in the squares and on the lawns which he overlooked as the 'bus lumbered wearily along was burnt to the colour of dust. Shepherd's Bush Green was a wretched desert, trampled brown, bordered with monotonous poplars, whose leaves hung motionless in air that was still, hot smoke. The foot passengers struggled wearily along the pavements, and the reek of the summer's end mingled with the breath of the brickfields made Darnell gasp, as if he were inhaling the poison of some foul sick-room.

He made but a slight inroad into the cold mutton that adorned the tea-table, and confessed that he felt rather 'done up' by the weather and the day's work.

'I have had a trying day, too,' said Mary. 'Alice has been very queer and troublesome all day, and I have had to speak to her quite seriously. You know I think her Sunday evenings out have a rather unsettling influence on the girl. But what is one to do?'

'Has she got a young man?'

'Of course: a grocer's assistant from the Goldhawk Road--Wilkin's, you know. I tried them when we settled here, but they were not very satisfactory.'

'What do they do with themselves all the evening? They have from five to ten, haven't they?'

'Yes; five, or sometimes half-past, when the water won't boil. Well, I believe they go for walks usually. Once or twice he has taken her to the City Temple, and the Sunday before last they walked up and down Oxford Street, and then sat in the Park. But it seems that last Sunday they went to tea with his mother at Putney. I should like to tell the old woman what I really think of her.'

'Why? What happened? Was she nasty to the girl?'

'No; that's just it. Before this, she has been very unpleasant on several occasions. When the young man first took Alice to see her--that was in March--the girl came away crying; she told me so herself. Indeed, she said she never wanted to see old Mrs. Murry again; and I told Alice that, if she had not exaggerated things, I could hardly blame her for feeling like that.'

'Why? What did she cry for?'

'Well, it seems that the old lady--she lives in quite a small cottage in some Putney back street--was so stately that she would hardly speak. She had borrowed a little girl from some neighbour's family, and had managed to dress her up to imitate a servant, and Alice said nothing could be sillier than to see that mite opening the door, with her black dress and her white cap and apron, and she hardly able to turn the handle, as Alice said. George (that's the young man's name) had told Alice that it was a little bit of a house; but he said the kitchen was comfortable, though very plain and old-fashioned. But, instead of going straight to the back, and sitting by a big fire on the old settle that they had brought up from the country, that child asked for their names (did you ever hear such nonsense?) and showed them into a little poky parlour, where old Mrs. Murry was sitting "like a duchess," by a fireplace full of coloured paper, and the room as cold as ice. And she was so grand that she would hardly speak to Alice.'

'That must have been very unpleasant.'

'Oh, the poor girl had a dreadful time. She began with: "Very pleased to make your acquaintance, Miss Dill. I know so very few persons in service." Alice imitates her mincing way of talking, but I can't do it. And then she went on to talk about her family, how they had farmed their own land for five hundred years--such stuff! George had told Alice all about it: they had had an old cottage with a good strip of garden and two fields somewhere in Essex, and that old woman talked almost as if they had been country gentry, and boasted about the Rector, Dr. Somebody, coming to see them so often, and of Squire Somebody Else always looking them up, as if they didn't visit them out of kindness. Alice told me it was as much as she could do to keep from laughing in Mrs. Murry's face, her young man having told her all about the place, and how small it was, and how the Squire had been so kind about buying it when old Murry died and George was a little boy, and his mother not able to keep things going. However, that silly old woman "laid it on thick," as you say, and the young man got more and more uncomfortable, especially when she went on to speak about marrying in one's own class, and how unhappy she had known young men to be who had married beneath them, giving some very pointed looks at Alice as she talked. And then such an amusing thing happened: Alice had noticed George looking about him in a puzzled sort of way, as if he couldn't make out something or other, and at last he burst out and asked his mother if she had been buying up the neighbours' ornaments, as he remembered the two green cut-glass vases on the mantelpiece at Mrs. Ellis's, and the wax flowers at Miss Turvey's. He was going on, but his mother scowled at him, and upset some books, which he had to pick up; but Alice quite understood she had been borrowing things from her neighbours, just as she had borrowed the little girl, so as to look grander. And then they had tea--water bewitched, Alice calls it--and very thin bread and butter, and rubbishy foreign pastry from the Swiss shop in the High Street--all sour froth and rancid fat, Alice declares. And then Mrs. Murry began boasting again about her family, and snubbing Alice and talking at her, till the girl came away quite furious, and very unhappy, too. I don't wonder at it, do you?'

'It doesn't sound very enjoyable, certainly,' said Darnell, looking dreamily at his wife. He had not been attending very carefully to the subject-matter of her story, but he loved to hear a voice that was incantation in his ears, tones that summoned before him the vision of a magic world.

'And has the young man's mother always been like this?' he said after a long pause, desiring that the music should continue.

'Always, till quite lately, till last Sunday in fact. Of course Alice spoke to George Murry at once, and said, like a sensible girl, that she didn't think it ever answered for a married couple to live with the man's mother, "especially," she went on, "as I can see your mother hasn't taken much of a fancy to me." He told her, in the usual style, it was only his mother's way, that she didn't really mean anything, and so on; but Alice kept away for a long time, and rather hinted, I think, that it might come to having to choose between her and his mother. And so affairs went on all through the spring and summer, and then, just before the August Bank Holiday, George spoke to Alice again about it, and told her how sorry the thought of any unpleasantness made him, and how he wanted his mother and her to get on with each other, and how she was only a bit old-fashioned and queer in her ways, and had spoken very nicely to him about her when there was nobody by. So the long and the short of it was that Alice said she might come with them on the Monday, when they had settled to go to Hampton Court--the girl was always talking about Hampton Court, and wanting to see it. You remember what a beautiful day it was, don't you?'

'Let me see,' said Darnell dreamily. 'Oh yes, of course--I sat out under the mulberry tree all day, and we had our meals there: it was quite a picnic. The caterpillars were a nuisance, but I enjoyed the day very much.' His ears were charmed, ravished with the grave, supernal melody, as of antique song, rather of the first made world in which all speech was descant, and all words were sacraments of might, speaking not to the mind but to the soul. He lay back in his chair, and said--

'Well, what happened to them?'

'My dear, would you believe it; but that wretched old woman behaved worse than ever. They met as had been arranged, at Kew Bridge, and got places, with a good deal of difficulty, in one of those char-à-banc things, and Alice thought she was going to enjoy herself tremendously. Nothing of the kind. They had hardly said "Good morning," when old Mrs. Murry began to talk about Kew Gardens, and how beautiful it must be there, and how much more convenient it was than Hampton, and no expense at all; just the trouble of walking over the bridge. Then she went on to say, as they were waiting for the char-à-banc, that she had always heard there was nothing to see at Hampton, except a lot of nasty, grimy old pictures, and some of them not fit for any decent woman, let alone girl, to look at, and she wondered why the Queen allowed such things to be shown, putting all kinds of notions into girls' heads that were light enough already; and as she said that she looked at Alice so nastily--horrid old thing--that, as she told me afterwards, Alice would have slapped her face if she hadn't been an elderly woman, and George's mother. Then she talked about Kew again, saying how wonderful the hot-houses were, with palms and all sorts of wonderful things, and a lily as big as a parlour table, and the view over the river. George was very good, Alice told me. He was quite taken aback at first, as the old woman had promised faithfully to be as nice as ever she could be; but then he said, gently but firmly, "Well, mother, we must go to Kew some other day, as Alice has set her heart on Hampton for to-day, and I want to see it myself!" All Mrs. Murry did was to snort, and look at the girl like vinegar, and just then the char-à-banc came up, and they had to scramble for their seats. Mrs. Murry grumbled to herself in an indistinct sort of voice all the way to Hampton Court. Alice couldn't very well make out what she said, but now and then she seemed to hear bits of sentences, like: Pity to grow old, if sons grow bold; and Honour thy father and mother; and Lie on the shelf, said the housewife to the old shoe, and the wicked son to his mother; and I gave you milk and you give me the go-by. Alice thought they must be proverbs (except the Commandment, of course), as George was always saying how old-fashioned his mother is; but she says there were so many of them, and all pointed at her and George, that she thinks now Mrs. Murry must have made them up as they drove along. She says it would be just like her to do it, being old-fashioned, and ill-natured too, and fuller of talk than a butcher on Saturday night.

Well, they got to Hampton at last, and Alice thought the place would please her, perhaps, and they might have some enjoyment. But she did nothing but grumble, and out loud too, so that people looked at them, and a woman said, so that they could hear, "Ah well, they'll be old themselves some day," which made Alice very angry, for, as she said, they weren't doing anything. When they showed her the chestnut avenue in Bushey Park, she said it was so long and straight that it made her quite dull to look at it, and she thought the deer (you know how pretty they are, really) looked thin and miserable, as if they would be all the better for a good feed of hog-wash, with plenty of meal in it. She said she knew they weren't happy by the look in their eyes, which seemed to tell her that their keepers beat them. It was the same with everything; she said she remembered market-gardens in Hammersmith and Gunnersbury that had a better show of flowers, and when they took her to the place where the water is, under the trees, she burst out with its being rather hard to tramp her off her legs to show her a common canal, with not so much as a barge on it to liven it up a bit. She went on like that the whole day, and Alice told me she was only too thankful to get home and get rid of her. Wasn't it wretched for the girl?'

'It must have been, indeed. But what happened last Sunday?'

'That's the most extraordinary thing of all. I noticed that Alice was rather queer in her manner this morning; she was a longer time washing up the breakfast things, and she answered me quite sharply when I called to her to ask when she would be ready to help me with the wash; and when I went into the kitchen to see about something, I noticed that she was going about her work in a sulky sort of way. So I asked her what was the matter, and then it all came out. I could scarcely believe my own ears when she mumbled out something about Mrs. Murry thinking she could do very much better for herself; but I asked her one question after another till I had it all out of her. It just shows one how foolish and empty-headed these girls are. I told her she was no better than a weather-cock. If you will believe me, that horrid old woman was quite another person when Alice went to see her the other night. Why, I can't think, but so she was. She told the girl how pretty she was; what a neat figure she had; how well she walked; and how she'd known many a girl not half so clever or well-looking earning her twenty-five or thirty pounds a year, and with good families. She seems to have gone into all sorts of details, and made elaborate calculations as to what she would be able to save, "with decent folks, who don't screw, and pinch, and lock up everything in the house," and then she went off into a lot of hypocritical nonsense about how fond she was of Alice, and how she could go to her grave in peace, knowing how happy her dear George would be with such a good wife, and about her savings from good wages helping to set up a little home, ending up with "And, if you take an old woman's advice, deary, it won't be long before you hear the marriage bells."'

'I see,' said Darnell; 'and the upshot of it all is, I suppose, that the girl is thoroughly dissatisfied?'

'Yes, she is so young and silly. I talked to her, and reminded her of how nasty old Mrs. Murry had been, and told her that she might change her place and change for the worse. I think I have persuaded her to think it over quietly, at all events. Do you know what it is, Edward? I have an idea. I believe that wicked old woman is trying to get Alice to leave us, that she may tell her son how changeable she is; and I suppose she would make up some of her stupid old proverbs: "A changeable wife, a troublesome life," or some nonsense of the kind. Horrid old thing!'

'Well, well,' said Darnell, 'I hope she won't go, for your sake. It would be such a bother for you, hunting for a fresh servant.'

He refilled his pipe and smoked placidly, refreshed somewhat after the emptiness and the burden of the day. The French window was wide open, and now at last there came a breath of quickening air, distilled by the night from such trees as still wore green in that arid valley. The song to which Darnell had listened in rapture, and now the breeze, which even in that dry, grim suburb still bore the word of the woodland, had summoned the dream to his eyes, and he meditated over matters that his lips could not express.

'She must, indeed, be a villainous old woman,' he said at length.

'Old Mrs. Murry? Of course she is; the mischievous old thing! Trying to take the girl from a comfortable place where she is happy.'

'Yes; and not to like Hampton Court! That shows how bad she must be, more than anything.'

'It is beautiful, isn't it?'

'I shall never forget the first time I saw it. It was soon after I went into the City; the first year. I had my holidays in July, and I was getting such a small salary that I couldn't think of going away to the seaside, or anything like that. I remember one of the other men wanted me to come with him on a walking tour in Kent. I should have liked that, but the money wouldn't run to it. And do you know what I did? I lived in Great College Street then, and the first day I was off, I stayed in bed till past dinner-time, and lounged about in an arm-chair with a pipe all the afternoon. I had got a new kind of tobacco--one and four for the two-ounce packet--much dearer than I could afford to smoke, and I was enjoying it immensely. It was awfully hot, and when I shut the window and drew down the red blind it grew hotter; at five o'clock the room was like an oven. But I was so pleased at not having to go into the City, that I didn't mind anything, and now and again I read bits from a queer old book that had belonged to my poor dad. I couldn't make out what a lot of it meant, but it fitted in somehow, and I read and smoked till teatime. Then I went out for a walk, thinking I should be better for a little fresh air before I went to bed; and I went wandering away, not much noticing where I was going, turning here and there as the fancy took me. I must have gone miles and miles, and a good many of them round and round, as they say they do in Australia if they lose their way in the bush; and I am sure I couldn't have gone exactly the same way all over again for any money. Anyhow, I was still in the streets when the twilight came on, and the lamp-lighters were trotting round from one lamp to another. It was a wonderful night: I wish you had been there, my dear.'

'I was quite a little girl then.'

'Yes, I suppose you were. Well, it was a wonderful night. I remember, I was walking in a little street of little grey houses all alike, with stucco copings and stucco door-posts; there were brass plates on a lot of the doors, and one had "Maker of Shell Boxes" on it, and I was quite pleased, as I had often wondered where those boxes and things that you buy at the seaside came from. A few children were playing about in the road with some rubbish or other, and men were singing in a small public-house at the corner, and I happened to look up, and I noticed what a wonderful colour the sky had turned. I have seen it since, but I don't think it has ever been quite what it was that night, a dark blue, glowing like a violet, just as they say the sky looks in foreign countries. I don't know why, but the sky or something made me feel quite queer; everything seemed changed in a way I couldn't understand. I remember, I told an old gentleman I knew then--a friend of my poor father's, he's been dead for five years, if not more--about how I felt, and he looked at me and said something about fairyland; I don't know what he meant, and I dare say I didn't explain myself properly. But, do you know, for a moment or two I felt as if that little back street was beautiful, and the noise of the children and the men in the public-house seemed to fit in with the sky and become part of it. You know that old saying about "treading on air" when one is glad! Well, I really felt like that as I walked, not exactly like air, you know, but as if the pavement was velvet or some very soft carpet. And then--I suppose it was all my fancy--the air seemed to smell sweet, like the incense in Catholic churches, and my breath came queer and catchy, as it does when one gets very excited about anything. I felt altogether stranger than I've ever felt before or since.'

Darnell stopped suddenly and looked up at his wife. She was watching him with parted lips, with eager, wondering eyes.

'I hope I'm not tiring you, dear, with all this story about nothing. You have had a worrying day with that stupid girl; hadn't you better go to bed?'

'Oh, no, please, Edward. I'm not a bit tired now. I love to hear you talk like that. Please go on.'

'Well, after I had walked a bit further, that queer sort of feeling seemed to fade away. I said a bit further, and I really thought I had been walking about five minutes, but I had looked at my watch just before I got into that little street, and when I looked at it again it was eleven o'clock. I must have done about eight miles. I could scarcely believe my own eyes, and I thought my watch must have gone mad; but I found out afterwards it was perfectly right. I couldn't make it out, and I can't now; I assure you the time passed as if I walked up one side of Edna Road and down the other. But there I was, right in the open country, with a cool wind blowing on me from a wood, and the air full of soft rustling sounds, and notes of birds from the bushes, and the singing noise of a little brook that ran under the road. I was standing on the bridge when I took out my watch and struck a wax light to see the time; and it came upon me suddenly what a strange evening it had been. It was all so different, you see, to what I had been doing all my life, particularly for the year before, and it almost seemed as if I couldn't be the man who had been going into the City every day in the morning and coming back from it every evening after writing a lot of uninteresting letters. It was like being pitched all of a sudden from one world into another. Well, I found my way back somehow or other, and as I went along I made up my mind how I'd spend my holiday. I said to myself, "I'll have a walking tour as well as Ferrars, only mine is to be a tour of London and its environs," and I had got it all settled when I let myself into the house about four o'clock in the morning, and the sun was shining, and the street almost as still as the wood at midnight!'

'I think that was a capital idea of yours. Did you have your tour? Did you buy a map of London?'

'I had the tour all right. I didn't buy a map; that would have spoilt it, somehow; to see everything plotted out, and named, and measured. What I wanted was to feel that I was going where nobody had been before. That's nonsense, isn't it? as if there could be any such places in London, or England either, for the matter of that.'

'I know what you mean; you wanted to feel as if you were going on a sort of voyage of discovery. Isn't that it?'

'Exactly, that's what I was trying to tell you. Besides, I didn't want to buy a map. I made a map.'

'How do you mean? Did you make a map out of your head?'

'I'll tell you about it afterwards. But do you really want to hear about my grand tour?'

'Of course I do; it must have been delightful. I call it a most original idea.'

'Well, I was quite full of it, and what you said just now about a voyage of discovery reminds me of how I felt then. When I was a boy I was awfully fond of reading of great travellers--I suppose all boys are--and of sailors who were driven out of their course and found themselves in latitudes where no ship had ever sailed before, and of people who discovered wonderful cities in strange countries; and all the second day of my holidays I was feeling just as I used to when I read these books. I didn't get up till pretty late. I was tired to death after all those miles I had walked; but when I had finished my breakfast and filled my pipe, I had a grand time of it. It was such nonsense, you know; as if there could be anything strange or wonderful in London.'

'Why shouldn't there be?'

'Well, I don't know; but I have thought afterwards what a silly lad I must have been. Anyhow, I had a great day of it, planning what I would do, half making-believe--just like a kid--that I didn't know where I might find myself, or what might happen to me. And I was enormously pleased to think it was all my secret, that nobody else knew anything about it, and that, whatever I might see, I would keep to myself. I had always felt like that about the books. Of course, I loved reading them, but it seemed to me that, if I had been a discoverer, I would have kept my discoveries a secret. If I had been Columbus, and, if it could possibly have been managed, I would have found America all by myself, and never have said a word about it to anybody. Fancy! how beautiful it would be to be walking about in one's own town, and talking to people, and all the while to have the thought that one knew of a great world beyond the seas, that nobody else dreamed of. I should have loved that!

'And that is exactly what I felt about the tour I was going to make. I made up my mind that nobody should know; and so, from that day to this, nobody has heard a word of it.'

'But you are going to tell me?'

'You are different. But I don't think even you will hear everything; not because I won't, but because I can't tell many of the things I saw.'

'Things you saw? Then you really did see wonderful, strange things in London?'

'Well, I did and I didn't. Everything, or pretty nearly everything, that I saw is standing still, and hundreds of thousands of people have looked at the same sights--there were many places that the fellows in the office knew quite well, I found out afterwards. And then I read a book called "London and its Surroundings." But (I don't know how it is) neither the men at the office nor the writers of the book seem to have seen the things that I did. That's why I stopped reading the book; it seemed to take the life, the real heart, out of everything, making it as dry and stupid as the stuffed birds in a museum.

'I thought about what I was going to do all that day, and went to bed early, so as to be fresh. I knew wonderfully little about London, really; though, except for an odd week now and then, I had spent all my life in town. Of course I knew the main streets--the Strand, Regent Street, Oxford Street, and so on--and I knew the way to the school I used to go to when I was a boy, and the way into the City. But I had just kept to a few tracks, as they say the sheep do on the mountains; and that made it all the easier for me to imagine that I was going to discover a new world.'

Darnell paused in the stream of his talk. He looked keenly at his wife to see if he were wearying her, but her eyes gazed at him with unabated interest--one would have almost said that they were the eyes of one who longed and half expected to be initiated into the mysteries, who knew not what great wonder was to be revealed. She sat with her back to the open window, framed in the sweet dusk of the night, as if a painter had made a curtain of heavy velvet behind her; and the work that she had been doing had fallen to the floor. She supported her head with her two hands placed on each side of her brow, and her eyes were as the wells in the wood of which Darnell dreamed in the night-time and in the day.

'And all the strange tales I had ever heard were in my head that morning,' he went on, as if continuing the thoughts that had filled his mind while his lips were silent. 'I had gone to bed early, as I told you, to get a thorough rest, and I had set my alarum clock to wake me at three, so that I might set out at an hour that was quite strange for the beginning of a journey. There was a hush in the world when I awoke, before the clock had rung to arouse me, and then a bird began to sing and twitter in the elm tree that grew in the next garden, and I looked out of the window, and everything was still, and the morning air breathed in pure and sweet, as I had never known it before. My room was at the back of the house, and most of the gardens had trees in them, and beyond these trees I could see the backs of the houses of the next street rising like the wall of an old city; and as I looked the sun rose, and the great light came in at my window, and the day began.

'And I found that when I was once out of the streets just about me that I knew, some of the queer feeling that had come to me two days before came back again. It was not nearly so strong, the streets no longer smelt of incense, but still there was enough of it to show me what a strange world I passed by. There were things that one may see again and again in many London streets: a vine or a fig tree on a wall, a lark singing in a cage, a curious shrub blossoming in a garden, an odd shape of a roof, or a balcony with an uncommon-looking trellis-work in iron. There's scarcely a street, perhaps, where you won't see one or other of such things as these; but that morning they rose to my eyes in a new light, as if I had on the magic spectacles in the fairy tale, and just like the man in the fairy tale, I went on and on in the new light. I remember going through wild land on a high place; there were pools of water shining in the sun, and great white houses in the middle of dark, rocking pines, and then on the turn of the height I came to a little lane that went aside from the main road, a lane that led to a wood, and in the lane was a little old shadowed house, with a bell turret in the roof, and a porch of trellis-work all dim and faded into the colour of the sea; and in the garden there were growing tall, white lilies, just as we saw them that day we went to look at the old pictures; they were shining like silver, and they filled the air with their sweet scent. It was from near that house I saw the valley and high places far away in the sun. So, as I say, I went "on and on," by woods and fields, till I came to a little town on the top of a hill, a town full of old houses bowing to the ground beneath their years, and the morning was so still that the blue smoke rose up straight into the sky from all the roof-tops, so still that I heard far down in the valley the song of a boy who was singing an old song through the streets as he went to school, and as I passed through the awakening town, beneath the old, grave houses, the church bells began to ring.

'It was soon after I had left this town behind me that I found the Strange Road. I saw it branching off from the dusty high road, and it looked so green that I turned aside into it, and soon I felt as if I had really come into a new country. I don't know whether it was one of the roads the old Romans made that my father used to tell me about; but it was covered with deep, soft turf, and the great tall hedges on each side looked as if they had not been touched for a hundred years; they had grown so broad and high and wild that they met overhead, and I could only get glimpses here and there of the country through which I was passing, as one passes in a dream. The Strange Road led me on and on, up and down hill; sometimes the rose bushes had grown so thick that I could scarcely make my way between them, and sometimes the road broadened out into a green, and in one valley a brook, spanned by an old wooden bridge, ran across it. I was tired, and I found a soft and shady place beneath an ash tree, where I must have slept for many hours, for when I woke up it was late in the afternoon. So I went on again, and at last the green road came out into the highway, and I looked up and saw another town on a high place with a great church in the middle of it, and when I went up to it there was a great organ sounding from within, and the choir was singing.'

There was a rapture in Darnell's voice as he spoke, that made his story well-nigh swell into a song, and he drew a long breath as the words ended, filled with the thought of that far-off summer day, when some enchantment had informed all common things, transmuting them into a great sacrament, causing earthly works to glow with the fire and the glory of the everlasting light.

And some splendour of that light shone on the face of Mary as she sat still against the sweet gloom of the night, her dark hair making her face more radiant. She was silent for a little while, and then she spoke--

'Oh, my dear, why have you waited so long to tell me these wonderful things? I think it is beautiful. Please go on.'

'I have always been afraid it was all nonsense,' said Darnell. 'And I don't know how to explain what I feel. I didn't think I could say so much as I have to-night.'

'And did you find it the same day after day?'

'All through the tour? Yes, I think every journey was a success. Of course, I didn't go so far afield every day; I was too tired. Often I rested all day long, and went out in the evening, after the lamps were lit, and then only for a mile or two. I would roam about old, dim squares, and hear the wind from the hills whispering in the trees; and when I knew I was within call of some great glittering street, I was sunk in the silence of ways where I was almost the only passenger, and the lamps were so few and faint that they seemed to give out shadows instead of light. And I would walk slowly, to and fro, perhaps for an hour at a time, in such dark streets, and all the time I felt what I told you about its being my secret--that the shadow, and the dim lights, and the cool of the evening, and trees that were like dark low clouds were all mine, and mine alone, that I was living in a world that nobody else knew of, into which no one could enter.

'I remembered one night I had gone farther. It was somewhere in the far west, where there are orchards and gardens, and great broad lawns that slope down to trees by the river. A great red moon rose that night through mists of sunset, and thin, filmy clouds, and I wandered by a road that passed through the orchards, till I came to a little hill, with the moon showing above it glowing like a great rose. Then I saw figures pass between me and the moon, one by one, in a long line, each bent double, with great packs upon their shoulders. One of them was singing, and then in the middle of the song I heard a horrible shrill laugh, in the thin cracked voice of a very old woman, and they disappeared into the shadow of the trees. I suppose they were people going to work, or coming from work in the gardens; but how like it was to a nightmare!

'I can't tell you about Hampton; I should never finish talking. I was there one evening, not long before they closed the gates, and there were very few people about. But the grey-red, silent, echoing courts, and the flowers falling into dreamland as the night came on, and the dark yews and shadowy-looking statues, and the far, still stretches of water beneath the avenues; and all melting into a blue mist, all being hidden from one's eyes, slowly, surely, as if veils were dropped, one by one, on a great ceremony! Oh! my dear, what could it mean? Far away, across the river, I heard a soft bell ring three times, and three times, and again three times, and I turned away, and my eyes were full of tears.

'I didn't know what it was when I came to it; I only found out afterwards that it must have been Hampton Court. One of the men in the office told me he had taken an A. B. C. girl there, and they had great fun. They got into the maze and couldn't get out again, and then they went on the river and were nearly drowned. He told me there were some spicy pictures in the galleries; his girl shrieked with laughter, so he said.'

Mary quite disregarded this interlude.

'But you told me you had made a map. What was it like?'

'I'll show it you some day, if you want to see it. I marked down all the places I had gone to, and made signs--things like queer letters--to remind me of what I had seen. Nobody but myself could understand it. I wanted to draw pictures, but I never learnt how to draw, so when I tried nothing was like what I wanted it to be. I tried to draw a picture of that town on the hill that I came to on the evening of the first day; I wanted to make a steep hill with houses on top, and in the middle, but high above them, the great church, all spires and pinnacles, and above it, in the air, a cup with rays coming from it. But it wasn't a success. I made a very strange sign for Hampton Court, and gave it a name that I made up out of my head.'

The Darnells avoided one another's eyes as they sat at breakfast the next morning. The air had lightened in the night, for rain had fallen at dawn; and there was a bright blue sky, with vast white clouds rolling across it from the south-west, and a fresh and joyous wind blew in at the open window; the mists had vanished. And with the mists there seemed to have vanished also the sense of strange things that had possessed Mary and her husband the night before; and as they looked out into the clear light they could scarcely believe that the one had spoken and the other had listened a few hours before to histories very far removed from the usual current of their thoughts and of their lives. They glanced shyly at one another, and spoke of common things, of the question whether Alice would be corrupted by the insidious Mrs. Murry, or whether Mrs. Darnell would be able to persuade the girl that the old woman must be actuated by the worst motives.

'And I think, if I were you,' said Darnell, as he went out, 'I should step over to the stores and complain of their meat. That last piece of beef was very far from being up to the mark--full of sinew.'

CHAPTER 3

It might have been different in the evening, and Darnell had matured a plan by which he hoped to gain much. He intended to ask his wife if she would mind having only one gas, and that a good deal lowered, on the pretext that his eyes were tired with work; he thought many things might happen if the room were dimly lit, and the window opened, so that they could sit and watch the night, and listen to the rustling murmur of the tree on the lawn. But his plans were made in vain, for when he got to the garden gate his wife, in tears, came forth to meet him.

'Oh, Edward,' she began, 'such a dreadful thing has happened! I never liked him much, but I didn't think he would ever do such awful things.'

'What do you mean? Who are you talking about? What has happened? Is it Alice's young man?'

'No, no. But come in, dear. I can see that woman opposite watching us: she's always on the look out.'

'Now, what is it?' said Darnell, as they sat down to tea. 'Tell me, quick! you've quite frightened me.'

'I don't know how to begin, or where to start. Aunt Marian has thought that there was something queer for weeks. And then she found--oh, well, the long and short of it is that Uncle Robert has been carrying on dreadfully with some horrid girl, and aunt has found out everything!'

'Lord! you don't say so! The old rascal! Why, he must be nearer seventy than sixty!'

'He's just sixty-five; and the money he has given her----'

The first shock of surprise over, Darnell turned resolutely to his mince.

'We'll have it all out after tea,' he said; 'I am not going to have my meals spoilt by that old fool of a Nixon. Fill up my cup, will you, dear?'

'Excellent mince this,' he went on, calmly. 'A little lemon juice and a bit of ham in it? I thought there was something extra. Alice all right to-day? That's good. I expect she's getting over all that nonsense.'

He went on calmly chattering in a manner that astonished Mrs. Darnell, who felt that by the fall of Uncle Robert the natural order had been inverted, and had scarcely touched food since the intelligence had arrived by the second post. She had started out to keep the appointment her aunt had made early in the morning, and had spent most of the day in a first-class waiting-room at Victoria Station, where she had heard all the story.

'Now,' said Darnell, when the table had been cleared, 'tell us all about it. How long has it been going on?'

'Aunt thinks now, from little things she remembers, that it must have been going on for a year at least. She says there has been a horrid kind of mystery about uncle's behaviour for a long time, and her nerves were quite shaken, as she thought he must be involved with Anarchists, or something dreadful of the sort.'

'What on earth made her think that?'

'Well, you see, once or twice when she was out walking with her husband, she has been startled by whistles, which seemed to follow them everywhere. You know there are some nice country walks at Barnet, and one in particular, in the fields near Totteridge, that uncle and aunt rather made a point of going to on fine Sunday evenings. Of course, this was not the first thing she noticed, but, at the time, it made a great impression on her mind; she could hardly get a wink of sleep for weeks and weeks.'

'Whistling?' said Darnell. 'I don't quite understand. Why should she be frightened by whistling?'

'I'll tell you. The first time it happened was one Sunday in last May. Aunt had a fancy they were being followed a Sunday or two before, but she didn't see or hear anything, except a sort of crackling noise in the hedge. But this particular Sunday they had hardly got through the stile into the fields, when she heard a peculiar kind of low whistle. She took no notice, thinking it was no concern of hers or her husband's, but as they went on she heard it again, and then again, and it followed them the whole walk, and it made her so uncomfortable, because she didn't know where it was coming from or who was doing it, or why. Then, just as they got out of the fields into the lane, uncle said he felt quite faint, and he thought he would try a little brandy at the "Turpin's Head," a small public-house there is there. And she looked at him and saw his face was quite purple--more like apoplexy, as she says, than fainting fits, which make people look a sort of greenish-white. But she said nothing, and thought perhaps uncle had a peculiar way of fainting of his own, as he always was a man to have his own way of doing everything. So she just waited in the road, and he went ahead and slipped into the public, and aunt says she thought she saw a little figure rise out of the dusk and slip in after him, but she couldn't be sure. And when uncle came out he looked red instead of purple, and said he felt much better; and so they went home quietly together, and nothing more was said. You see, uncle had said nothing about the whistling, and aunt had been so frightened that she didn't dare speak, for fear they might be both shot.

'She wasn't thinking anything more about it, when two Sundays afterwards the very same thing happened just as it had before. This time aunt plucked up a spirit, and asked uncle what it could be. And what do you think he said? "Birds, my dear, birds." Of course aunt said to him that no bird that ever flew with wings made a noise like that: sly, and low, with pauses in between; and then he said that many rare sorts of birds lived in North Middlesex and Hertfordshire. "Nonsense, Robert," said aunt, "how can you talk so, considering it has followed us all the way, for a mile or more?" And then uncle told her that some birds were so attached to man that they would follow one about for miles sometimes; he said he had just been reading about a bird like that in a book of travels. And do you know that when they got home he actually showed her a piece in the "Hertfordshire Naturalist" which they took in to oblige a friend of theirs, all about rare birds found in the neighbourhood, all the most outlandish names, aunt says, that she had never heard or thought of, and uncle had the impudence to say that it must have been a Purple Sandpiper, which, the paper said, had "a low shrill note, constantly repeated." And then he took down a book of Siberian Travels from the bookcase and showed her a page which told how a man was followed by a bird all day long through a forest. And that's what Aunt Marian says vexes her more than anything almost; to think that he should be so artful and ready with those books, twisting them to his own wicked ends. But, at the time, when she was out walking, she simply couldn't make out what he meant by talking about birds in that random, silly sort of way, so unlike him, and they went on, that horrible whistling following them, she looking straight ahead and walking fast, really feeling more huffy and put out than frightened. And when they got to the next stile, she got over and turned round, and "lo and behold," as she says, there was no Uncle Robert to be seen! She felt herself go quite white with alarm, thinking of that whistle, and making sure he'd been spirited away or snatched in some way or another, and she had just screamed out "Robert" like a mad woman, when he came quite slowly round the corner, as cool as a cucumber, holding something in his hand. He said there were some flowers he could never pass, and when aunt saw that he had got a dandelion torn up by the roots, she felt as if her head were going round.'

Mary's story was suddenly interrupted. For ten minutes Darnell had been writhing in his chair, suffering tortures in his anxiety to avoid wounding his wife's feelings, but the episode of the dandelion was too much for him, and he burst into a long, wild shriek of laughter, aggravated by suppression into the semblance of a Red Indian's war-whoop. Alice, who was washing-up in the scullery, dropped some three shillings' worth of china, and the neighbours ran out into their gardens wondering if it were murder. Mary gazed reproachfully at her husband.

'How can you be so unfeeling, Edward?' she said, at length, when Darnell had passed into the feebleness of exhaustion. 'If you had seen the tears rolling down poor Aunt Marian's cheeks as she told me, I don't think you would have laughed. I didn't think you were so hard-hearted.'

'My dear Mary,' said Darnell, faintly, through sobs and catching of the breath, 'I am awfully sorry. I know it's very sad, really, and I'm not unfeeling; but it is such an odd tale, now, isn't it? The Sandpiper, you know, and then the dandelion!'

His face twitched and he ground his teeth together. Mary looked gravely at him for a moment, and then she put her hands to her face, and Darnell could see that she also shook with merriment.

'I am as bad as you,' she said, at last. 'I never thought of it in that way. I'm glad I didn't, or I should have laughed in Aunt Marian's face, and I wouldn't have done that for the world. Poor old thing; she cried as if her heart would break. I met her at Victoria, as she asked me, and we had some soup at a confectioner's. I could scarcely touch it; her tears kept dropping into the plate all the time; and then we went to the waiting-room at the station, and she cried there terribly.'

'Well,' said Darnell, 'what happened next? I won't laugh any more.'

'No, we mustn't; it's much too horrible for a joke. Well, of course aunt went home and wondered and wondered what could be the matter, and tried to think it out, but, as she says, she could make nothing of it. She began to be afraid that uncle's brain was giving way through overwork, as he had stopped in the City (as he said) up to all hours lately, and he had to go to Yorkshire (wicked old story-teller!), about some very tiresome business connected with his leases. But then she reflected that however queer he might be getting, even his queerness couldn't make whistles in the air, though, as she said, he was always a wonderful man. So she had to give that up; and then she wondered if there were anything the matter with her, as she had read about people who heard noises when there was really nothing at all. But that wouldn't do either, because though it might account for the whistling, it wouldn't account for the dandelion or the Sandpiper, or for fainting fits that turned purple, or any of uncle's queerness. So aunt said she could think of nothing but to read the Bible every day from the beginning, and by the time she got into Chronicles she felt rather better, especially as nothing had happened for three or four Sundays. She noticed uncle seemed absent-minded, and not as nice to her as he might be, but she put that down to too much work, as he never came home before the last train, and had a hansom twice all the way, getting there between three and four in the morning. Still, she felt it was no good bothering her head over what couldn't be made out or explained anyway, and she was just settling down, when one Sunday evening it began all over again, and worse things happened. The whistling followed them just as it did before, and poor aunt set her teeth and said nothing to uncle, as she knew he would only tell her stories, and they were walking on, not saying a word, when something made her look back, and there was a horrible boy with red hair, peeping through the hedge just behind, and grinning. She said it was a dreadful face, with something unnatural about it, as if it had been a dwarf, and before she had time to have a good look, it popped back like lightning, and aunt all but fainted away.'

'A red-headed boy?' said Darnell. 'I thought----What an extraordinary story this is. I've never heard of anything so queer. Who was the boy?'

'You will know in good time,' said Mrs. Darnell. 'It is very strange, isn't it?'

'Strange!' Darnell ruminated for a while.

'I know what I think, Mary,' he said at length. 'I don't believe a word of it. I believe your aunt is going mad, or has gone mad, and that she has delusions. The whole thing sounds to me like the invention of a lunatic.'

'You are quite wrong. Every word is true, and if you will let me go on, you will understand how it all happened.'

'Very good, go ahead.'

'Let me see, where was I? Oh, I know, aunt saw the boy grinning in the hedge. Yes, well, she was dreadfully frightened for a minute or two; there was something so queer about the face, but then she plucked up a spirit and said to herself, "After all, better a boy with red hair than a big man with a gun," and she made up her mind to watch Uncle Robert closely, as she could see by his look he knew all about it; he seemed as if he were thinking hard and puzzling over something, as if he didn't know what to do next, and his mouth kept opening and shutting, like a fish's. So she kept her face straight, and didn't say a word, and when he said something to her about the fine sunset, she took no notice. "Don't you hear what I say, Marian?" he said, speaking quite crossly, and bellowing as if it were to somebody in the next field. So aunt said she was very sorry, but her cold made her so deaf, she couldn't hear much. She noticed uncle looked quite pleased, and relieved too, and she knew he thought she hadn't heard the whistling. Suddenly uncle pretended to see a beautiful spray of honeysuckle high up in the hedge, and he said he must get it for aunt, only she must go on ahead, as it made him nervous to be watched. She said she would, but she just stepped aside behind a bush where there was a sort of cover in the hedge, and found she could see him quite well, though she scratched her face terribly with poking it into a rose bush. And in a minute or two out came the boy from behind the hedge, and she saw uncle and him talking, and she knew it was the same boy, as it wasn't dark enough to hide his flaming red head. And uncle put out his hand as if to catch him, but he just darted into the bushes and vanished. Aunt never said a word at the time, but that night when they got home she charged uncle with what she'd seen and asked him what it all meant. He was quite taken aback at first, and stammered and stuttered and said a spy wasn't his notion of a good wife, but at last he made her swear secrecy, and told her that he was a very high Freemason, and that the boy was an emissary of the order who brought him messages of the greatest importance. But aunt didn't believe a word of it, as an uncle of hers was a mason, and he never behaved like that. It was then she began to be afraid that it was really Anarchists, or something of the kind, and every time the bell rang she thought that uncle had been found out, and the police had come for him.'

'What nonsense! As if a man with house property would be an Anarchist.'

'Well, she could see there must be some horrible secret, and she didn't know what else to think. And then she began to have the things through the post.'

'Things through the post! What do you mean by that?'

'All sorts of things; bits of broken bottle-glass, packed carefully as if it were jewellery; parcels that unrolled and unrolled worse than Chinese boxes, and then had "cat" in large letters when you came to the middle; old artificial teeth, a cake of red paint, and at last cockroaches.'

'Cockroaches by post! Stuff and nonsense; your aunt's mad.'

'Edward, she showed me the box; it was made to hold cigarettes, and there were three dead cockroaches inside. And when she found a box of exactly the same kind, half-full of cigarettes, in uncle's great-coat pocket, then her head began to turn again.'

Darnell groaned, and stirred uneasily in his chair, feeling that the tale of Aunt Marian's domestic troubles was putting on the semblance of an evil dream.

'Anything else?' he asked.

'My dear, I haven't repeated half the things poor aunt told me this afternoon. There was the night she thought she saw a ghost in the shrubbery. She was anxious about some chickens that were just due to hatch out, so she went out after dark with some egg and bread-crumbs, in case they might be out. And just before her she saw a figure gliding by the rhododendrons. It looked like a short, slim man dressed as they used to be hundreds of years ago; she saw the sword by his side, and the feather in his cap. She thought she should have died, she said, and though it was gone in a minute, and she tried to make out it was all her fancy, she fainted when she got into the house. Uncle was at home that night, and when she came to and told him he ran out, and stayed out for half-an-hour or more, and then came in and said he could find nothing; and the next minute aunt heard that low whistle just outside the window, and uncle ran out again.'

'My dear Mary, do let us come to the point. What on earth does it all lead to?'

'Haven't you guessed? Why, of course it was that girl all the time.'

'Girl? I thought you said it was a boy with a red head?'

'Don't you see? She's an actress, and she dressed up. She won't leave uncle alone. It wasn't enough that he was with her nearly every evening in the week, but she must be after him on Sundays too. Aunt found a letter the horrid thing had written, and so it has all come out. Enid Vivian she calls herself, though I don't suppose she has any right to one name or the other. And the question is, what is to be done?'

'Let us talk of that again. I'll have a pipe, and then we'll go to bed.'

They were almost asleep when Mary said suddenly--

'Doesn't it seem queer, Edward? Last night you were telling me such beautiful things, and to-night I have been talking about that disgraceful old man and his goings on.'

'I don't know,' answered Darnell, dreamily. 'On the walls of that great church upon the hill I saw all kinds of strange grinning monsters, carved in stone.'

The misdemeanours of Mr. Robert Nixon brought in their train consequences strange beyond imagination. It was not that they continued to develop on the somewhat fantastic lines of these first adventures which Mrs. Darnell had related; indeed, when 'Aunt Marian' came over to Shepherd's Bush, one Sunday afternoon, Darnell wondered how he had had the heart to laugh at the misfortunes of a broken-hearted woman.

He had never seen his wife's aunt before, and he was strangely surprised when Alice showed her into the garden where they were sitting on the warm and misty Sunday in September. To him, save during these latter days, she had always been associated with ideas of splendour and success: his wife had always mentioned the Nixons with a tinge of reverence; he had heard, many times, the epic of Mr. Nixon's struggles and of his slow but triumphant rise. Mary had told the story as she had received it from her parents, beginning with the flight to

London from some small, dull, and unprosperous town in the flattest of the Midlands, long ago, when a young man from the country had great chances of fortune. Robert Nixon's father had been a grocer in the High Street, and in after days the successful coal merchant and builder loved to tell of that dull provincial life, and while he glorified his own victories, he gave his hearers to understand that he came of a race which had also known how to achieve. That had been long ago, he would explain: in the days when that rare citizen who desired to go to London or to York was forced to rise in the dead of night, and make his way, somehow or other, by ten miles of quagmirish, wandering lanes to the Great North Road, there to meet the 'Lightning' coach, a vehicle which stood to all the countryside as the visible and tangible embodiment of tremendous speed--'and indeed,' as Nixon would add, 'it was always up to time, which is more than can be said of the Dunham Branch Line nowadays!' It was in this ancient Dunham that the Nixons had waged successful trade for perhaps a hundred years, in a shop with bulging bay windows looking on the market-place. There was no competition, and the townsfolk, and well-to-do farmers, the clergy and the country families, looked upon the house of Nixon as an institution fixed as the town hall (which stood on Roman pillars) and the parish church. But the change came: the railway crept nearer and nearer, the farmers and the country gentry became less well-to-do; the tanning, which was the local industry, suffered from a great business which had been established in a larger town, some twenty miles away, and the profits of the Nixons grew less and less. Hence the hegira of Robert, and he would dilate on the poorness of his beginnings, how he saved, by little and little, from his sorry wage of City clerk, and how he and a fellow clerk, 'who had come into a hundred pounds,' saw an opening in the coal trade--and filled it. It was at this stage of Robert's fortunes, still far from magnificent, that Miss Marian Reynolds had encountered him, she being on a visit to friends in Gunnersbury. Afterwards, victory followed victory; Nixon's wharf became a landmark to bargemen; his power stretched abroad, his dusky fleets went outwards to the sea, and inward by all the far reaches of canals. Lime, cement, and bricks were added to his merchandise, and at last he hit upon the great stroke--that extensive taking up of land in the north of London. Nixon himself ascribed this coup to native sagacity, and the possession of capital; and there were also obscure rumours to the effect that some one or other had been 'done' in the course of the transaction. However that might be, the Nixons grew wealthy to excess, and Mary had often told her husband of the state in which they dwelt, of their liveried servants, of the glories of their drawing-room, of their broad lawn, shadowed by a splendid and ancient cedar. And so Darnell had somehow been led into conceiving the lady of this demesne as a personage of no small pomp. He saw her, tall, of dignified port and presence, inclining, it might be, to some measure of obesity, such a measure as was not unbefitting in an elderly lady of position, who lived well and lived at ease. He even imagined a slight ruddiness of complexion, which went very well with hair that was beginning to turn grey, and when he heard the door-bell ring, as he sat under the mulberry on the Sunday afternoon, he bent forward to catch sight of this stately figure, clad, of course, in the richest, blackest silk, girt about with heavy chains of gold.

He started with amazement when he saw the strange presence that followed the servant into the garden. Mrs. Nixon was a little, thin old woman, who bent as she feebly trotted after Alice; her eyes were on the ground, and she did not lift them when the Darnells rose to greet her. She glanced to the right, uneasily, as she shook hands with Darnell, to the left when Mary kissed her, and when she was placed on the garden seat with a cushion at her back, she looked away at the back of the houses in the next street. She was dressed in black, it was true, but even Darnell could see that her gown was old and shabby, that the fur trimming of her cape and the fur boa which was twisted about her neck were dingy and disconsolate, and had all the melancholy air which fur wears when it is seen in a second-hand clothes-shop in a back street. And her gloves--they were black kid, wrinkled with much wear, faded to a bluish hue at the finger-tips, which showed signs of painful mending. Her hair, plastered over her forehead, looked dull and colourless, though some greasy matter had evidently been used with a view of producing a becoming gloss, and on it perched an antique bonnet, adorned with black pendants that rattled paralytically one against the other.

And there was nothing in Mrs. Nixon's face to correspond with the imaginary picture that Darnell had made of her. She was sallow, wrinkled, pinched; her nose ran to a sharp point, and her red-rimmed eyes were a queer water-grey, that seemed to shrink alike from the light and from encounter with the eyes of others. As she sat beside his wife on the green garden-seat, Darnell, who occupied a wicker-chair brought out from the drawing-room, could not help feeling that this shadowy and evasive figure, muttering replies to Mary's polite questions, was almost impossibly remote from his conceptions of the rich and powerful aunt, who could give away a hundred pounds as a mere birthday gift. She would say little at first; yes, she was feeling rather tired, it had been so hot all the way, and she had been afraid to put on lighter things as one never knew at this time of year what it might be like in the evenings; there were apt to be cold mists when the sun went down, and she didn't care to risk bronchitis.

'I thought I should never get here,' she went on, raising her voice to an odd querulous pipe. 'I'd no notion it was such an out-of-the-way place, it's so many years since I was in this neighbourhood.'

She wiped her eyes, no doubt thinking of the early days at Turnham Green, when she married Nixon; and when the pocket-handkerchief had done its office she replaced it in a shabby black bag which she clutched rather than carried. Darnell noticed, as he watched her, that the bag seemed full, almost to bursting, and he speculated idly as to the nature of its contents: correspondence, perhaps, he thought, further proofs of Uncle Robert's treacherous and wicked dealings. He grew quite uncomfortable, as he sat and saw her glancing all the while furtively away from his wife and himself, and presently he got up and strolled away to the other end of the garden, where he lit his pipe and walked to and fro on the gravel walk, still astounded at the gulf between the real and the imagined woman.

Presently he heard a hissing whisper, and he saw Mrs. Nixon's head inclining to his wife's. Mary rose and came towards him.

'Would you mind sitting in the drawing-room, Edward?' she murmured. 'Aunt says she can't bring herself to discuss such a delicate matter before you. I dare say it's quite natural.'

'Very well, but I don't think I'll go into the drawing-room. I feel as if a walk would do me good. You mustn't be frightened if I am a little late,' he said; 'if I don't get back before your aunt goes, say good-bye to her for me.'

He strolled into the main road, where the trams were humming to and fro. He was still confused and perplexed, and he tried to account for a certain relief he felt in removing himself from the presence of Mrs. Nixon. He told himself that her grief at her husband's ruffianly conduct was worthy of all pitiful respect, but at the same time, to his shame, he had felt a certain physical aversion from her as she sat in his garden in her dingy black, dabbing her red-rimmed eyes with a damp pocket-handkerchief. He had been to the Zoo when he was a lad, and he still remembered how he had shrunk with horror at the sight of certain reptiles slowly crawling over one another in their slimy pond. But he was enraged at the similarity between the two sensations, and he walked briskly on that level and monotonous road, looking about him at the unhandsome spectacle of suburban London keeping Sunday.

There was something in the tinge of antiquity which still exists in Acton that soothed his mind and drew it away from those unpleasant contemplations, and when at last he had penetrated rampart after rampart of brick, and heard no more the harsh shrieks and laughter of the people who were enjoying themselves, he found a way into a little sheltered field, and sat down in peace beneath a tree, whence he could look out on a pleasant valley. The sun sank down beneath the hills, the clouds changed into the likeness of blossoming rose-gardens; and he still sat there in the gathering darkness till a cool breeze blew upon him, and he rose with a sigh, and turned back to the brick ramparts and the glimmering streets, and the noisy idlers sauntering to and fro in the procession of their dismal festival. But he was murmuring to himself some words that seemed a magic song, and it was with uplifted heart that he let himself into his house.

Mrs. Nixon had gone an hour and a half before his return, Mary told him. Darnell sighed with relief, and he and his wife strolled out into the garden and sat down side by side.

They kept silence for a time, and at last Mary spoke, not without a nervous tremor in her voice.

'I must tell you, Edward,' she began, 'that aunt has made a proposal which you ought to hear. I think we should consider it.'

'A proposal? But how about the whole affair? Is it still going on?'

'Oh, yes! She told me all about it. Uncle is quite unrepentant. It seems he has taken a flat somewhere in town for that woman, and furnished it in the most costly manner. He simply laughs at aunt's reproaches, and says he means to have some fun at last. You saw how broken she was?'

'Yes; very sad. But won't he give her any money? Wasn't she very badly dressed for a woman in her position?'

'Aunt has no end of beautiful things, but I fancy she likes to hoard them; she has a horror of spoiling her dresses. It isn't for want of money, I assure you, as uncle settled a very large sum on her two years ago, when he was everything that could be desired as a husband. And that brings me to what I want to say. Aunt would like to live with us. She would pay very liberally. What do you say?'

'Would like to live with us?' exclaimed Darnell, and his pipe dropped from his hand on to the grass. He was stupefied by the thought of Aunt Marian as a boarder, and sat staring vacantly before him, wondering what new monster the night would next produce.

'I knew you wouldn't much like the idea,' his wife went on. 'But I do think, dearest, that we ought not to refuse without very serious consideration. I am afraid you did not take to poor aunt very much.'

Darnell shook his head dumbly.

'I thought you didn't; she was so upset, poor thing, and you didn't see her at her best. She is really so good. But listen to me, dear. Do you think we have the right to refuse her offer? I told you she has money of her own, and I am sure she would be dreadfully offended if we said we wouldn't have her. And what would become of me if anything happened to you? You know we have very little saved.'

Darnell groaned.

'It seems to me,' he said, 'that it would spoil everything. We are so happy, Mary dear, by ourselves. Of course I am extremely sorry for your aunt. I think she is very much to be pitied. But when it comes to having her always here----'

'I know, dear. Don't think I am looking forward to the prospect; you know I don't want anybody but you. Still, we ought to think of the future, and besides we shall be able to live so very much better. I shall be able to give you all sorts of nice things that I know you ought to have after all that hard work in the City. Our income would be doubled.'

'Do you mean she would pay us £150 a year?'

'Certainly. And she would pay for the spare room being furnished, and any extra she might want. She told me, specially, that if a friend or two came now and again to see her, she would gladly bear the cost of a fire in the drawing-room, and give something towards the gas bill, with a few shillings for the girl for any additional trouble. We should certainly be more than twice as well off as we are now. You see, Edward, dear, it's not the sort of offer we are likely to have again. Besides, we must think of the future, as I said. Do you know aunt took a great fancy to you?'

He shuddered and said nothing, and his wife went on with her argument.

'And, you see, it isn't as if we should see so very much of her. She will have her breakfast in bed, and she told me she would often go up to her room in the evening directly after dinner. I thought that very nice and considerate. She quite understands that we shouldn't like to have a third person always with us. Don't you think, Edward, that, considering everything, we ought to say we will have her?'

'Oh, I suppose so,' he groaned. 'As you say, it's a very good offer, financially, and I am afraid it would be very imprudent to refuse. But I don't like the notion, I confess.'

'I am so glad you agree with me, dear. Depend upon it, it won't be half so bad as you think. And putting our own advantage on one side, we shall really be doing poor aunt a very great kindness. Poor old dear, she cried bitterly after you were gone; she said she had made up her mind not to stay any longer in Uncle Robert's house, and she didn't know where to go, or what would become of her, if we refused to take her in. She quite broke down.'

'Well, well; we will try it for a year, anyhow. It may be as you say; we shan't find it quite so bad as it seems now. Shall we go in?'

He stooped for his pipe, which lay as it had fallen, on the grass. He could not find it, and lit a wax match which showed him the pipe, and close beside it, under the seat, something that looked like a page torn from a book. He wondered what it could be, and picked it up.

The gas was lit in the drawing-room, and Mrs. Darnell, who was arranging some notepaper, wished to write at once to Mrs. Nixon, cordially accepting her proposal, when she was startled by an exclamation from her husband.

'What is the matter?' she said, startled by the tone of his voice. 'You haven't hurt yourself?'

'Look at this,' he replied, handing her a small leaflet; 'I found it under the garden seat just now.'

Mary glanced with bewilderment at her husband and read as follows:--

THE NEW AND CHOSEN SEED OF ABRAHAM
PROPHECIES TO BE FULFILLED IN THE PRESENT YEAR

1. The Sailing of a Fleet of One hundred and Forty and Four Vessels for Tarshish and the Isles.

2. Destruction of the Power of the Dog, including all the instruments of anti-Abrahamic legislation.

3. Return of the Fleet from Tarshish, bearing with it the gold of Arabia, destined to be the Foundation of the New City of Abraham.

4. The Search for the Bride, and the bestowing of the Seals on the Seventy and Seven.

5. The Countenance of FATHER to become luminous, but with a greater glory than the face of Moses.

6. The Pope of Rome to be stoned with stones in the valley called Berek-Zittor.

7. FATHER to be acknowledged by Three Great Rulers. Two Great Rulers will deny FATHER, and will immediately perish in the Effluvia of FATHER'S Indignation.

8. Binding of the Beast with the Little Horn, and all Judges cast down.

9. Finding of the Bride in the Land of Egypt, which has been revealed to FATHER as now existing in the western part of London.

10. Bestowal of the New Tongue on the Seventy and Seven, and on the One Hundred and Forty and Four. FATHER proceeds to the Bridal Chamber.

11. Destruction of London and rebuilding of the City called No, which is the New City of Abraham.

12. FATHER united to the Bride, and the present Earth removed to the Sun for the space of half an hour.

Mrs. Darnell's brow cleared as she read matter which seemed to her harmless if incoherent. From her husband's voice she had been led to fear something more tangibly unpleasant than a vague catena of prophecies.

'Well,' she said, 'what about it?'

'What about it? Don't you see that your aunt dropped it, and that she must be a raging lunatic?'

'Oh, Edward! don't say that. In the first place, how do you know that aunt dropped it at all? It might easily have blown over from any of the other gardens. And, if it were hers, I don't think you should call her a lunatic. I don't believe, myself, that there are any real prophets now; but there are many good people who think quite differently. I knew an old lady once who, I am sure, was very good, and she took in a paper every week that was full of prophecies and things very like this. Nobody called her mad, and I have heard father say that she had one of the sharpest heads for business he had ever come across.'

'Very good; have it as you like. But I believe we shall both be sorry.'

They sat in silence for some time. Alice came in after her 'evening out,' and they sat on, till Mrs. Darnell said she was tired and wanted to go to bed.

Her husband kissed her. 'I don't think I will come up just yet,' he said; 'you go to sleep, dearest. I want to think things over. No, no; I am not going to change my mind: your aunt shall come, as I said. But there are one or two things I should like to get settled in my mind.'

He meditated for a long while, pacing up and down the room. Light after light was extinguished in Edna Road, and the people of the suburb slept all around him, but still the gas was alight in Darnell's drawing-room, and he walked softly up and down the floor. He was thinking that about the life of Mary and himself, which had been so quiet, there seemed to be gathering on all sides grotesque and fantastic shapes, omens of confusion and disorder, threats of madness; a strange company from another world. It was as if into the quiet, sleeping streets of some little ancient town among the hills there had come from afar the sound of drum and pipe, snatches of wild song, and there had burst into the market-place the mad company of the players, strangely bedizened, dancing a furious measure to their hurrying music, drawing forth the citizens from their sheltered homes and peaceful lives, and alluring them to mingle in the significant figures of their dance.

Yet afar and near (for it was hidden in his heart) he beheld the glimmer of a sure and constant star. Beneath, darkness came on, and mists and shadows closed about the town. The red, flickering flame of torches was kindled in the midst of it. The song grew louder, with more insistent, magical tones, surging and falling in unearthly modulations, the very speech of incantation; and the drum beat madly, and the pipe shrilled to a scream, summoning all to issue forth, to leave their peaceful hearths; for a strange rite was preconized in their midst. The streets that were wont to be so still, so hushed with the cool and tranquil veils of darkness, asleep beneath the patronage of the evening star, now danced with glimmering lanterns, resounded with the cries of those who hurried forth, drawn as by a magistral spell; and the songs swelled and triumphed, the reverberant beating of the drum grew louder, and in the midst of the awakened town the players, fantastically arrayed, performed their interlude under the red blaze of torches. He knew not whether they were players, men that would vanish suddenly as they came, disappearing by the track that climbed the hill; or whether they were indeed magicians, workers of great and efficacious spells, who knew the secret word by which the earth may be transformed into the hall of Gehenna, so that they that gazed and listened, as at a passing spectacle, should be entrapped by the sound and the sight presented to them, should be drawn into the elaborated figures of that mystic dance, and so should be whirled away into those unending mazes on the wild hills that were abhorred, there to wander for evermore.

But Darnell was not afraid, because of the Daystar that had risen in his heart. It had dwelt there all his life, and had slowly shone forth with clearer and clearer light, and he began to see that though his earthly steps might be in the ways of the ancient town that was beset by the Enchanters, and resounded with their songs and their processions, yet he dwelt also in that serene and secure world of brightness, and from a great and unutterable height looked on the confusion of the mortal pageant, beholding mysteries in which he was no true actor, hearing magic songs that could by no means draw him down from the battlements of the high and holy city.

His heart was filled with a great joy and a great peace as he lay down beside his wife and fell asleep, and in the morning, when he woke up, he was glad.

CHAPTER 4

In a haze as of a dream Darnell's thoughts seemed to move through the opening days of the next week. Perhaps nature had not intended that he should be practical or much given to that which is usually called 'sound common sense,' but his training had made him desirous of good, plain qualities of the mind, and he uneasily strove to account to himself for his strange mood of the Sunday night, as he had often endeavoured to interpret the fancies of his boyhood and early manhood. At first he was annoyed by his want of success; the morning paper, which he always secured as the 'bus delayed at Uxbridge Road Station, fell from his hands unread, while he vainly reasoned, assuring himself that the threatened incursion of a whimsical old woman, though tiresome enough, was no rational excuse for those curious hours of meditation in which his thoughts seemed to have dressed themselves in unfamiliar, fantastic habits, and to parley with him in a strange speech, and yet a speech that he had understood.

With such arguments he perplexed his mind on the long, accustomed ride up the steep ascent of Holland Park, past the incongruous hustle of Notting Hill Gate, where in one direction a road shows the way to the snug, somewhat faded bowers and retreats of Bayswater, and in another one sees the portal of the murky region of the slums. The customary companions of his morning's journey were in the seats about him; he heard the hum of their talk, as they disputed concerning politics, and the man next to him, who came from Acton, asked him what he thought of the Government now. There was a discussion, and a loud and excited one, just in front, as to whether rhubarb was a fruit or vegetable, and in his ear he heard Redman, who was a near neighbour, praising the economy of 'the wife.'

'I don't know how she does it. Look here; what do you think we had yesterday? Breakfast: fish-cakes, beautifully fried--rich, you know, lots of herbs, it's a receipt of her aunt's; you should just taste 'em. Coffee, bread, butter, marmalade, and, of course, all the usual etceteras. Dinner: roast beef, Yorkshire, potatoes, greens, and horse-radish sauce, plum tart, cheese. And where will you get a better dinner than that? Well, I call it wonderful, I really do.'

But in spite of these distractions he fell into a dream as the 'bus rolled and tossed on its way Citywards, and still he strove to solve the enigma of his vigil of the night before, and as the shapes of trees and green lawns and houses passed before his eyes, and as he saw the procession moving on the pavement, and while the murmur of the streets sounded in his ears, all was to him strange and unaccustomed, as if he moved through the avenues of some city in a foreign land. It was, perhaps, on these mornings, as he rode to his mechanical work, that vague and floating fancies that must have long haunted his brain began to shape themselves, and to put on the form of definite conclusions, from which he could no longer escape, even if he had wished it. Darnell had received what is called a sound commercial education, and would therefore have found very great difficulty in putting into articulate speech any thought that was worth thinking; but he grew certain on these mornings that the 'common sense' which he had always heard exalted as man's supremest faculty was, in all probability, the smallest and least-considered item in the equipment of an ant of average intelligence. And with this, as an almost necessary corollary, came a firm belief that the whole fabric of life in which he moved was sunken, past all thinking, in the grossest absurdity; that he and all his friends and acquaintances and fellow-workers were interested in matters in which men were never meant to be interested, were pursuing aims which they were never meant to pursue, were, indeed, much like fair stones of an altar serving as a pigsty wall. Life, it seemed to him, was a great search for--he knew not what; and in the process of the ages one by one the true marks upon the ways had been shattered, or buried, or the meaning of the words had been slowly forgotten; one by one the signs had been turned awry, the true entrances had been thickly overgrown, the very way itself had been diverted from the heights to the depths, till at last the race of pilgrims had become hereditary stone-breakers and ditch-scourers on a track that led to destruction--if it led anywhere at all. Darnell's heart thrilled with a strange and trembling joy, with a sense that was all new, when it came to his mind that this great loss might not be a hopeless one, that perhaps the difficulties were by no means insuperable. It might be, he considered, that the stone-breaker had merely to throw down his hammer and set out, and the way would be plain before him; and a single step would free the delver in rubbish from the foul slime of the ditch.

It was, of course, with difficulty and slowly that these things became clear to him. He was an English City clerk, 'flourishing' towards the end of the nineteenth century, and the rubbish heap that had been accumulating for some centuries could not be cleared away in an instant. Again and again the spirit of nonsense that had been implanted in him as in his fellows assured him that the true world was the visible and tangible world, the world in which good and faithful letter-copying was exchangeable for a certain quantum of bread, beef, and house-room, and that the man who copied letters well, did not beat his wife, nor lose money foolishly, was a good man, fulfilling the end for which he had been made. But in spite of these arguments, in spite of their acceptance by all who were about him, he had the grace to perceive the utter falsity and absurdity of the whole position. He was fortunate in his entire ignorance of sixpenny 'science,' but if the whole library had been projected into his brain it would not have moved him to 'deny in the darkness that which he had known in the light.' Darnell knew by experience that man is made a mystery for mysteries and visions, for the realization in his consciousness of ineffable bliss, for a great joy that transmutes the whole world, for a joy that surpasses all joys and overcomes all sorrows. He knew this certainly, though he knew it dimly; and he was apart from other men, preparing himself for a great experiment.

With such thoughts as these for his secret and concealed treasure, he was able to bear the threatened invasion of Mrs. Nixon with something approaching indifference. He knew, indeed, that her presence between his wife and himself would be unwelcome to him, and he was not without grave doubts as to the woman's sanity; but after all, what did it matter? Besides, already a faint glimmering light had risen within him that showed the profit of self-negation, and in this matter he had preferred his wife's will to his own. Et non sua poma; to his astonishment he found a delight in denying himself his own wish, a process that he had always regarded as thoroughly detestable. This was a state of things which he could not in the least understand; but, again, though a member of a most hopeless class, living in the most hopeless surroundings that the world has ever seen, though he knew as much of the askesis as of Chinese metaphysics; again, he had the grace not to deny the light that had begun to glimmer in his soul.

And he found a present reward in the eyes of Mary, when she welcomed him home after his foolish labours in the cool of the evening. They sat together, hand in hand, under the mulberry tree, at the coming of the dusk, and as the ugly walls about them became obscure and vanished into the formless world of shadows, they seemed to be freed from the bondage of Shepherd's Bush, freed to wander in that undisfigured, undefiled world that lies beyond the walls. Of this region Mary knew little or nothing by experience, since her relations had always been of one mind with the modern world, which has for the true country an instinctive and most significant horror and dread. Mr. Reynolds had also shared in another odd superstition of these later days--that it is necessary to leave London at least once a year; consequently Mary had some knowledge of various seaside resorts on the south and east coasts, where Londoners gather in hordes, turn the sands into one vast, bad music-hall, and derive, as they say, enormous benefit from the change. But experiences such as these give but little knowledge of the country in its true and occult sense; and yet Mary, as she sat in the dusk beneath the whispering tree, knew something of the secret of the wood, of the valley shut in by high hills, where the sound of pouring water always echoes from the clear brook. And to Darnell these were nights of great dreams; for it was the hour of the work, the time of transmutation, and he who could not understand the miracle, who could scarcely believe in it, yet knew, secretly and half consciously, that the water was being changed into the wine of a new life. This was ever the inner music of his dreams, and to it he added on these still and sacred nights the far-off memory of that time long ago when, a child, before the world had overwhelmed him, he journeyed down to the old grey house in the west, and for a whole month heard the murmur of the forest through his bedroom window, and when the wind was hushed, the washing of the tides about the reeds; and sometimes awaking very early he had heard the strange cry of a bird as it rose from its nest among the reeds, and had looked out and had seen the valley whiten to the dawn, and the winding river whiten as it swam down to the sea. The memory of all this had faded and become shadowy as he grew older and the chains of common life were riveted firmly about his soul; all the atmosphere by which he was surrounded was well-nigh fatal to such thoughts, and only now and again in half-conscious moments or in sleep he had revisited that valley in the far-off west, where the breath of the wind was an incantation, and every leaf and stream and hill spoke of great and ineffable mysteries. But now the broken vision was in great part restored to him, and looking with love in his wife's eyes he saw the gleam of water-pools in the still forest, saw the mists rising in the evening, and heard the music of the winding river.

They were sitting thus together on the Friday evening of the week that had begun with that odd and half-forgotten visit of Mrs. Nixon, when, to Darnell's annoyance, the door-bell gave a discordant peal, and Alice with some disturbance of manner came out and announced that a gentleman wished to see the master. Darnell went into the drawing-room, where Alice had lit one gas so that it flared and burnt with a rushing sound, and in this distorting light there waited a stout, elderly gentleman, whose countenance was altogether unknown to him. He stared blankly, and hesitated, about to speak, but the visitor began.

'You don't know who I am, but I expect you'll know my name. It's Nixon.'

He did not wait to be interrupted. He sat down and plunged into narrative, and after the first few words, Darnell, whose mind was not altogether unprepared, listened without much astonishment.

'And the long and the short of it is,' Mr. Nixon said at last, 'she's gone stark, staring mad, and we had to put her away to-day--poor thing.'

His voice broke a little, and he wiped his eyes hastily, for though stout and successful he was not unfeeling, and he was fond of his wife. He had spoken quickly, and had gone lightly over many details which might have interested specialists in certain kinds of mania, and Darnell was sorry for his evident distress.

'I came here,' he went on after a brief pause, 'because I found out she had been to see you last Sunday, and I knew the sort of story she must have told.'

Darnell showed him the prophetic leaflet which Mrs. Nixon had dropped in the garden. 'Did you know about this?' he said.

'Oh, him,' said the old man, with some approach to cheerfulness; 'oh yes, I thrashed him black and blue the day before yesterday.'

'Isn't he mad? Who is the man?'

'He's not mad, he's bad. He's a little Welsh skunk named Richards. He's been running some sort of chapel over at New Barnet for the last few years, and my poor wife--she never could find the parish church good enough for her--had been going to his damned schism shop for the last twelve-month. It was all that finished her off. Yes; I thrashed him the day before yesterday, and I'm not afraid of a summons either. I know him, and he knows I know him.'

Old Nixon whispered something in Darnell's ear, and chuckled faintly as he repeated for the third time his formula--

'I thrashed him black and blue the day before yesterday.'

Darnell could only murmur condolences and express his hope that Mrs. Nixon might recover.

The old man shook his head.

'I'm afraid there's no hope of that,' he said. 'I've had the best advice, but they couldn't do anything, and told me so.'

Presently he asked to see his niece, and Darnell went out and prepared Mary as well as he could. She could scarcely take in the news that her aunt was a hopeless maniac, for Mrs. Nixon, having been extremely stupid all her days, had naturally succeeded in passing with her relations as typically sensible. With the Reynolds family, as with the great majority of us, want of imagination is always equated with sanity, and though many of us have never heard of Lombroso we are his ready-made converts. We have always believed that poets are mad, and if statistics unfortunately show that few poets have really been inhabitants of lunatic asylums, it is soothing to learn that nearly all poets have had whooping-cough, which is doubtless, like intoxication, a minor madness.

'But is it really true?' she asked at length. 'Are you certain uncle is not deceiving you? Aunt seemed so sensible always.'

She was helped at last by recollecting that Aunt Marian used to get up very early of mornings, and then they went into the drawing-room and talked to the old man. His evident kindliness and honesty grew upon Mary, in spite of a lingering belief in her aunt's fables, and when he left, it was with a promise to come to see them again.

Mrs. Darnell said she felt tired, and went to bed; and Darnell returned to the garden and began to pace to and fro, collecting his thoughts. His immeasurable relief at the intelligence that, after all, Mrs. Nixon was not coming to live with them taught him that, despite his submission, his dread of the event had been very great. The weight was removed, and now he was free to consider his life without reference to the grotesque intrusion that he had feared. He sighed for joy, and as he paced to and fro he savoured the scent of the night, which, though it came faintly to him in that brick-bound suburb, summoned to his mind across many years the odour of the world at night as he had known it in that short sojourn of his boyhood; the odour that rose from the earth when the flame of the sun had gone down beyond the mountain, and the afterglow had paled in the sky and on the fields. And as he recovered as best he could these lost dreams of an enchanted land, there came to him other images of his childhood, forgotten and yet not forgotten, dwelling unheeded in dark places of the memory, but ready to be summoned forth. He remembered one fantasy that had long haunted him. As he lay half asleep in the forest on one hot afternoon of that memorable visit to the country, he had 'made believe' that a little companion had come to him out of the blue mists and the green light beneath the leaves--a white girl with long black hair, who had played with him and whispered her secrets in his ear, as his father lay sleeping under a tree; and from that summer afternoon, day by day, she had been beside him; she had visited him in the wilderness of London, and even in recent years there had come to him now and again the sense of her presence, in the midst of the heat and turmoil of the City. The last visit he remembered well; it was a few weeks before he married, and from the depths of some futile task he had looked up with puzzled eyes, wondering why the close air suddenly grew scented with green leaves, why the murmur of the trees and the wash of the river on the reeds came to his ears; and then that sudden rapture to which he had given a name and an individuality possessed him utterly. He knew then how the dull flesh of man can be like fire; and now, looking back from a new standpoint on this and other experiences, he realized how all that was real in his life had been unwelcomed, uncherished by him, had come to him, perhaps, in virtue of merely negative qualities on his part. And yet, as he reflected, he saw that there had been a chain of witnesses all through his life: again and again voices had whispered in his ear words in a strange language that he now recognized as his native tongue; the common street had not been lacking in visions of the true land of his birth; and in all the passing and repassing of the world he saw that there had been emissaries ready to guide his feet on the way of the great journey.

A week or two after the visit of Mr. Nixon, Darnell took his annual holiday.

There was no question of Walton-on-the-Naze, or of anything of the kind, as he quite agreed with his wife's longing for some substantial sum put by against the evil day. But the weather was still fine, and he lounged away the time in his garden beneath the tree, or he sauntered out on long aimless walks in the western purlieus of London, not unvisited by that old sense of some great ineffable beauty, concealed by the dim and dingy veils of grey interminable streets. Once, on a day of heavy rain he went to the 'box-room,' and began to turn over the papers in the old hair trunk—scraps and odds and ends of family history, some of them in his father's handwriting, others in faded ink, and there were a few ancient pocket-books, filled with manuscript of a still earlier time, and in these the ink was glossier and blacker than any writing fluids supplied by stationers of later days. Darnell had hung up the portrait of the ancestor in this room, and had bought a solid kitchen table and a chair; so that Mrs. Darnell, seeing him looking over his old documents, half thought of naming the room 'Mr. Darnell's study.' He had not glanced at these relics of his family for many years, but from the hour when the rainy morning sent him to them, he remained constant to research till the end of the holidays. It was a new interest, and he began to fashion in his mind a faint picture of his forefathers, and of their life in that grey old house in the river valley, in the western land of wells and streams and dark and ancient woods. And there were stranger things than mere notes on family history amongst that odd litter of old disregarded papers, and when he went back to his work in the City some of the men fancied that he was in some vague manner changed in appearance; but he only laughed when they asked him where he had been and what he had been doing with himself. But Mary noticed that every evening he spent at least an hour in the box-room; she was rather sorry at the waste of time involved in reading old papers about dead people. And one afternoon, as they were out together on a somewhat dreary walk towards Acton, Darnell stopped at a hopeless second-hand bookshop, and after scanning the rows of shabby books in the window, went in and purchased two volumes. They proved to be a Latin dictionary and grammar, and she was surprised to hear her husband declare his intention of acquiring the Latin language.

But, indeed, all his conduct impressed her as indefinably altered; and she began to be a little alarmed, though she could scarcely have formed her fears in words. But she knew that in some way that was all indefined and beyond the grasp of her thought their lives had altered since the summer, and no single thing wore quite the same aspect as before. If she looked out into the dull street with its rare loiterers, it was the same and yet it had altered, and if she opened the window in the early morning the wind that entered came with a changed breath that spoke some message that she could not understand. And day by day passed by in the old course, and not even the four walls were altogether familiar, and the voices of men and women sounded with strange notes, with the echo, rather, of a music that came over unknown hills. And day by day as she went about her household work, passing from shop to shop in those dull streets that were a network, a fatal labyrinth of grey desolation on every side, there came to her sense half-seen images of some other world, as if she walked in a dream, and every moment must bring her to light and to awakening, when the grey should fade, and regions long desired should appear in glory. Again and again it seemed as if that which was hidden would be shown even to the sluggish testimony of sense; and as she went to and fro from street to street of that dim and weary suburb, and looked on those grey material walls, they seemed as if a light glowed behind them, and again and again the mystic fragrance of incense was blown to her nostrils from across the verge of that world which is not so much impenetrable as ineffable, and to her ears came the dream of a chant that spoke of hidden choirs about all her ways. She struggled against these impressions, refusing her assent to the testimony of them, since all the pressure of credited opinion for three hundred years has been directed towards stamping out real knowledge, and so effectually has this been accomplished that we can only recover the truth through much anguish. And so Mary passed the days in a strange perturbation, clinging to common things and common thoughts, as if she feared that one morning she would wake up in an unknown world to a changed life. And Edward Darnell went day by day to his labour and returned in the evening, always with that shining of light within his eyes and upon his face, with the gaze of wonder that was greater day by day, as if for him the veil grew thin and soon would disappear.

From these great matters both in herself and in her husband Mary shrank back, afraid, perhaps, that if she began the question the answer might be too wonderful. She rather taught herself to be troubled over little things; she asked herself what attraction there could be in the old records over which she supposed Edward to be poring night after night in the cold room upstairs. She had glanced over the papers at Darnell's invitation, and could see but little interest in them; there were one or two sketches, roughly done in pen and ink, of the old house in the west: it looked a shapeless and fantastic place, furnished with strange pillars and stranger ornaments on the projecting porch; and on one side a roof dipped down almost to the earth, and in the centre there was something that might almost be a tower rising above the rest of the building. Then there were documents that seemed all names and dates, with here and there a coat of arms done in the margin, and she came upon a string of uncouth Welsh names linked together by the word 'ap' in a chain that looked endless. There was a paper covered with signs and figures that meant nothing to her, and then there were the pocket-books, full of old-fashioned writing, and much of it in Latin, as her husband told her--it was a collection as void of significance as a treatise on conic sections, so far as Mary was concerned. But night after night Darnell shut himself up with the musty rolls, and more than ever when he rejoined her he bore upon his face the blazonry of some great adventure. And one night she asked him what interested him so much in the papers he had shown her.

He was delighted with the question. Somehow they had not talked much together for the last few weeks, and he began to tell her of the records of the old race from which he came, of the old strange house of grey stone between the forest and the river. The family went back and back, he said, far into the dim past, beyond the Normans, beyond the Saxons, far into the Roman days, and for many hundred years they had been petty kings, with a strong fortress high up on the hill, in the heart of the forest; and even now the great mounds remained, whence one could look through the trees towards the mountain on one side and across the yellow sea on the other. The real name of the family was not Darnell; that was assumed by one Iolo ap Taliesin ap Iorwerth in the sixteenth century--why, Darnell did not seem to understand. And then he told her how the race had dwindled in prosperity, century by century, till at last there was nothing left but the grey house and a few acres of land bordering the river.

'And do you know, Mary,' he said, 'I suppose we shall go and live there some day or other. My great-uncle, who has the place now, made money in business when he was a young man, and I believe he will leave it all to me. I know I am the only relation he has. How strange it would be. What a change from the life here.'

'You never told me that. Don't you think your great-uncle might leave his house and his money to somebody he knows really well? You haven't seen him since you were a little boy, have you?'

'No; but we write once a year. And from what I have heard my father say, I am sure the old man would never leave the house out of the family. Do you think you would like it?'

'I don't know. Isn't it very lonely?'

'I suppose it is. I forget whether there are any other houses in sight, but I don't think there are any at all near. But what a change! No City, no streets, no people passing to and fro; only the sound of the wind and the sight of the green leaves and the green hills, and the song of the voices of the earth.'... He checked himself suddenly, as if he feared that he was about to tell some secret that must not yet be uttered; and indeed, as he spoke of the change from the little street in Shepherd's Bush to that ancient house in the woods of the far west, a change seemed already to possess himself, and his voice put on the modulation of an antique chant. Mary looked at him steadily and touched his arm, and he drew a long breath before he spoke again.

'It is the old blood calling to the old land,' he said. 'I was forgetting that I am a clerk in the City.'

It was, doubtless, the old blood that had suddenly stirred in him; the resurrection of the old spirit that for many centuries had been faithful to secrets that are now disregarded by most of us, that now day by day was quickened more and more in his heart, and grew so strong that it was hard to conceal. He was indeed almost in the position of the man in the tale, who, by a sudden electric shock, lost the vision of the things about him in the London streets, and gazed instead upon the sea and shore of an island in the Antipodes; for Darnell only clung with an effort to the interests and the atmosphere which, till lately, had seemed all the world to him; and the grey house and the wood and the river, symbols of the other sphere, intruded as it were into the landscape of the London suburb.

But he went on, with more restraint, telling his stories of far-off ancestors, how one of them, the most remote of all, was called a saint, and was supposed to possess certain mysterious secrets often alluded to in the papers as the 'Hidden Songs of Iolo Sant.' And then with an abrupt transition he recalled memories of his father and of the strange, shiftless life in dingy lodgings in the backwaters of London, of the dim stucco streets that were his first recollections, of forgotten squares in North London, and of the figure of his father, a grave bearded man who seemed always in a dream, as if he too sought for the vision of a land beyond the strong walls, a land where there were deep orchards and many shining hills, and fountains and water-pools gleaming under the leaves of the wood.

'I believe my father earned his living,' he went on, 'such a living as he did earn, at the Record Office and the British Museum. He used to hunt up things for lawyers and country parsons who wanted old deeds inspected. He never made much, and we were always moving from one lodging to another--always to out-of-the-way places where everything seemed to have run to seed. We never knew our neighbours--we moved too often for that--but my father had about half a dozen friends, elderly men like himself, who used to come to see us pretty often; and then, if there was any money, the lodging-house servant would go out for beer, and they would sit and smoke far into the night.

'I never knew much about these friends of his, but they all had the same look, the look of longing for something hidden. They talked of mysteries that I never understood, very little of their own lives, and when they did speak of ordinary affairs one could tell that they thought such matters as money and the want of it were unimportant trifles. When I grew up and went into the City, and met other young fellows and heard their way of talking, I wondered whether my father and his friends were not a little queer in their heads; but I know better now.'

So night after night Darnell talked to his wife, seeming to wander aimlessly from the dingy lodging-houses, where he had spent his boyhood in the company of his father and the other seekers, to the old house hidden in that far western valley, and the old race that had so long looked at the setting of the sun over the mountain. But in truth there was one end in all that he spoke, and Mary felt that beneath his words, however indifferent they might seem, there was hidden a purpose, that they were to embark on a great and marvellous adventure.

So day by day the world became more magical; day by day the work of separation was being performed, the gross accidents were being refined away. Darnell neglected no instruments that might be useful in the work; and now he neither lounged at home on Sunday mornings, nor did he accompany his wife to the Gothic blasphemy which pretended to be a church. They had discovered a little church of another fashion in a back street, and Darnell, who had found in one of the old notebooks the maxim Incredibilia sola Credenda, soon perceived how high and glorious a thing was that service at which he assisted. Our stupid ancestors taught us that we could become wise by studying books on 'science,' by meddling with test-tubes, geological specimens, microscopic preparations, and the like; but they who have cast off these follies know that they must read not 'science' books, but mass-books, and that the soul is made wise by the contemplation of mystic ceremonies and elaborate and curious rites. In such things Darnell found a wonderful mystery language, which spoke at once more secretly and more directly than the formal creeds; and he saw that, in a sense, the whole world is but a great ceremony or sacrament, which teaches under visible forms a hidden and transcendent doctrine. It was thus that he found in the ritual of the church a perfect image of the world; an image purged, exalted, and illuminate, a holy house built up of shining and translucent stones, in which the burning torches were more significant than the wheeling stars, and the fuming incense was a more certain token than the rising of the mist. His soul went forth with the albed procession in its white and solemn order, the mystic dance that signifies rapture and a joy above all joys, and when he beheld Love slain and rise again victorious he knew that he witnessed, in a figure, the consummation of all things, the Bridal of all Bridals, the mystery that is beyond all mysteries, accomplished from the foundation of the world. So day by day the house of his life became more magical.

And at the same time he began to guess that if in the New Life there are new and unheard-of joys, there are also new and unheard-of dangers. In his manuscript books which professed to deliver the outer sense of those mysterious 'Hidden Songs of Iolo Sant' there was a little chapter that bore the heading: Fons Sacer non in communem Vsum convertendus est, and by diligence, with much use of the grammar and dictionary, Darnell was able to construe the by no means complex Latin of his ancestor. The special book which contained the chapter in question was one of the most singular in the collection, since it bore the title Terra de Iolo, and on the surface, with an ingenious concealment of its real symbolism, it affected to give an account of the orchards, fields, woods, roads, tenements, and waterways in the possession of Darnell's ancestors. Here, then, he read of the Holy Well, hidden in the Wistman's Wood--Sylva Sapientum--'a fountain of abundant water, which no heats of summer can ever dry, which no flood can ever defile, which is as a water of life, to them that thirst for life, a stream of cleansing to them that would be pure, and a medicine of such healing virtue that by it, through the might of God and the intercession of His saints, the most grievous wounds are made whole.' But the water of this well was to be kept sacred perpetually, it was not to be used for any common purpose, nor to satisfy any bodily thirst; but ever to be esteemed as holy, 'even as the water which the priest hath hallowed.' And in the margin a comment in a later hand taught Darnell something of the meaning of these prohibitions. He was warned not to use the Well of Life as a mere luxury of mortal life, as a new sensation, as a means of making the insipid cup of everyday existence more palatable. 'For,' said the commentator, 'we are not called to sit as the spectators in a theatre, there to watch the play performed before us, but we are rather summoned to stand in the very scene itself, and there fervently to enact our parts in a great and wonderful mystery.'

Darnell could quite understand the temptation that was thus indicated. Though he had gone but a little way on the path, and had barely tested the over-runnings of that mystic well, he was already aware of the enchantment that was transmuting all the world about him, informing his life with a strange significance and romance.

London seemed a city of the Arabian Nights, and its labyrinths of streets an enchanted maze; its long avenues of lighted lamps were as starry systems, and its immensity became for him an image of the endless universe. He could well imagine how pleasant it might be to linger in such a world as this, to sit apart and dream, beholding the strange pageant played before him; but the Sacred Well was not for common use, it was for the cleansing of the soul, and the healing of the grievous wounds of the spirit. There must be yet another transformation: London had become Bagdad; it must at last be transmuted to Syon, or in the phrase of one of his old documents, the City of the Cup.

And there were yet darker perils which the Iolo MSS. (as his father had named the collection) hinted at more or less obscurely. There were suggestions of an awful region which the soul might enter, of a transmutation that was unto death, of evocations which could summon the utmost forces of evil from their dark places--in a word, of that sphere which is represented to most of us under the crude and somewhat childish symbolism of Black Magic. And here again he was not altogether without a dim comprehension of what was meant. He found himself recalling an odd incident that had happened long ago, which had remained all the years in his mind unheeded, amongst the many insignificant recollections of his childhood, and now rose before him, clear and distinct and full of meaning. It was on that memorable visit to the old house in the west, and the whole scene returned, with its smallest events, and the voices seemed to sound in his ears. It was a grey, still day of heavy heat that he remembered: he had stood on the lawn after breakfast, and wondered at the great peace and silence of the world. Not a leaf stirred in the trees on the lawn, not a whisper came from the myriad leaves of the wood; the flowers gave out sweet and heavy odours as if they breathed the dreams of the summer night; and far down the valley, the winding river was like dim silver under that dim and silvery sky, and the far hills and woods and fields vanished in the mist. The stillness of the air held him as with a charm; he leant all the morning against the rails that parted the lawn from the meadow, breathing the mystic breath of summer, and watching the fields brighten as with a sudden blossoming of shining flowers as the high mist grew thin for a moment before the hidden sun. As he watched thus, a man weary with heat, with some glance of horror in his eyes, passed him on his way to the house; but he stayed at his post till the old bell in the turret rang, and they dined all together, masters and servants, in the dark cool room that looked towards the still leaves of the wood. He could see that his uncle was upset about something, and when they had finished dinner he heard him tell his father that there was trouble at a farm; and it was settled that they should all drive over in the afternoon to some place with a strange name. But when the time came Mr. Darnell was too deep in old books and tobacco smoke to be stirred from his corner, and Edward and his uncle went alone in the dog-cart. They drove swiftly down the narrow lane, into the road that followed the winding river, and crossed the bridge at Caermaen by the mouldering Roman walls, and then, skirting the deserted, echoing village, they came out on a broad white turnpike road, and the limestone dust followed them like a cloud. Then, suddenly, they turned to the north by such a road as Edward had never seen before. It was so narrow that there was barely room for the cart to pass, and the footway was of rock, and the banks rose high above them as they slowly climbed the long, steep way, and the untrimmed hedges on either side shut out the light. And the ferns grew thick and green upon the banks, and hidden wells dripped down upon them; and the old man told him how the lane in winter was a torrent of swirling water, so that no one could pass by it. On they went, ascending and then again descending, always in that deep hollow under the wild woven boughs, and the boy wondered vainly what the country was like on either side. And now the air grew darker, and the hedge on one bank was but the verge of a dark and rustling wood, and the grey limestone rocks had changed to dark-red earth flecked with green patches and veins of marl, and suddenly in the stillness from the depths of the wood a bird began to sing a melody that charmed the heart into another world, that sang to the child's soul of the blessed faery realm beyond the woods of the earth, where the wounds of man are healed. And so at last, after many turnings and windings, they came to a high bare land where the lane broadened out into a kind of common, and along the edge of this place there were scattered three or four old cottages, and one of them was a little tavern. Here they stopped, and a man came out and tethered the tired horse to a post and gave him water; and old Mr. Darnell took the child's hand and led him by a path across the fields. The boy could see the country now, but it was all a strange, undiscovered land; they were in the heart of a wilderness of hills and valleys that he had never looked upon, and they were going down a wild, steep hillside, where the narrow path wound in and out amidst gorse and towering bracken, and the sun gleaming out for a moment, there was a gleam of white water far below in a narrow valley, where a little brook poured and rippled from stone to stone. They went down the hill, and through a brake, and then, hidden in dark-green orchards, they came upon a long, low whitewashed house, with a stone roof strangely coloured by the growth of moss and lichens. Mr. Darnell knocked at a heavy oaken door, and they came into a dim room where but little light entered through the thick glass in the deep-set window. There were heavy beams in the ceiling, and a great fireplace sent out an odour of burning wood that

Darnell never forgot, and the room seemed to him full of women who talked all together in frightened tones. Mr. Darnell beckoned to a tall, grey old man, who wore corduroy knee-breeches, and the boy, sitting on a high straight-backed chair, could see the old man and his uncle passing to and fro across the window-panes, as they walked together on the garden path. The women stopped their talk for a moment, and one of them brought him a glass of milk and an apple from some cold inner chamber; and then, suddenly, from a room above there rang out a shrill and terrible shriek, and then, in a young girl's voice, a more terrible song. It was not like anything the child had ever heard, but as the man recalled it to his memory, he knew to what song it might be compared--to a certain chant indeed that summons the angels and archangels to assist in the great Sacrifice. But as this song chants of the heavenly army, so did that seem to summon all the hierarchy of evil, the hosts of Lilith and Samael; and the words that rang out with such awful modulations--neumata inferorum--were in some unknown tongue that few men have ever heard on earth.

The women glared at one another with horror in their eyes, and he saw one or two of the oldest of them clumsily making an old sign upon their breasts. Then they began to speak again, and he remembered fragments of their talk.

'She has been up there,' said one, pointing vaguely over her shoulder.

'She'd never know the way,' answered another. 'They be all gone that went there.'

'There be nought there in these days.'

'How can you tell that, Gwenllian? 'Tis not for us to say that.'

'My great-grandmother did know some that had been there,' said a very old woman. 'She told me how they was taken afterwards.'

And then his uncle appeared at the door, and they went their way as they had come. Edward Darnell never heard any more of it, nor whether the girl died or recovered from her strange attack; but the scene had haunted his mind in boyhood, and now the recollection of it came to him with a certain note of warning, as a symbol of dangers that might be in the way.

* * * * *

It would be impossible to carry on the history of Edward Darnell and of Mary his wife to a greater length, since from this point their legend is full of impossible events, and seems to put on the semblance of the stories of the Graal. It is certain, indeed, that in this world they changed their lives, like King Arthur, but this is a work which no chronicler has cared to describe with any amplitude of detail. Darnell, it is true, made a little book, partly consisting of queer verse which might have been written by an inspired infant, and partly made up of 'notes and exclamations' in an odd dog-Latin which he had picked up from the 'Iolo MSS.', but it is to be feared that this work, even if published in its entirety, would cast but little light on a perplexing story. He called this piece of literature 'In Exitu Israel,' and wrote on the title page the motto, doubtless of his own composition, 'Nunc certe scio quod omnia legenda; omnes historiæ, omnes fabulæ, omnis Scriptura sint de ME narrata.' It is only too evident that his Latin was not learnt at the feet of Cicero; but in this dialect he relates the great history of the 'New Life' as it was manifested to him. The 'poems' are even stranger. One, headed (with an odd reminiscence of old-fashioned books) 'Lines written on looking down from a Height in London on a Board School suddenly lit up by the Sun' begins thus:--

One day when I was all alone I found a wondrous little stone, It lay forgotten on the road Far from the ways of man's abode. When on this stone mine eyes I cast I saw my Treasure found at last. I pressed it hard against my face, I covered it with my embrace, I hid it in a secret place. And every day I went to see This stone that was my ecstasy; And worshipped it with flowers rare, And secret words and sayings fair. O stone, so rare and red and wise O fragment of far Paradise, O Star, whose light is life! O Sea, Whose ocean is infinity! Thou art a fire that ever burns, And all the world to wonder turns; And all the dust of the dull day By thee is changed and purged away, So that, where'er I look, I see A world of a Great Majesty. The sullen river rolls all gold, The desert park's a faery wold, When on the trees the wind is borne I hear the sound of Arthur's horn I see no town of grim grey ways, But a great city all ablaze With burning torches, to light up The pinnacles that shrine the Cup. Ever the magic wine is poured, Ever the Feast shines on the board, Ever the song is borne on high That chants the holy Magistry-- Etc. etc. etc.

From such documents as these it is clearly impossible to gather any very definite information. But on the last page Darnell has written--

'So I awoke from a dream of a London suburb, of daily labour, of weary, useless little things; and as my eyes were opened I saw that I was in an ancient wood, where a clear well rose into grey film and vapour beneath a misty, glimmering heat. And a form came towards me from the hidden places of the wood, and my love and I were united by the well.'

The Inmost Light

CHAPTER 1

One evening in autumn, when the deformities of London were veiled in faint blue mist, and its vistas and far-reaching streets seemed splendid, Mr. Charles Salisbury was slowly pacing down Rupert Street, drawing nearer to his favourite restaurant by slow degrees. His eyes were downcast in study of the pavement, and thus it was that as he passed in at the narrow door a man who had come up from the lower end of the street jostled against him.

'I beg your pardon--wasn't looking where I was going. Why, it's Dyson!'

'Yes, quite so. How are you, Salisbury?'

'Quite well. But where have you been, Dyson? I don't think I can have seen you for the last five years?'

'No; I dare say not. You remember I was getting rather hard up when you came to my place at Charlotte Street?'

'Perfectly. I think I remember your telling me that you owed five weeks' rent, and that you had parted with your watch for a comparatively small sum.'

'My dear Salisbury, your memory is admirable. Yes, I was hard up. But the curious thing is that soon after you saw me I became harder up. My financial state was described by a friend as "stone broke." I don't approve of slang, mind you, but such was my condition. But suppose we go in; there might be other people who would like to dine--it's a human weakness, Salisbury.'

'Certainly; come along. I was wondering as I walked down whether the corner table were taken. It has a velvet back, you know.'

'I know the spot; it's vacant. Yes, as I was saying, I became even harder up.'

'What did you do then?' asked Salisbury, disposing of his hat, and settling down in the corner of the seat, with a glance of fond anticipation at the menu.

'What did I do? Why, I sat down and reflected. I had a good classical education, and a positive distaste for business of any kind: that was the capital with which I faced the world. Do you know, I have heard people describe olives as nasty! What lamentable Philistinism! I have often thought, Salisbury, that I could write genuine poetry under the influence of olives and red wine. Let us have Chianti; it may not be very good, but the flasks are simply charming.'

'It is pretty good here. We may as well have a big flask.'

'Very good. I reflected, then, on my want of prospects, and I determined to embark in literature.'

'Really; that was strange. You seem in pretty comfortable circumstances, though.'

'Though! What a satire upon a noble profession. I am afraid, Salisbury, you haven't a proper idea of the dignity of an artist. You see me sitting at my desk--or at least you can see me if you care to call-- with pen and ink, and simple nothingness before me, and if you come again in a few hours you will (in all probability) find a creation!'

'Yes, quite so. I had an idea that literature was not remunerative.'

'You are mistaken; its rewards are great. I may mention, by the way, that shortly after you saw me I succeeded to a small income. An uncle died, and proved unexpectedly generous.'

'Ah, I see. That must have been convenient.'

'It was pleasant--undeniably pleasant. I have always considered it in the light of an endowment of my researches. I told you I was a man of letters; it would, perhaps, be more correct to describe myself as a man of science.'

'Dear me, Dyson, you have really changed very much in the last few years. I had a notion, don't you know, that you were a sort of idler about town, the kind of man one might meet on the north side of Piccadilly every day from May to July.'

'Exactly. I was even then forming myself, though all unconsciously. You know my poor father could not afford to send me to the University. I used to grumble in my ignorance at not having completed my education. That was the folly of youth, Salisbury; my University was Piccadilly. There I began to study the great science which still occupies me.'

'What science do you mean?'

'The science of the great city; the physiology of London; literally and metaphysically the greatest subject that the mind of man can conceive. What an admirable salmi this is; undoubtedly the final end of the pheasant. Yet I feel sometimes positively overwhelmed with the thought of the vastness and complexity of London. Paris a man may get to understand thoroughly with a reasonable amount of study; but London is always a mystery. In Paris you may say: "Here live the actresses, here the Bohemians, and the Ratés"; but it is different in London. You may point out a street, correctly enough, as the abode of washerwomen; but, in that second floor, a man may be studying Chaldee roots, and in the garret over the way a forgotten artist is dying by inches.'

'I see you are Dyson, unchanged and unchangeable,' said Salisbury, slowly sipping his Chianti. 'I think you are misled by a too fervid imagination; the mystery of London exists only in your fancy. It seems to me a dull place enough. We seldom hear of a really artistic crime in London, whereas I believe Paris abounds in that sort of thing.'

'Give me some more wine. Thanks. You are mistaken, my dear fellow, you are really mistaken. London has nothing to be ashamed of in the way of crime. Where we fail is for want of Homers, not Agamemnons. Carent quia vate sacro, you know.'

'I recall the quotation. But I don't think I quite follow you.'

'Well, in plain language, we have no good writers in London who make a speciality of that kind of thing. Our common reporter is a dull dog; every story that he has to tell is spoilt in the telling. His idea of horror and of what excites horror is so lamentably deficient. Nothing will content the fellow but blood, vulgar red blood, and when he can get it he lays it on thick, and considers that he has produced a telling article. It's a poor notion. And, by some curious fatality, it is the most commonplace and brutal murders which always attract the most attention and get written up the most. For instance, I dare say that you never heard of the Harlesden case?'

'No; no, I don't remember anything about it.'

'Of course not. And yet the story is a curious one. I will tell it you over our coffee. Harlesden, you know, or I expect you don't know, is quite on the out-quarters of London; something curiously different from your fine old crusted suburb like Norwood or Hampstead, different as each of these is from the other. Hampstead, I mean, is where you look for the head of your great China house with his three acres of land and pine-houses, though of late there is the artistic substratum; while Norwood is the home of the prosperous middle-class family who took the house "because it was near the Palace," and sickened of the Palace six months afterwards; but Harlesden is a place of no character. It's too new to have any character as yet. There are the rows of red houses and the rows of white houses and the bright green Venetians, and the blistering doorways, and the little backyards they call gardens, and a few feeble shops, and then, just as you think you're going to grasp the physiognomy of the settlement, it all melts away.'

'How the dickens is that? the houses don't tumble down before one's eyes, I suppose!'

'Well, no, not exactly that. But Harlesden as an entity disappears.

Your street turns into a quiet lane, and your staring houses into elm trees, and the back-gardens into green meadows. You pass instantly from town to country; there is no transition as in a small country town, no soft gradations of wider lawns and orchards, with houses gradually becoming less dense, but a dead stop. I believe the people who live there mostly go into the City. I have seen once or twice a laden 'bus bound thitherwards. But however that may be, I can't conceive a greater loneliness in a desert at midnight than there is there at midday. It is like a city of the dead; the streets are glaring and desolate, and as you pass it suddenly strikes you that this too is part of London. Well, a year or two ago there was a doctor living there; he had set up his brass plate and his red lamp at the very end of one of those shining streets, and from the back of the house, the fields stretched away to the north. I don't know what his reason was in settling down in such an out-of-the-way place, perhaps Dr. Black, as we will call him, was a far-seeing man and looked ahead. His relations, so it appeared afterwards, had lost sight of him for many years and didn't even know he was a doctor, much less where he lived. However, there he was settled in Harlesden, with some fragments of a practice, and an uncommonly pretty wife. People used to see them walking out together in the summer evenings soon after they came to Harlesden, and, so far as could be observed, they seemed a very affectionate couple. These walks went on through the autumn, and then ceased; but, of course, as the days grew dark and the weather cold, the lanes near Harlesden might be expected to lose many of their attractions. All through the winter nobody saw anything of Mrs. Black; the doctor used to reply to his patients' inquiries that she was a "little out of sorts, would be better, no doubt, in the spring." But the spring came, and the summer, and no Mrs. Black appeared, and at last people began to rumour and talk amongst themselves, and all sorts of queer things were said at "high teas," which you may possibly have heard are the only form of entertainment known in such suburbs. Dr. Black began to surprise some very odd looks cast in his direction, and the practice, such as it was, fell off before his eyes. In short, when the neighbours whispered about the matter, they whispered that Mrs. Black was dead, and that the doctor had made away with her. But this wasn't the case; Mrs. Black was seen alive in June. It was a Sunday afternoon, one of those few exquisite days that an English climate offers, and half London had strayed out into the fields, north, south, east, and west to smell the scent of the white May, and to see if the wild roses were yet in blossom in the hedges. I had gone out myself early in the morning, and had had a long ramble, and somehow or other as I was steering homeward I found myself in this very Harlesden we have been talking about. To be exact, I had a glass of beer in the "General Gordon," the most flourishing house in the neighbourhood, and as I was wandering rather aimlessly about, I saw an uncommonly tempting gap in a hedgerow, and resolved to explore the meadow beyond. Soft grass is very grateful to the feet after the infernal grit strewn on suburban sidewalks, and after walking about for some time I thought I should like to sit down on a bank and have a smoke. While I was getting out my pouch, I looked up in the direction of the houses, and as I looked I felt my breath caught back, and my teeth began to chatter, and the stick I had in one hand snapped in two with the grip I gave it. It was as if I had had an electric current down my spine, and yet for some moment of time which seemed long, but which must have been very short, I caught myself wondering what on earth was the matter. Then I knew what had made my very heart shudder and my bones grind together in an agony. As I glanced up I had looked straight towards the last house in the row before me, and in an upper window of that house I had seen for some short fraction of a second a face. It was the face of a woman, and yet it was not human. You and I, Salisbury, have heard in our time, as we sat in our seats in church in sober English fashion, of a lust that cannot be satiated and of a fire that is unquenchable, but few of us have any notion what these words mean. I hope you never may, for as I saw that face at the window, with the blue sky above me and the warm air playing in gusts about me, I knew I had looked into another world--looked through the window of a commonplace, brand-new house, and seen hell open before me. When the first shock was over, I thought once or twice that I should have fainted; my face streamed with a cold sweat, and my breath came and went in sobs, as if I had been half drowned. I managed to get up at last, and walked round to the street, and there I saw the name "Dr. Black" on the post by the front gate. As fate or my luck would have it, the door opened and a man came down the steps as I passed by. I had no doubt it was the doctor himself. He was of a type rather common in London; long and thin, with a pasty face and a dull black moustache. He gave me a look as we passed each other on the pavement, and though it was merely the casual glance which one foot-passenger bestows on another, I felt convinced in my mind that here was an ugly customer to deal with. As you may imagine, I went my way a good deal puzzled and horrified too by what I had seen; for I had paid another visit to the "General Gordon," and had got together a good deal of the common gossip of the place about the Blacks. I didn't mention the fact that I had seen a woman's face in the window; but I heard that Mrs. Black had been much admired for her beautiful golden hair, and round what had struck me with such a nameless terror, there was a mist of flowing yellow hair, as it were an aureole of glory round the visage of a satyr. The whole thing bothered me in an indescribable manner; and when I got home I tried my best to think of the impression I had received as an illusion, but it was no use.

I knew very well I had seen what I have tried to describe to you, and I was morally certain that I had seen Mrs. Black. And then there was the gossip of the place, the suspicion of foul play, which I knew to be false, and my own conviction that there was some deadly mischief or other going on in that bright red house at the corner of Devon Road: how to construct a theory of a reasonable kind out of these two elements. In short, I found myself in a world of mystery; I puzzled my head over it and filled up my leisure moments by gathering together odd threads of speculation, but I never moved a step towards any real solution, and as the summer days went on the matter seemed to grow misty and indistinct, shadowing some vague terror, like a nightmare of last month. I suppose it would before long have faded into the background of my brain--I should not have forgotten it, for such a thing could never be forgotten--but one morning as I was looking over the paper my eye was caught by a heading over some two dozen lines of small type. The words I had seen were simply, "The Harlesden Case," and I knew what I was going to read. Mrs. Black was dead. Black had called in another medical man to certify as to cause of death, and something or other had aroused the strange doctor's suspicions and there had been an inquest and post-mortem. And the result? That, I will confess, did astonish me considerably; it was the triumph of the unexpected. The two doctors who made the autopsy were obliged to confess that they could not discover the faintest trace of any kind of foul play; their most exquisite tests and reagents failed to detect the presence of poison in the most infinitesimal quantity. Death, they found, had been caused by a somewhat obscure and scientifically interesting form of brain disease. The tissue of the brain and the molecules of the grey matter had undergone a most extraordinary series of changes; and the younger of the two doctors, who has some reputation, I believe, as a specialist in brain trouble, made some remarks in giving his evidence which struck me deeply at the time, though I did not then grasp their full significance. He said: "At the commencement of the examination I was astonished to find appearances of a character entirely new to me, notwithstanding my somewhat large experience. I need not specify these appearances at present, it will be sufficient for me to state that as I proceeded in my task I could scarcely believe that the brain before me was that of a human being at all." There was some surprise at this statement, as you may imagine, and the coroner asked the doctor if he meant to say that the brain resembled that of an animal. "No," he replied, "I should not put it in that way. Some of the appearances I noticed seemed to point in that direction, but others, and these were the more surprising, indicated a nervous organization of a wholly different character from that either of man or the lower animals." It was a curious thing to say, but of course the jury brought in a verdict of death from natural causes, and, so far as the public was concerned, the case came to an end. But after I had read what the doctor said I made up my mind that I should like to know a good deal more, and I set to work on what seemed likely to prove an interesting investigation. I had really a good deal of trouble, but I was successful in a measure. Though why--my dear fellow, I had no notion at the time. Are you aware that we have been here nearly four hours? The waiters are staring at us. Let's have the bill and be gone.'

The two men went out in silence, and stood a moment in the cool air, watching the hurrying traffic of Coventry Street pass before them to the accompaniment of the ringing bells of hansoms and the cries of the newsboys; the deep far murmur of London surging up ever and again from beneath these louder noises.

'It is a strange case, isn't it?' said Dyson at length. 'What do you think of it?'

'My dear fellow, I haven't heard the end, so I will reserve my opinion. When will you give me the sequel?'

'Come to my rooms some evening; say next Thursday. Here's the address. Good-night; I want to get down to the Strand.' Dyson hailed a passing hansom, and Salisbury turned northward to walk home to his lodgings.

CHAPTER 2

Mr. Salisbury, as may have been gathered from the few remarks which he had found it possible to introduce in the course of the evening, was a young gentleman of a peculiarly solid form of intellect, coy and retiring before the mysterious and the uncommon, with a constitutional dislike of paradox. During the restaurant dinner he had been forced to listen in almost absolute silence to a strange tissue of improbabilities strung together with the ingenuity of a born meddler in plots and mysteries, and it was with a feeling of weariness that he crossed Shaftesbury Avenue, and dived into the recesses of Soho, for his lodgings were in a modest neighbourhood to the north of Oxford Street. As he walked he speculated on the probable fate of Dyson, relying on literature, unbefriended by a thoughtful relative, and could not help concluding that so much subtlety united to a too vivid imagination would in all likelihood have been rewarded with a pair of sandwich-boards or a super's banner. Absorbed in this train of thought, and admiring the perverse dexterity which could transmute the face of a sickly woman and a case of brain disease into the crude elements of romance, Salisbury strayed on through the dimly-lighted streets, not noticing the gusty wind which drove sharply round corners and whirled the stray rubbish of the pavement into the air in eddies, while black clouds gathered over the sickly yellow moon. Even a stray drop or two of rain blown into his face did not rouse him from his meditations, and it was only when with a sudden rush the storm tore down upon the street that he began to consider the expediency of finding some shelter. The rain, driven by the wind, pelted down with the violence of a thunderstorm, dashing up from the stones and hissing through the air, and soon a perfect torrent of water coursed along the kennels and accumulated in pools over the choked-up drains. The few stray passengers who had been loafing rather than walking about the street had scuttered away, like frightened rabbits, to some invisible places of refuge, and though Salisbury whistled loud and long for a hansom, no hansom appeared. He looked about him, as if to discover how far he might be from the haven of Oxford Street, but strolling carelessly along, he had turned out of his way, and found himself in an unknown region, and one to all appearance devoid even of a public-house where shelter could be bought for the modest sum of twopence. The street lamps were few and at long intervals, and burned behind grimy glasses with the sickly light of oil, and by this wavering glimmer Salisbury could make out the shadowy and vast old houses of which the street was composed. As he passed along, hurrying, and shrinking from the full sweep of the rain, he noticed the innumerable bell-handles, with names that seemed about to vanish of old age graven on brass plates beneath them, and here and there a richly carved penthouse overhung the door, blackening with the grime of fifty years. The storm seemed to grow more and more furious; he was wet through, and a new hat had become a ruin, and still Oxford Street seemed as far off as ever; it was with deep relief that the dripping man caught sight of a dark archway which seemed to promise shelter from the rain if not from the wind. Salisbury took up his position in the driest corner and looked about him; he was standing in a kind of passage contrived under part of a house, and behind him stretched a narrow footway leading between blank walls to regions unknown. He had stood there for some time, vainly endeavouring to rid himself of some of his superfluous moisture, and listening for the passing wheel of a hansom, when his attention was aroused by a loud noise coming from the direction of the passage behind, and growing louder as it drew nearer. In a couple of minutes he could make out the shrill, raucous voice of a woman, threatening and renouncing, and making the very stones echo with her accents, while now and then a man grumbled and expostulated. Though to all appearance devoid of romance, Salisbury had some relish for street rows, and was, indeed, somewhat of an amateur in the more amusing phases of drunkenness; he therefore composed himself to listen and observe with something of the air of a subscriber to grand opera. To his annoyance, however, the tempest seemed suddenly to be composed, and he could hear nothing but the impatient steps of the woman and the slow lurch of the man as they came towards him. Keeping back in the shadow of the wall, he could see the two drawing nearer; the man was evidently drunk, and had much ado to avoid frequent collision with the wall as he tacked across from one side to the other, like some bark beating up against a wind. The woman was looking straight in front of her, with tears streaming from her eyes, but suddenly as they went by the flame blazed up again, and she burst forth into a torrent of abuse, facing round upon her companion.

'You low rascal, you mean, contemptible cur,' she went on, after an incoherent storm of curses, 'you think I'm to work and slave for you always, I suppose, while you're after that Green Street girl and drinking every penny you've got? But you're mistaken, Sam--indeed, I'll bear it no longer. Damn you, you dirty thief, I've done with you and your master too, so you can go your own errands, and I only hope they'll get you into trouble.'

The woman tore at the bosom of her dress, and taking something out that looked like paper, crumpled it up and flung it away. It fell at Salisbury's feet. She ran out and disappeared in the darkness, while the man lurched slowly into the street, grumbling indistinctly to himself in a perplexed tone of voice. Salisbury looked out after him and saw him maundering along the pavement, halting now and then and swaying indecisively, and then starting off at some fresh tangent. The sky had cleared, and white fleecy clouds were fleeting across the moon, high in the heaven. The light came and went by turns, as the clouds passed by, and, turning round as the clear, white rays shone into the passage, Salisbury saw the little ball of crumpled paper which the woman had cast down. Oddly curious to know what it might contain, he picked it up and put it in his pocket, and set out afresh on his journey.

CHAPTER 3

Salisbury was a man of habit. When he got home, drenched to the skin, his clothes hanging lank about him, and a ghastly dew besmearing his hat, his only thought was of his health, of which he took studious care. So, after changing his clothes and encasing himself in a warm dressing-gown, he proceeded to prepare a sudorific in the shape of a hot gin and water, warming the latter over one of those spirit-lamps which mitigate the austerities of the modern hermit's life. By the time this preparation had been exhibited, and Salisbury's disturbed feelings had been soothed by a pipe of tobacco, he was able to get into bed in a happy state of vacancy, without a thought of his adventure in the dark archway, or of the weird fancies with which Dyson had seasoned his dinner. It was the same at breakfast the next morning, for Salisbury made a point of not thinking of any thing until that meal was over; but when the cup and saucer were cleared away, and the morning pipe was lit, he remembered the little ball of paper, and began fumbling in the pockets of his wet coat. He did not remember into which pocket he had put it, and as he dived now into one and now into another, he experienced a strange feeling of apprehension lest it should not be there at all, though he could not for the life of him have explained the importance he attached to what was in all probability mere rubbish. But he sighed with relief when his fingers touched the crumpled surface in an inside pocket, and he drew it out gently and laid it on the little desk by his easy-chair with as much care as if it had been some rare jewel. Salisbury sat smoking and staring at his find for a few minutes, an odd temptation to throw the thing in the fire and have done with it struggling with as odd a speculation as to its possible contents, and as to the reason why the infuriated woman should have flung a bit of paper from her with such vehemence. As might be expected, it was the latter feeling that conquered in the end, and yet it was with something like repugnance that he at last took the paper and unrolled it, and laid it out before him. It was a piece of common dirty paper, to all appearance torn out of a cheap exercise-book, and in the middle were a few lines written in a queer cramped hand. Salisbury bent his head and stared eagerly at it for a moment, drawing a long breath, and then fell back in his chair gazing blankly before him, till at last with a sudden revulsion he burst into a peal of laughter, so long and loud and uproarious that the landlady's baby on the floor below awoke from sleep and echoed his mirth with hideous yells. But he laughed again and again, and took the paper up to read a second time what seemed such meaningless nonsense.

'Q. has had to go and see his friends in Paris,' it began. 'Traverse Handle S. "Once around the grass, and twice around the lass, and thrice around the maple tree."'

Salisbury took up the paper and crumpled it as the angry woman had done, and aimed it at the fire. He did not throw it there, however, but tossed it carelessly into the well of the desk, and laughed again. The sheer folly of the thing offended him, and he was ashamed of his own eager speculation, as one who pores over the high-sounding announcements in the agony column of the daily paper, and finds nothing but advertisement and triviality. He walked to the window, and stared out at the languid morning life of his quarter; the maids in slatternly print dresses washing door-steps, the fish-monger and the butcher on their rounds, and the tradesmen standing at the doors of their small shops, drooping for lack of trade and excitement. In the distance a blue haze gave some grandeur to the prospect, but the view as a whole was depressing, and would only have interested a student of the life of London, who finds something rare and choice in its very aspect. Salisbury turned away in disgust, and settled himself in the easy-chair, upholstered in a bright shade of green, and decked with yellow gimp, which was the pride and attraction of the apartments. Here he composed himself to his morning's occupation--the perusal of a novel that dealt with sport and love in a manner that suggested the collaboration of a stud-groom and a ladies' college. In an ordinary way, however, Salisbury would have been carried on by the interest of the story up to lunch-time, but this morning he fidgeted in and out of his chair, took the book up and laid it down again, and swore at last to himself and at himself in mere irritation. In point of fact the jingle of the paper found in the archway had 'got into his head,' and do what he would he could not help muttering over and over, 'Once around the grass, and twice around the lass, and thrice around the maple tree.' It became a positive pain, like the foolish burden of a music-hall song, everlastingly quoted, and sung at all hours of the day and night, and treasured by the street-boys as an unfailing resource for six months together. He went out into the streets, and tried to forget his enemy in the jostling of the crowds and the roar and clatter of the traffic, but presently he would find himself stealing quietly aside, and pacing some deserted byway, vainly puzzling his brains, and trying to fix some meaning to phrases that were meaningless. It was a positive relief when Thursday came, and he remembered that he had made an appointment to go and see Dyson; the flimsy reveries of the self-styled man of letters appeared entertaining when compared with this ceaseless iteration, this maze of thought from which there seemed no possibility of escape. Dyson's abode was in one of the quietest of the quiet streets that led down from the Strand to the river, and when Salisbury passed from the narrow stairway into his friend's room, he saw that the uncle had been beneficent indeed. The floor glowed and flamed with all the colours of the East; it was, as Dyson pompously remarked, 'a sunset in a dream,' and the lamplight, the twilight of London streets, was shut out with strangely worked curtains, glittering here and there with threads of gold. In the shelves of an oak armoire stood jars and plates of old French china, and the black and white of etchings not to be found in the Haymarket or in Bond Street, stood out against the splendour of a Japanese paper. Salisbury sat down on the settle by the hearth, and sniffed the mingled fumes of incense and tobacco, wondering and dumb before all this splendour after the green rep and the oleographs, the gilt-framed mirror, and the lustres of his own apartment.

'I am glad you have come,' said Dyson. 'Comfortable little room, isn't it? But you don't look very well, Salisbury. Nothing disagreed with you, has it?'

'No; but I have been a good deal bothered for the last few days. The fact is I had an odd kind of--of--adventure, I suppose I may call it, that night I saw you, and it has worried me a good deal. And the provoking part of it is that it's the merest nonsense--but, however, I will tell you all about it, by and by. You were going to let me have the rest of that odd story you began at the restaurant.'

'Yes. But I am afraid, Salisbury, you are incorrigible. You are a slave to what you call matter of fact. You know perfectly well that in your heart you think the oddness in that case is of my making, and that it is all really as plain as the police reports. However, as I have begun, I will go on. But first we will have something to drink, and you may as well light your pipe.'

Dyson went up to the oak cupboard, and drew from its depths a rotund bottle and two little glasses, quaintly gilded.

'It's Benedictine,' he said. 'You'll have some, won't you?'

Salisbury assented, and the two men sat sipping and smoking reflectively for some minutes before Dyson began.

'Let me see,' he said at last, 'we were at the inquest, weren't we? No, we had done with that. Ah, I remember. I was telling you that on the whole I had been successful in my inquiries, investigation, or whatever you like to call it, into the matter. Wasn't that where I left off?'

'Yes, that was it. To be precise, I think "though" was the last word you said on the matter.'

'Exactly. I have been thinking it all over since the other night, and I have come to the conclusion that that "though" is a very big "though" indeed. Not to put too fine a point on it, I have had to confess that what I found out, or thought I found out, amounts in reality to nothing. I am as far away from the heart of the case as ever. However, I may as well tell you what I do know. You may remember my saying that I was impressed a good deal by some remarks of one of the doctors who gave evidence at the inquest. Well, I determined that my first step must be to try if I could get something more definite and intelligible out of that doctor. Somehow or other I managed to get an introduction to the man, and he gave me an appointment to come and see him. He turned out to be a pleasant, genial fellow; rather young and not in the least like the typical medical man, and he began the conference by offering me whisky and cigars. I didn't think it worth while to beat about the bush, so I began by saying that part of his evidence at the Harlesden Inquest struck me as very peculiar, and I gave him the printed report, with the sentences in question underlined. He just glanced at the slip, and gave me a queer look. "It struck you as peculiar, did it?" said he. "Well, you must remember that the Harlesden case was very peculiar. In fact, I think I may safely say that in some features it was unique--quite unique." "Quite so," I replied, "and that's exactly why it interests me, and why I want to know more about it. And I thought that if anybody could give me any information it would be you. What is your opinion of the matter?"

'It was a pretty downright sort of question, and my doctor looked rather taken aback.

'"Well," he said, "as I fancy your motive in inquiring into the question must be mere curiosity, I think I may tell you my opinion with tolerable freedom. So, Mr., Mr. Dyson? if you want to know my theory, it is this: I believe that Dr. Black killed his wife."

'"But the verdict," I answered, "the verdict was given from your own evidence."

'"Quite so; the verdict was given in accordance with the evidence of my colleague and myself, and, under the circumstances, I think the jury acted very sensibly. In fact, I don't see what else they could have done. But I stick to my opinion, mind you, and I say this also. I don't wonder at Black's doing what I firmly believe he did. I think he was justified."

'"Justified! How could that be?" I asked. I was astonished, as you may imagine, at the answer I had got. The doctor wheeled round his chair and looked steadily at me for a moment before he answered.

"'I suppose you are not a man of science yourself? No; then it would be of no use my going into detail. I have always been firmly opposed myself to any partnership between physiology and psychology. I believe that both are bound to suffer. No one recognizes more decidedly than I do the impassable gulf, the fathomless abyss that separates the world of consciousness from the sphere of matter. We know that every change of consciousness is accompanied by a rearrangement of the molecules in the grey matter; and that is all. What the link between them is, or why they occur together, we do not know, and most authorities believe that we never can know. Yet, I will tell you that as I did my work, the knife in my hand, I felt convinced, in spite of all theories, that what lay before me was not the brain of a dead woman--not the brain of a human being at all. Of course I saw the face; but it was quite placid, devoid of all expression. It must have been a beautiful face, no doubt, but I can honestly say that I would not have looked in that face when there was life behind it for a thousand guineas, no, nor for twice that sum."

"'My dear sir,' I said, 'you surprise me extremely. You say that it was not the brain of a human being. What was it then?'"

"'The brain of a devil.' He spoke quite coolly, and never moved a muscle. 'The brain of a devil,' he repeated, 'and I have no doubt that Black found some way of putting an end to it. I don't blame him if he did. Whatever Mrs. Black was, she was not fit to stay in this world. Will you have anything more? No? Good-night, good-night.'"

'It was a queer sort of opinion to get from a man of science, wasn't it? When he was saying that he would not have looked on that face when alive for a thousand guineas, or two thousand guineas, I was thinking of the face I had seen, but I said nothing. I went again to Harlesden, and passed from one shop to another, making small purchases, and trying to find out whether there was anything about the Blacks which was not already common property, but there was very little to hear. One of the tradesmen to whom I spoke said he had known the dead woman well; she used to buy of him such quantities of grocery as were required for their small household, for they never kept a servant, but had a charwoman in occasionally, and she had not seen Mrs. Black for months before she died. According to this man Mrs. Black was "a nice lady," always kind and considerate, and so fond of her husband and he of her, as every one thought. And yet, to put the doctor's opinion on one side, I knew what I had seen. And then after thinking it all over, and putting one thing with another, it seemed to me that the only person likely to give me much assistance would be Black himself, and I made up my mind to find him. Of course he wasn't to be found in Harlesden; he had left, I was told, directly after the funeral. Everything in the house had been sold, and one fine day Black got into the train with a small portmanteau, and went, nobody knew where. It was a chance if he were ever heard of again, and it was by a mere chance that I came across him at last. I was walking one day along Gray's Inn Road, not bound for anywhere in particular, but looking about me, as usual, and holding on to my hat, for it was a gusty day in early March, and the wind was making the treetops in the Inn rock and quiver. I had come up from the Holborn end, and I had almost got to Theobald's Road when I noticed a man walking in front of me, leaning on a stick, and to all appearance very feeble. There was something about his look that made me curious, I don't know why, and I began to walk briskly with the idea of overtaking him, when of a sudden his hat blew off and came bounding along the pavement to my feet. Of course I rescued the hat, and gave it a glance as I went towards its owner. It was a biography in itself; a Piccadilly maker's name in the inside, but I don't think a beggar would have picked it out of the gutter. Then I looked up and saw Dr. Black of Harlesden waiting for me. A queer thing, wasn't it? But, Salisbury, what a change! When I saw Dr. Black come down the steps of his house at Harlesden he was an upright man, walking firmly with well-built limbs; a man, I should say, in the prime of his life. And now before me there crouched this wretched creature, bent and feeble, with shrunken cheeks, and hair that was whitening fast, and limbs that trembled and shook together, and misery in his eyes. He thanked me for bringing him his hat, saying, "I don't think I should ever have got it, I can't run much now. A gusty day, sir, isn't it?" and with this he was turning away, but by little and little I contrived to draw him into the current of conversation, and we walked together eastward. I think the man would have been glad to get rid of me; but I didn't intend to let him go, and he stopped at last in front of a miserable house in a miserable street. It was, I verily believe, one of the most wretched quarters I have ever seen: houses that must have been sordid and hideous enough when new, that had gathered foulness with every year, and now seemed to lean and totter to their fall. "I live up there," said Black, pointing to the tiles, "not in the front--in the back. I am very quiet there. I won't ask you to come in now, but perhaps some other day----" I caught him up at that, and told him I should be only too glad to come and see him. He gave me an odd sort of glance, as if he were wondering what on earth I or anybody else could care about him, and I left him fumbling with his latch-key. I think you will say I did pretty well when I tell you that within a few weeks I had made myself an intimate friend of Black's. I shall never forget the first time I went to his room; I hope I shall never see such abject, squalid misery again. The foul paper, from which all pattern or trace of a pattern had long vanished, subdued and penetrated with the grime of the evil street, was hanging in mouldering pennons from the wall. Only at the end of the room was it possible to stand upright, and the sight of the wretched bed and the odour of corruption that pervaded the place made me turn faint and sick. Here I found him munching a piece of bread; he seemed surprised to find that I had kept my promise, but he gave me his chair and sat on the bed while we talked. I used to go to see him often, and we had long conversations together, but he never mentioned Harlesden or his wife. I fancy that he supposed me ignorant of the matter, or thought that if I had heard of it, I should never connect the respectable Dr. Black of Harlesden with a poor garreteer in the backwoods of London. He was a strange man, and as we sat together smoking, I often wondered whether he were mad or sane, for I think the wildest dreams of Paracelsus and the Rosicrucians would appear plain and sober fact compared with the theories I have heard him earnestly advance in that grimy den of his. I once ventured to hint something of the sort to him. I suggested that something he had said was in flat contradiction to all science and all experience. "No," he answered, "not all experience, for mine counts for something. I am no dealer in unproved theories; what I say I have proved for myself, and at a terrible cost. There is a region of knowledge which you will never know, which wise men seeing from afar off shun like the plague, as well they may, but into that region I have gone. If you knew, if you could even dream of what may be done, of what one or two men have done in this quiet world of ours, your very soul would shudder and faint within you. What you have heard from me has been but the merest husk and outer covering of true science--that science which means death, and that which is more awful than death, to those who gain it. No, when men say that there are strange things in the world, they little know the awe and the terror that dwell always with them and about them." There was a sort of fascination about the man that drew me to him, and I was quite sorry to have to leave London for a month or two; I missed his odd talk. A few days after I came back to town I thought I would look him up, but when I gave the two rings at the bell that used to summon him, there was no answer. I rang and rang again, and was just turning to go away, when the door opened and a dirty woman asked me what I wanted. From her look I fancy she took me for a plain-clothes officer after one of her lodgers, but when I inquired if Mr. Black were in, she gave me a stare of another kind. "There's no Mr. Black lives here," she said. "He's gone. He's dead this six weeks. I always thought he was a bit queer in his head, or else had been and got into some trouble or other. He used to go out every morning from ten till one, and one Monday morning we heard him come in, and go into his room and shut the door, and a few minutes after, just as we was a-sitting down to our dinner, there was such a scream that I thought I should have gone right off. And then we heard a stamping, and down he came, raging and cursing most dreadful, swearing he had been robbed of something that was worth millions. And then he just dropped down in the passage, and we thought he was dead. We got him up to his room, and put him on his bed, and I just sat there and waited, while my 'usband he went for the doctor. And there was the winder wide open, and a little tin box he had lying on the floor open and empty, but of course nobody could possible have got in at the winder, and as for him having anything that was worth anything, it's nonsense, for he was often weeks and weeks behind with his rent, and my 'usband he threatened often and often to turn him into the street, for, as he said, we've got a living to myke like other people--and, of course, that's true; but, somehow, I didn't like to do it, though he was an odd kind of a man, and I fancy had been better off. And then the doctor came and looked at him, and said as he couldn't do nothing, and that night he died as I was a-sitting by his bed; and I can tell you that, with one thing and another, we lost money by him, for the few bits of clothes as he had were worth next to nothing when they came to be sold." I gave the woman half a sovereign for her trouble, and went home thinking of Dr. Black and the epitaph she had made him, and wondering at his strange fancy that he had been robbed. I take it that he had very little to fear on that score, poor fellow; but I suppose that he was really mad, and died in a sudden access of his mania. His landlady said that once or twice when she had had occasion to go into his room (to dun the poor wretch for his rent, most likely), he would keep her at the door for about a minute, and that when she came in she would find him putting away his tin box in the corner by the window; I suppose he had become possessed with the idea of some great treasure, and fancied himself a wealthy man in the midst of all his misery. Explicit, my tale is ended, and you see that though I knew Black, I know nothing of his wife or of the history of her death.--That's the Harlesden case, Salisbury, and I think it interests me all the more deeply because there does not seem the shadow of a possibility that I or any one else will ever know more about it. What do you think of it?'

'Well, Dyson, I must say that I think you have contrived to surround the whole thing with a mystery of your own making. I go for the doctor's solution: Black murdered his wife, being himself in all probability an undeveloped lunatic.'

'What? Do you believe, then, that this woman was something too awful, too terrible to be allowed to remain on the earth? You will remember that the doctor said it was the brain of a devil?'

'Yes, yes, but he was speaking, of course, metaphorically. It's really quite a simple matter if you only look at it like that.'

'Ah, well, you may be right; but yet I am sure you are not. Well, well, it's no good discussing it any more. A little more Benedictine? That's right; try some of this tobacco. Didn't you say that you had been bothered by something--something which happened that night we dined together?'

'Yes, I have been worried, Dyson, worried a great deal. I----But it's such a trivial matter--indeed, such an absurdity--that I feel ashamed to trouble you with it.'

'Never mind, let's have it, absurd or not.'

With many hesitations, and with much inward resentment of the folly of the thing, Salisbury told his tale, and repeated reluctantly the absurd intelligence and the absurder doggerel of the scrap of paper, expecting to hear Dyson burst out into a roar of laughter.

'Isn't it too bad that I should let myself be bothered by such stuff as that?' he asked, when he had stuttered out the jingle of once, and twice, and thrice.

Dyson listened to it all gravely, even to the end, and meditated for a few minutes in silence.

'Yes,' he said at length, 'it was a curious chance, your taking shelter in that archway just as those two went by. But I don't know that I should call what was written on the paper nonsense; it is bizarre certainly, but I expect it has a meaning for somebody. Just repeat it again, will you, and I will write it down. Perhaps we might find a cipher of some sort, though I hardly think we shall.'

Again had the reluctant lips of Salisbury slowly to stammer out the rubbish that he abhorred, while Dyson jotted it down on a slip of paper.

'Look over it, will you?' he said, when it was done; 'it may be important that I should have every word in its place. Is that all right?'

'Yes; that is an accurate copy. But I don't think you will get much out of it. Depend upon it, it is mere nonsense, a wanton scribble. I must be going now, Dyson. No, no more; that stuff of yours is pretty strong. Good-night.'

'I suppose you would like to hear from me, if I did find out anything?'

'No, not I; I don't want to hear about the thing again. You may regard the discovery, if it is one, as your own.'

'Very well. Good-night.'

CHAPTER 4

A good many hours after Salisbury had returned to the company of the green rep chairs, Dyson still sat at his desk, itself a Japanese romance, smoking many pipes, and meditating over his friend's story. The bizarre quality of the inscription which had annoyed Salisbury was to him an attraction, and now and again he took it up and scanned thoughtfully what he had written, especially the quaint jingle at the end. It was a token, a symbol, he decided, and not a cipher, and the woman who had flung it away was in all probability entirely ignorant of its meaning; she was but the agent of the 'Sam' she had abused and discarded, and he too was again the agent of some one unknown, possibly of the individual styled Q, who had been forced to visit his French friends. But what to make of 'Traverse Handle S.' Here was the root and source of the enigma, and not all the tobacco of Virginia seemed likely to suggest any clue here. It seemed almost hopeless, but Dyson regarded himself as the Wellington of mysteries, and went to bed feeling assured that sooner or later he would hit upon the right track For the next few days he was deeply engaged in his literary labours, labours which were a profound mystery even to the most intimate of his friends, who searched the railway bookstalls in vain for the result of so many hours spent at the Japanese bureau in company with strong tobacco and black tea. On this occasion Dyson confined himself to his room for four days, and it was with genuine relief that he laid down his pen and went out into the streets in quest of relaxation and fresh air. The gas-lamps were being lighted, and the fifth edition of the evening papers was being howled through the streets, and Dyson, feeling that he wanted quiet, turned away from the clamorous Strand, and began to trend away to the north-west. Soon he found himself in streets that echoed to his footsteps, and crossing a broad new thoroughfare, and verging still to the west, Dyson discovered that he had penetrated to the depths of Soho. Here again was life; rare vintages of France and Italy, at prices which seemed contemptibly small, allured the passer-by; here were cheeses, vast and rich, here olive oil, and here a grove of Rabelaisian sausages; while in a neighbouring shop the whole Press of Paris appeared to be on sale. In the middle of the roadway a strange miscellany of nations sauntered to and fro, for there cab and hansom rarely ventured; and from window over window the inhabitants looked forth in pleased contemplation of the scene. Dyson made his way slowly along, mingling with the crowd on the cobble-stones, listening to the queer babel of French and German, and Italian and English, glancing now and again at the shop-windows with their levelled batteries of bottles, and had almost gained the end of the street, when his attention was arrested by a small shop at the corner, a vivid contrast to its neighbours. It was the typical shop of the poor quarter; a shop entirely English. Here were vended tobacco and sweets, cheap pipes of clay and cherry-wood; penny exercise-books and penholders jostled for precedence with comic songs, and story papers with appalling cuts showed that romance claimed its place beside the actualities of the evening paper, the bills of which fluttered at the doorway. Dyson glanced up at the name above the door, and stood by the kennel trembling, for a sharp pang, the pang of one who has made a discovery, had for a moment left him incapable of motion. The name over the shop was Travers. Dyson looked up again, this time at the corner of the wall above the lamp-post, and read in white letters on a blue ground the words 'Handel Street, W. C.,' and the legend was repeated in fainter letters just below. He gave a little sigh of satisfaction, and without more ado walked boldly into the shop, and stared full in the face the fat man who was sitting behind the counter. The fellow rose to his feet, and returned the stare a little curiously, and then began in stereotyped phrase--

'What can I do for you, sir?'

Dyson enjoyed the situation and a dawning perplexity on the man's face. He propped his stick carefully against the counter and leaning over it, said slowly and impressively--

'Once around the grass, and twice around the lass, and thrice around the maple-tree.'

Dyson had calculated on his words producing an effect, and he was not disappointed. The vendor of miscellanies gasped, open-mouthed like a fish, and steadied himself against the counter. When he spoke, after a short interval, it was in a hoarse mutter, tremulous and unsteady.

'Would you mind saying that again, sir? I didn't quite catch it.'

'My good man, I shall most certainly do nothing of the kind. You heard what I said perfectly well. You have got a clock in your shop, I see; an admirable timekeeper, I have no doubt. Well, I give you a minute by your own clock.'

The man looked about him in a perplexed indecision, and Dyson felt that it was time to be bold.

'Look here, Travers, the time is nearly up. You have heard of Q, I think. Remember, I hold your life in my hands. Now!'

Dyson was shocked at the result of his own audacity. The man shrank and shrivelled in terror, the sweat poured down a face of ashy white, and he held up his hands before him.

'Mr. Davies, Mr. Davies, don't say that--don't for Heaven's sake. I didn't know you at first, I didn't indeed. Good God! Mr. Davies, you wouldn't ruin me? I'll get it in a moment.'

'You had better not lose any more time.'

The man slunk piteously out of his own shop, and went into a back parlour. Dyson heard his trembling fingers fumbling with a bunch of keys, and the creak of an opening box. He came back presently with a small package neatly tied up in brown paper in his hands, and, still full of terror, handed it to Dyson.

'I'm glad to be rid of it,' he said. 'I'll take no more jobs of this sort.'

Dyson took the parcel and his stick, and walked out of the shop with a nod, turning round as he passed the door. Travers had sunk into his seat, his face still white with terror, with one hand over his eyes, and Dyson speculated a good deal as he walked rapidly away as to what queer chords those could be on which he had played so roughly. He hailed the first hansom he could see and drove home, and when he had lit his hanging lamp, and laid his parcel on the table, he paused for a moment, wondering on what strange thing the lamplight would soon shine. He locked his door, and cut the strings, and unfolded the paper layer after layer, and came at last to a small wooden box, simply but solidly made. There was no lock, and Dyson had simply to raise the lid, and as he did so he drew a long breath and started back. The lamp seemed to glimmer feebly like a single candle, but the whole room blazed with light--and not with light alone, but with a thousand colours, with all the glories of some painted window; and upon the walls of his room and on the familiar furniture, the glow flamed back and seemed to flow again to its source, the little wooden box. For there upon a bed of soft wool lay the most splendid jewel, a jewel such as Dyson had never dreamed of, and within it shone the blue of far skies, and the green of the sea by the shore, and the red of the ruby, and deep violet rays, and in the middle of all it seemed aflame as if a fountain of fire rose up, and fell, and rose again with sparks like stars for drops. Dyson gave a long deep sigh, and dropped into his chair, and put his hands over his eyes to think. The jewel was like an opal, but from a long experience of the shop-windows he knew there was no such thing as an opal one-quarter or one-eighth of its size. He looked at the stone again, with a feeling that was almost awe, and placed it gently on the table under the lamp, and watched the wonderful flame that shone and sparkled in its centre, and then turned to the box, curious to know whether it might contain other marvels. He lifted the bed of wool on which the opal had reclined, and saw beneath, no more jewels, but a little old pocket-book, worn and shabby with use. Dyson opened it at the first leaf, and dropped the book again appalled. He had read the name of the owner, neatly written in blue ink:

STEVEN BLACK, M. D., Oranmore, Devon Road, Harlesden.

It was several minutes before Dyson could bring himself to open the book a second time; he remembered the wretched exile in his garret; and his strange talk, and the memory too of the face he had seen at the window, and of what the specialist had said, surged up in his mind, and as he held his finger on the cover, he shivered, dreading what might be written within. When at last he held it in his hand, and turned the pages, he found that the first two leaves were blank, but the third was covered with clear, minute writing, and Dyson began to read with the light of the opal flaming in his eyes.

CHAPTER 5

'Ever since I was a young man'--the record began--'I devoted all my leisure and a good deal of time that ought to have been given to other studies to the investigation of curious and obscure branches of knowledge. What are commonly called the pleasures of life had never any attractions for me, and I lived alone in London, avoiding my fellow-students, and in my turn avoided by them as a man self-absorbed and unsympathetic. So long as I could gratify my desire of knowledge of a peculiar kind, knowledge of which the very existence is a profound secret to most men, I was intensely happy, and I have often spent whole nights sitting in the darkness of my room, and thinking of the strange world on the brink of which I trod. My professional studies, however, and the necessity of obtaining a degree, for some time forced my more obscure employment into the background, and soon after I had qualified I met Agnes, who became my wife. We took a new house in this remote suburb, and I began the regular routine of a sober practice, and for some months lived happily enough, sharing in the life about me, and only thinking at odd intervals of that occult science which had once fascinated my whole being. I had learnt enough of the paths I had begun to tread to know that they were beyond all expression difficult and dangerous, that to persevere meant in all probability the wreck of a life, and that they led to regions so terrible, that the mind of man shrinks appalled at the very thought. Moreover, the quiet and the peace I had enjoyed since my marriage had wiled me away to a great extent from places where I knew no peace could dwell. But suddenly--I think indeed it was the work of a single night, as I lay awake on my bed gazing into the darkness--suddenly, I say, the old desire, the former longing, returned, and returned with a force that had been intensified ten times by its absence; and when the day dawned and I looked out of the window, and saw with haggard eyes the sunrise in the east, I knew that my doom had been pronounced; that as I had gone far, so now I must go farther with unfaltering steps. I turned to the bed where my wife was sleeping peacefully, and lay down again, weeping bitter tears, for the sun had set on our happy life and had risen with a dawn of terror to us both. I will not set down here in minute detail what followed; outwardly I went about the day's labour as before, saying nothing to my wife. But she soon saw that I had changed; I spent my spare time in a room which I had fitted up as a laboratory, and often I crept upstairs in the grey dawn of the morning, when the light of many lamps still glowed over London; and each night I had stolen a step nearer to that great abyss which I was to bridge over, the gulf between the world of consciousness and the world of matter. My experiments were many and complicated in their nature, and it was some months before I realized whither they all pointed, and when this was borne in upon me in a moment's time, I felt my face whiten and my heart still within me. But the power to draw back, the power to stand before the doors that now opened wide before me and not to enter in, had long ago been absent; the way was closed, and I could only pass onward. My position was as utterly hopeless as that of the prisoner in an utter dungeon, whose only light is that of the dungeon above him; the doors were shut and escape was impossible. Experiment after experiment gave the same result, and I knew, and shrank even as the thought passed through my mind, that in the work I had to do there must be elements which no laboratory could furnish, which no scales could ever measure. In that work, from which even I doubted to escape with life, life itself must enter; from some human being there must be drawn that essence which men call the soul, and in its place (for in the scheme of the world there is no vacant chamber)--in its place would enter in what the lips can hardly utter, what the mind cannot conceive without a horror more awful than the horror of death itself. And when I knew this, I knew also on whom this fate would fall; I looked into my wife's eyes. Even at that hour, if I had gone out and taken a rope and hanged myself, I might have escaped, and she also, but in no other way. At last I told her all. She shuddered, and wept, and called on her dead mother for help, and asked me if I had no mercy, and I could only sigh. I concealed nothing from her; I told her what she would become, and what would enter in where her life had been; I told her of all the shame and of all the horror. You who will read this when I am dead--if indeed I allow this record to survive,--you who have opened the box and have seen what lies there, if you could understand what lies hidden in that opal! For one night my wife consented to what I asked of her, consented with the tears running down her beautiful face, and hot shame flushing red over her neck and breast, consented to undergo this for me. I threw open the window, and we looked together at the sky and the dark earth for the last time; it was a fine star-light night, and there was a pleasant breeze blowing, and I kissed her on her lips, and her tears ran down upon my face. That night she came down to my laboratory, and there, with shutters bolted and barred down, with curtains drawn thick and close, so that the very stars might be shut out from the sight of that room, while the crucible hissed and boiled over the lamp, I did what had to be done, and led out what was no longer a woman. But on the table the opal flamed and sparkled with such light as no eyes of man have ever gazed on, and the rays of the flame that was within it flashed and glittered, and shone even to my heart. My wife had only asked one thing of me; that when there came at last what I had told her, I would kill her. I have kept that promise.'

* * * * *

There was nothing more. Dyson let the little pocket-book fall, and turned and looked again at the opal with its flaming inmost light, and then with unutterable irresistible horror surging up in his heart, grasped the jewel, and flung it on the ground, and trampled it beneath his heel. His face was white with terror as he turned away, and for a moment stood sick and trembling, and then with a start he leapt across the room and steadied himself against the door. There was an angry hiss, as of steam escaping under great pressure, and as he gazed, motionless, a volume of heavy yellow smoke was slowly issuing from the very centre of the jewel, and wreathing itself in snake-like coils above it. And then a thin white flame burst forth from the smoke, and shot up into the air and vanished; and on the ground there lay a thing like a cinder, black and crumbling to the touch.

The Shining Pyramid

CHAPTER 1. THE ARROW-HEAD CHARACTER

"Haunted, you said?"

"Yes, haunted. Don't you remember, when I saw you three years ago, you told me about your place in the west with the ancient woods hanging all about it, and the wild, domed hills, and the ragged land? It has always remained a sort of enchanted picture in my mind as I sit at my desk and hear the traffic rattling in the street in the midst of whirling London. But when did you come up?"

"The fact is, Dyson, I have only just got out of the train. I drove to the station early this morning and caught the 10.45."

"Well, I am very glad you looked in on me. How have you been getting on since we last met? There is no Mrs. Vaughan, I suppose?"

"No," said Vaughan, "I am still a hermit, like yourself. I have done nothing but loaf about."

Vaughan had lit his pipe and sat in the elbow chair, fidgeting and glancing about him in a somewhat dazed and restless manner. Dyson had wheeled round his chair when his visitor entered and sat with one arm fondly reclining on the desk of his bureau, and touching the litter of manuscript.

"And you are still engaged in the old task?" said Vaughan, pointing to the pile of papers and the teeming pigeon-holes.

"Yes, the vain pursuit of literature, as idle as alchemy, and as entrancing. But you have come to town for some time I suppose; what shall we do to-night?"

"Well, I rather wanted you to try a few days with me down in the west. It would do you a lot of good, I'm sure."

"You are very kind, Vaughan, but London in September is hard to leave. Doré could not have designed anything more wonderful and mystic than Oxford Street as I saw it the other evening; the sunset flaming, the blue haze transmuting the plain street into a road 'far in the spiritual city.'"

"I should like you to come down though. You would enjoy roaming over our hills. Does this racket go on all day and all night? It quite bewilders me; I wonder how you can work through it. I am sure you would revel in the great peace of my old home among the woods."

Vaughan lit his pipe again, and looked anxiously at Dyson to see if his inducements had had any effect, but the man of letters shook his head, smiling, and vowed in his heart a firm allegiance to the streets.

"You cannot tempt me," he said.

"Well, you may be right. Perhaps, after all, I was wrong to speak of the peace of the country. There, when a tragedy does occur, it is like a stone thrown into a pond; the circles of disturbance keep on widening, and it seems as if the water would never be still again."

"Have you ever any tragedies where you are?"

"I can hardly say that. But I was a good deal disturbed about a month ago by something that happened; it may or may not have been a tragedy in the usual sense of the word."

"What was the occurrence?"

"Well, the fact is a girl disappeared in a way which seems highly mysterious. Her parents, people of the name of Trevor, are well-to-do farmers, and their eldest daughter Annie was a sort of village beauty; she was really remarkably handsome. One afternoon she thought she would go and see her aunt, a widow who farms her own land, and as the two houses are only about five or six miles apart, she started off, telling her parents she would take the short cut over the hills. She never got to her aunt's, and she never was seen again. That's putting it in a few words."

"What an extraordinary thing! I suppose there are no disused mines, are there, on the hills? I don't think you quite run to anything so formidable as a precipice?"

"No; the path the girl must have taken had no pitfalls of any description; it is just a track over wild, bare hillside, far, even, from a byroad. One may walk for miles without meeting a soul, but it is all perfectly safe."

"And what do people say about it?"

"Oh, they talk nonsense--among themselves. You have no notion as to how superstitious English cottagers are in out-of-the-way parts like mine. They are as bad as the Irish, every whit, and even more secretive."

"But what do they say?"

"Oh, the poor girl is supposed to have 'gone with the fairies,' or to have been 'taken by the fairies.' Such stuff!" he went on, "one would laugh if it were not for the real tragedy of the case."

Dyson looked somewhat interested.

"Yes," he said, "'fairies' certainly strike a little curiously on the ear in these days. But what do the police say? I presume they do not accept the fairy-tale hypothesis?"

"No; but they seem quite at fault. What I am afraid of is that Annie Trevor must have fallen in with some scoundrels on her way. Castletown is a large seaport, you know, and some of the worst of the foreign sailors occasionally desert their ships and go on the tramp up and down the country. Not many years ago a Spanish sailor named Garcia murdered a whole family for the sake of plunder that was not worth sixpence. They are hardly human, some of these fellows, and I am dreadfully afraid the poor girl must have come to an awful end."

"But no foreign sailor was seen by anyone about the country?"

"No; there is certainly that; and of course country people are quick to notice anyone whose appearance and dress are a little out of the common. Still it seems as if my theory were the only possible explanation."

"There are no data to go upon," said Dyson, thoughtfully. "There was no question of a love affair, or anything of the kind, I suppose?"

"Oh, no, not a hint of such a thing. I am sure if Annie were alive she would have contrived to let her mother know of her safety."

"No doubt, no doubt. Still it is barely possible that she is alive and yet unable to communicate with her friends. But all this must have disturbed you a good deal."

"Yes, it did; I hate a mystery, and especially a mystery which is probably the veil of horror. But frankly, Dyson, I want to make a clean breast of it; I did not come here to tell you all this."

"Of course not," said Dyson, a little surprised at Vaughan's uneasy manner. "You came to have a chat on more cheerful topics."

"No, I did not. What I have been telling you about happened a month ago, but something which seems likely to affect me more personally has taken place within the last few days, and to be quite plain, I came up to town with the idea that you might be able to help me. You recollect that curious case you spoke to me about at our last meeting; something about a spectacle-maker."

"Oh, yes, I remember that. I know I was quite proud of my acumen at the time; even to this day the police have no idea why those peculiar yellow spectacles were wanted. But, Vaughan, you really look quite put out; I hope there is nothing serious?"

"No, I think I have been exaggerating, and I want you to reassure me. But what has happened is very odd."

"And what has happened?"

"I am sure that you will laugh at me, but this is the story. You must know there is a path, a right of way, that goes through my land, and to be precise, close to the wall of the kitchen garden. It is not used by many people; a woodman now and again finds it useful, and five or six children who go to school in the village pass twice a day. Well, a few days ago I was taking a walk about the place before breakfast, and I happened to stop to fill my pipe just by the large doors in the garden wall. The wood, I must tell you, comes to within a few feet of the wall, and the track I spoke of runs right in the shadow of the trees. I thought the shelter from a brisk wind that was blowing rather pleasant, and I stood there smoking with my eyes on the ground. Then something caught my attention. Just under the wall, on the short grass, a number of small flints were arranged in a pattern; something like this": and Mr. Vaughan caught at a pencil and piece of paper, and dotted down a few strokes.

"You see," he went on, "there were, I should think, twelve little stones neatly arranged in lines, and spaced at equal distances, as I have shewn it on the paper. They were pointed stones, and the points were very carefully directed one way."

"Yes," said Dyson, without much interest, "no doubt the children you have mentioned had been playing there on their way from school. Children, as you know, are very fond of making such devices with oyster shells or flints or flowers, or with whatever comes in their way."

"So I thought; I just noticed these flints were arranged in a sort of pattern and then went on. But the next morning I was taking the same round, which, as a matter of fact, is habitual with me, and again I saw at the same spot a device in flints. This time it was really a curious pattern; something like the spokes of a wheel, all meeting at a common centre, and this centre formed by a device which looked like a bowl; all, you understand, done in flints."

"You are right," said Dyson, "that seems odd enough. Still it is reasonable that your half-a-dozen school children are responsible for these fantasies in stone."

"Well, I thought I would set the matter at rest. The children pass the gate every evening at half-past five, and I walked by at six, and found the device just as I had left it in the morning. The next day I was up and about at a quarter to seven, and I found the whole thing had been changed. There was a pyramid outlined in flints upon the grass. The children I saw going by an hour and a half later, and they ran past the spot without glancing to right or left. In the evening I watched them going home, and this morning when I got to the gate at six o'clock there was a thing like a half moon waiting for me."

"So then the series runs thus: firstly ordered lines, then the device of the spokes and the bowl, then the pyramid, and finally, this morning, the half moon. That is the order, isn't it?"

"Yes; that is right. But do you know it has made me feel very uneasy? I suppose it seems absurd, but I can't help thinking that some kind of signalling is going on under my nose, and that sort of thing is disquieting."

"But what have you to dread? You have no enemies?"

"No; but I have some very valuable old plate."

"You are thinking of burglars then?" said Dyson, with an accent of considerable interest, "but you must know your neighbours. Are there any suspicious characters about?"

"Not that I am aware of. But you remember what I told you of the sailors."

"Can you trust your servants?"

"Oh, perfectly. The plate is preserved in a strong room; the butler, an old family servant, alone knows where the key is kept. There is nothing wrong there. Still, everybody is aware that I have a lot of old silver, and all country folks are given to gossip. In that way information may have got abroad in very undesirable quarters."

"Yes, but I confess there seems something a little unsatisfactory in the burglar theory. Who is signalling to whom? I cannot see my way to accepting such an explanation. What put the plate into your head in connection with these flint signs, or whatever one may call them?"

"It was the figure of the Bowl," said Vaughan. "I happen to possess a very large and very valuable Charles II punch-bowl. The chasing is really exquisite, and the thing is worth a lot of money. The sign I described to you was exactly the same shape as my punch-bowl."

"A queer coincidence certainly. But the other figures or devices: you have nothing shaped like a pyramid?"

"Ah, you will think that queerer. As it happens, this punch-bowl of mine, together with a set of rare old ladles, is kept in a mahogany chest of a pyramidal shape. The four sides slope upwards, the narrow towards the top."

"I confess all this interests me a good deal," said Dyson. "Let us go on then. What about the other figures; how about the Army, as we may call the first sign, and the Crescent or Half-moon?"

"Ah, there is no reference that I can make out of these two. Still, you see I have some excuse for curiosity at all events. I should be very vexed to lose any of the old plate; nearly all the pieces have been in the family for generations. And I cannot get it out of my head that some scoundrels mean to rob me, and are communicating with one another every night."

"Frankly," said Dyson, "I can make nothing of it; I am as much in the dark as yourself. Your theory seems certainly the only possible explanation, and yet the difficulties are immense."

He leaned back in his chair, and the two men faced each other, frowning, and perplexed by so bizarre a problem.

"By the way," said Dyson, after a long pause, "what is your geological formation down there?"

Mr. Vaughan looked up, a good deal surprised by the question.

"Old red sandstone and limestone, I believe," he said. "We are just beyond the coal measures, you know."

"But surely there are no flints either in the sandstone or the limestone?"

"No, I never see any flints in the fields. I confess that did strike me as a little curious."

"I should think so! It is very important. By the way, what size were the flints used in making these devices?"

"I happen to have brought one with me; I took it this morning."

"From the Half-moon?"

"Exactly. Here it is."

He handed over a small flint, tapering to a point, and about three inches in length.

Dyson's face blazed up with excitement as he took the thing from Vaughan.

"Certainly," he said, after a moment's pause, "you have some curious neighbours in your country. I hardly think they can harbour any designs on your punch-bowl. Do you know this is a flint arrowhead of vast antiquity, and not only that, but an arrow-head of a unique kind? I have seen specimens from all parts of the world, but there are features about this thing that are quite peculiar."

He laid down his pipe, and took out a book from a drawer.

"We shall just have time to catch the 5.45 to Castletown," he said.

CHAPTER 2. THE EYES ON THE WALL

Mr. Dyson drew in a long breath of the air of the hills and felt all the enchantment of the scene about him. It was very early morning, and he stood on the terrace in the front of the house. Vaughan's ancestor had built on the lower slope of a great hill, in the shelter of a deep and ancient wood that gathered on three sides about the house, and on the fourth side, the south-west, the land fell gently away and sank to the valley, where a brook wound in and out in mystic esses, and the dark and gleaming alders tracked the stream's course to the eye. On the terrace in that sheltered place no wind blew, and far beyond, the trees were still. Only one sound broke in upon the silence, and Dyson heard the noise of the brook singing far below, the song of clear and shining water rippling over the stones, whispering and murmuring as it sank to dark deep pools. Across the stream, just below the house, rose a grey stone bridge, vaulted and buttressed, a fragment of the Middle Ages, and then beyond the bridge the hills rose again, vast and rounded like bastions, covered here and there with dark woods and thickets of undergrowth, but the heights were all bare of trees, showing only grey turf and patches of bracken, touched here and there with the gold of fading fronds. Dyson looked to the north and south, and still he saw the wall of the hills, and the ancient woods, and the stream drawn in and out between them; all grey and dim with morning mist beneath a grey sky in a hushed and haunted air.

Mr. Vaughan's voice broke in upon the silence.

"I thought you would be too tired to be about so early," he said. "I see you are admiring the view. It is very pretty, isn't it, though I suppose old Meyrick Vaughan didn't think much about the scenery when he built the house. A queer grey, old place, isn't it?"

"Yes, and how it fits into the surroundings; it seems of a piece with the grey hills and the grey bridge below."

"I am afraid I have brought you down on false pretences, Dyson," said Vaughan, as they began to walk up and down the terrace. "I have been to the place, and there is not a sign of anything this morning."

"Ah, indeed. Well, suppose we go round together."

They walked across the lawn and went by a path through the ilex shrubbery to the back of the house. There Vaughan pointed out the track leading down to the valley and up to the heights above the wood, and presently they stood beneath the garden wall, by the door.

"Here, you see, it was," said Vaughan, pointing to a spot on the turf. "I was standing just where you are now that morning I first saw the flints."

"Yes, quite so. That morning it was the Army, as I call it; then the Bowl, then the Pyramid, and yesterday, the Half-moon. What a queer old stone that is," he went on, pointing to a block of limestone rising out of the turf just beneath the wall.

"It looks like a sort of dwarf pillar, but I suppose it is natural."

"Oh, yes, I think so. I imagine it was brought here, though, as we stand on the red sandstone. No doubt it was used as a foundation stone for some older building."

"Very likely." Dyson was peering about him attentively, looking from the ground to the wall, and from the wall to the deep wood that hung almost over the garden and made the place dark even in the morning.

"Look here," said Dyson at length, "it is certainly a case of children this time. Look at that."

He was bending down and staring at the dull red surface of the mellowed bricks of the wall Vaughan came up and looked hard where Dyson's finger was pointing, and could scarcely distinguish a faint mark in deeper red.

"What is it?" he said. "I can make nothing of it."

"Look a little more closely. Don't you see it is an attempt to draw the human eye?"

"Ah, now I see what you mean. My sight is not very sharp. Yes, so it is, it is meant for an eye, no doubt, as you say. I thought the children learnt drawing at school."

"Well, it is an odd eye enough. Do you notice the peculiar almond shape; almost like the eye of a Chinaman?"

Dyson looked meditatively at the work of the undeveloped artist, and scanned the wall again, going down on his knees in the minuteness of his inquisition.

"I should like very much," he said at length, "to know how a child in this out of the way place could have any idea of the shape of the Mongolian eye. You see the average child has a very distinct impression of the subject; he draws a circle, or something like a circle, and puts a dot in the centre. I don't think any child imagines that the eye is really made like that; it's just a convention of infantile art. But this almond-shaped thing puzzles me extremely. Perhaps it may be derived from a gilt Chinaman on a tea-canister in the grocer's shop. Still that's hardly likely."

"But why are you so sure it was done by a child?"

"Why! Look at the height. These old-fashioned bricks are little more than two inches thick; there are twenty courses from the ground to the sketch if we call it so; that gives a height of three and a half feet. Now, just imagine you are going to draw something on this wall. Exactly; your pencil, if you had one, would touch the wall somewhere on the level with your eyes, that is, more than five feet from the ground. It seems, therefore, a very simple deduction to conclude that this eye on the wall was drawn by a child about ten years old."

"Yes, I had not thought of that. Of course one of the children must have done it."

"I suppose so; and yet as I said, there is something singularly unchildlike about those two lines, and the eyeball itself, you see, is almost an oval. To my mind, the thing has an odd, ancient air; and a touch that is not altogether pleasant. I cannot help fancying that if we could see a whole face from the same hand it would not be altogether agreeable. However, that is nonsense, after all, and we are not getting farther in our investigations. It is odd that the flint series has come to such an abrupt end."

The two men walked away towards the house, and as they went in at the porch there was a break in the grey sky, and a gleam of sunshine on the grey hill before them.

All the day Dyson prowled meditatively about the fields and woods surrounding the house. He was thoroughly and completely puzzled by the trivial circumstances he proposed to elucidate, and now he again took the flint arrow-head from his pocket, turning it over and examining it with deep attention. There was something about the thing that was altogether different from the specimens he had seen at the museums and private collections; the shape was of a distinct type, and around the edge there was a line of little punctured dots, apparently a suggestion of ornament. Who, thought Dyson, could possess such things in so remote a place; and who, possessing the flints, could have put them to the fantastic use of designing meaningless figures under Vaughan's garden wall? The rank absurdity of the whole affair offended him unutterably; and as one theory after another rose in his mind only to be rejected, he felt strongly tempted to take the next train back to town. He had seen the silver plate which Vaughan treasured, and had inspected the punch-bowl, the gem of the collection, with close attention; and what he saw and his interview with the butler convinced him that a plot to rob the strong box was out of the limits of enquiry.

The chest in which the bowl was kept, a heavy piece of mahogany, evidently dating from the beginning of the century, was certainly strongly suggestive of a pyramid, and Dyson was at first inclined to the inept manoeuvres of the detective, but a little sober thought convinced him of the impossibility of the burglary hypothesis, and he cast wildly about for something more satisfying. He asked Vaughan if there were any gypsies in the neighbourhood, and heard that the Romany had not been seen for years. This dashed him a good deal, as he knew the gypsy habit of leaving queer hieroglyphics on the line of march, and had been much elated when the thought occurred to him. He was facing Vaughan by the old-fashioned hearth when he put the question, and leaned back in his chair in disgust at the destruction of his theory.

"It is odd," said Vaughan, "but the gypsies never trouble us here. Now and then the farmers find traces of fires in the wildest part of the hills, but nobody seems to know who the fire-lighters are."

"Surely that looks like gypsies?"

"No, not in such places as those. Tinkers and gypsies and wanderers of all sorts stick to the roads and don't go very far from the farm-houses."

"Well, I can make nothing of it. I saw the children going by this afternoon, and, as you say, they ran straight on. So we shall have no more eyes on the wall at all events."

"No, I must waylay them one of these days and find out who is the artist."

The next morning when Vaughan strolled in his usual course from the lawn to the back of the house he found Dyson already awaiting him by the garden door and evidently in a state of high excitement, for he beckoned furiously with his hand, and gesticulated violently.

"What is it?" asked Vaughan. "The flints again?"

"No; but look here, look at the wall. There; don't you see it?"

"There's another of those eyes!"

"Exactly. Drawn, you see, at a little distance from the first, almost on the same level, but slightly lower."

"What on earth is one to make of it? It couldn't have been done by the children; it wasn't there last night, and they won't pass for another hour. What can it mean?"

"I think the very devil is at the bottom of all this," said Dyson. "Of course, one cannot resist the conclusion that these infernal almond eyes are to be set down to the same agency as the devices in the arrow-heads; and where that conclusion is to lead us is more than I can tell. For my part, I have to put a strong check on my imagination, or it would run wild."

"Vaughan," he said, as they turned away from the wall, "has it struck you that there is one point--a very curious point--in common between the figures done in flints and the eyes drawn on the wall?"

"What is that?" asked Vaughan, on whose face there had fallen a certain shadow of indefinite dread.

"It is this. We know that the signs of the Army, the Bowl, the Pyramid, and the Half-moon must have been done at night. Presumably they were meant to be seen at night. Well, precisely the same reasoning applies to those eyes on the wall."

"I do not quite see your point."

"Oh, surely. The nights are dark just now, and have been very cloudy, I know, since I came down. Moreover, those overhanging trees would throw that wall into deep shadow even on a clear night."

"Well?"

"What struck me was this. What very peculiarly sharp eyesight, they, whoever 'they' are, must have to be able to arrange arrow-heads in intricate order in the blackest shadow of the wood, and then draw the eyes on the wall without a trace of bungling, or a false line."

"I have read of persons confined in dungeons for many years who have been able to see quite well in the dark," said Vaughan.

"Yes," said Dyson, "there was the abbé in Monte Cristo. But it is a singular point."

CHAPTER 3. THE SEARCH FOR THE BOWL

"Who was that old man that touched his hat to you just now?" said Dyson, as they came to the bend of the lane near the house.

"Oh, that was old Trevor. He looks very broken, poor old fellow."

"Who is Trevor?"

"Don't you remember? I told you the story that afternoon I came to your rooms--about a girl named Annie Trevor, who disappeared in the most inexplicable manner about five weeks ago. That was her father."

"Yes, yes, I recollect now. To tell the truth I had forgotten all about it. And nothing has been heard of the girl?"

"Nothing whatever. The police are quite at fault."

"I am afraid I did not pay very much attention to the details you gave me. Which way did the girl go?"

"Her path would take her right across those wild hills above the house; the nearest point in the track must be about two miles from here."

"Is it near that little hamlet I saw yesterday?"

"You mean Croesyceiliog, where the children came from? No; it goes more to the north."

"Ah, I have never been that way."

They went into the house, and Dyson shut himself up in his room, sunk deep in doubtful thought, but yet with the shadow of a suspicion growing within him that for a while haunted his brain, all vague and fantastic, refusing to take definite form. He was sitting by the open window and looking out on the valley and saw, as if in a picture, the intricate winding of the brook, the grey bridge, and the vast hills rising beyond; all still and without a breath of wind to stir the mystic hanging woods, and the evening sunshine glowed warm on the bracken, and down below a faint mist, pure white, began to rise from the stream. Dyson sat by the window as the day darkened and the huge bastioned hills loomed vast and vague, and the woods became dim and more shadowy; and the fancy that had seized him no longer appeared altogether impossible. He passed the rest of the evening in a reverie, hardly hearing what Vaughan said; and when he took his candle in the hall, he paused a moment before bidding his friend goodnight.

"I want a good rest," he said. "I have got some work to do tomorrow."

"Some writing, you mean?"

"No. I am going to look for the Bowl."

"The Bowl! If you mean my punch-bowl, that is safe in the chest."

"I don't mean the punch-bowl. You may take my word for it that your plate has never been threatened. No; I will not bother you with any suppositions. We shall in all probability have something much stronger than suppositions before long. Good-night, Vaughan."

The next morning Dyson set off after breakfast. He took the path by the garden-wall, and noted that there were now eight of the weird almond eyes dimly outlined on the brick.

"Six days more," he said to himself, but as he thought over the theory he had formed, he shrank, in spite of strong conviction, from such a wildly incredible fancy. He struck up through the dense shadows of the wood, and at length came out on the bare hillside, and climbed higher and higher over the slippery turf, keeping well to the north, and following the indications given him by Vaughan.

As he went on, he seemed to mount ever higher above the world of human life and customary things; to his right he looked at a fringe of orchard and saw a faint blue smoke rising like a pillar; there was the hamlet from which the children came to school, and there the only sign of life, for the woods embowered and concealed Vaughan's old grey house. As he reached what seemed the summit of the hill, he realised for the first time the desolate loneliness and strangeness of the land; there was nothing but grey sky and grey hill, a high, vast plain that seemed to stretch on for ever and ever, and a faint glimpse of a blue-peaked mountain far away and to the north. At length he came to the path, a slight track scarcely noticeable, and from its position and by what Vaughan had told him he knew that it was the way the lost girl, Annie Trevor, must have taken. He followed the path on the bare hilltop, noticing the great limestone rocks that cropped out of the turf, grim and hideous, and of an aspect as forbidding as an idol of the South Seas; and suddenly he halted, astonished, although he had found what he searched for. Almost without warning the ground shelved suddenly away on all sides, and Dyson looked down into a circular depression, which might well have been a Roman amphitheatre, and the ugly crags of limestone rimmed it round as if with a broken wall. Dyson walked round the hollow, and noted the position of the stones, and then turned on his way home.

"This," he thought to himself, "is more than curious. The Bowl is discovered, but where is the Pyramid?"

"My dear Vaughan," he said, when he got back, "I may tell you that I have found the Bowl, and that is all I shall tell you for the present. We have six days of absolute inaction before us; there is really nothing to be done."

CHAPTER 4. THE SECRET OF THE PYRAMID

"I have just been round the garden," said Vaughan one morning. "I have been counting those infernal eyes, and I find there are fourteen of them. For heaven's sake, Dyson, tell me what the meaning of it all is."

"I should be very sorry to attempt to do so. I may have guessed this or that, but I always make it a principle to keep my guesses to myself. Besides, it is really not worth while anticipating events; you will remember my telling you that we had six days of inaction before us? Well, this is the sixth day, and the last of idleness. To-night I propose we take a stroll."

"A stroll! Is that all the action you mean to take?"

"Well, it may show you some very curious things. To be plain, I want you to start with me at nine o'clock this evening for the hills. We may have to be out all night, so you had better wrap up well, and bring some of that brandy."

"Is it a joke?" asked Vaughan, who was bewildered with strange events and strange surmises.

"No, I don't think there is much joke in it. Unless I am much mistaken we shall find a very serious explanation of the puzzle. You will come with me, I am sure?"

"Very good. Which way do you want to go?"

"By the path you told me of; the path Annie Trevor is supposed to have taken."

Vaughan looked white at the mention of the girl's name

"I did not think you were on that track," he said. "I thought it was the affair of those devices in flint and of the eyes on the wall that you were engaged on. It's no good saying any more, but I will go with you."

At a quarter to nine that evening the two men set out, taking the path through the wood, and up the hill-side. It was a dark and heavy night, the sky was thick with clouds, and the valley full of mist, and all the way they seemed to walk in a world of shadow and gloom, hardly speaking, and afraid to break the haunted silence. They came out at last on the steep hill-side, and instead of the oppression of the wood there was the long, dim sweep of the turf, and higher, the fantastic limestone rocks hinted horror through the darkness, and the wind sighed as it passed across the mountain to the sea, and in its passage beat chill about their hearts. They seemed to walk on and on for hours, and the dim outline of the hill still stretched before them, and the haggard rocks still loomed through the darkness, when suddenly Dyson whispered, drawing his breath quickly, and coming close to his companion,

"Here," he said, "we will lie down. I do not think there is anything yet."

"I know the place," said Vaughan, after a moment. "I have often been by in the daytime. The country people are afraid to come here, I believe; it is supposed to be a fairies' castle, or something of the kind. But why on earth have we come here?"

"Speak a little lower," said Dyson. "It might not do us any good if we are overheard."

"Overheard here! There is not a soul within three miles of us."

"Possibly not; indeed, I should say certainly not. But there might be a body somewhat nearer."

"I don't understand you in the least," said Vaughan, whispering to humour Dyson, "but why have we come here?"

"Well, you see this hollow before us is the Bowl. I think we had better not talk even in whispers."

They lay full length upon the turf; the rock between their faces and the Bowl, and now and again, Dyson, slouching his dark, soft hat over his forehead, put out the glint of an eye, and in a moment drew back, not daring to take a prolonged view. Again he laid an ear to the ground and listened, and the hours went by, and the darkness seemed to blacken, and the faint sigh of the wind was the only sound.

Vaughan grew impatient with this heaviness of silence, this watching for indefinite terror; for to him there was no shape or form of apprehension, and he began to think the whole vigil a dreary farce.

"How much longer is this to last?" he whispered to Dyson, and Dyson who had been holding his breath in the agony of attention put his mouth to Vaughan's ear and said:

"Will you listen?" with pauses between each syllable, and in the voice with which the priest pronounces the awful words.

Vaughan caught the ground with his hands, and stretched forward, wondering what he was to hear. At first there was nothing, and then a low and gentle noise came very softly from the Bowl, a faint sound, almost indescribable, but as if one held the tongue against the roof of the mouth and expelled the breath. He listened eagerly and presently the noise grew louder, and became a strident and horrible hissing as if the pit beneath boiled with fervent heat, and Vaughan, unable to remain in suspense any longer, drew his cap half over his face in imitation of Dyson, and looked down to the hollow below.

It did, in truth, stir and seethe like an infernal caldron. The whole of the sides and bottom tossed and writhed with vague and restless forms that passed to and fro without the sound of feet, and gathered thick here and there and seemed to speak to one another in those tones of horrible sibilance, like the hissing of snakes, that he had heard. It was as if the sweet turf and the cleanly earth had suddenly become quickened with some foul writhing growth. Vaughan could not draw back his face, though he felt Dyson's finger touch him, but he peered into the quaking mass and saw faintly that there were things like faces and human limbs, and yet he felt his inmost soul chill with the sure belief that no fellow soul or human thing stirred in all that tossing and hissing host. He looked aghast, choking back sobs of horror, and at length the loathsome forms gathered thickest about some vague object in the middle of the hollow, and the hissing of their speech grew more venomous, and he saw in the uncertain light the abominable limbs, vague and yet too plainly seen, writhe and intertwine, and he thought he heard, very faint, a low human moan striking through the noise of speech that was not of man. At his heart something seemed to whisper ever "the worm of corruption, the worm that dieth not," and grotesquely the image was pictured to his imagination of a piece of putrid offal stirring through and through with bloated and horrible creeping things. The writhing of the dusky limbs continued, they seemed clustered round the dark form in the middle of the hollow, and the sweat dripped and poured off Vaughan's forehead, and fell cold on his hand beneath his face.

Then, it seemed done in an instant, the loathsome mass melted and fell away to the sides of the Bowl, and for a moment Vaughan saw in the middle of the hollow the tossing of human arms. But a spark gleamed beneath, a fire kindled, and as the voice of a woman cried out loud in a shrill scream of utter anguish and terror, a great pyramid of flame spired up like a bursting of a pent fountain, and threw a blaze of light upon the whole mountain. In that instant Vaughan saw the myriads beneath; the things made in the form of men but stunted like children hideously deformed, the faces with the almond eyes burning with evil and unspeakable lusts; the ghastly yellow of the mass of naked flesh; and then as if by magic the place was empty, while the fire roared and crackled, and the flames shone abroad.

"You have seen the Pyramid," said Dyson in his ear, "the Pyramid of fire."

CHAPTER 5. THE LITTLE PEOPLE

"Then you recognise the thing?"

"Certainly. It is a brooch that Annie Trevor used to wear on Sundays; I remember the pattern. But where did you find it? You don't mean to say that you have discovered the girl?"

"My dear Vaughan, I wonder you have not guessed where I found the brooch. You have not forgotten last night already?"

"Dyson," said the other, speaking very seriously, " I have been turning it over in my mind this morning while you have been out. I have thought about what I saw, or perhaps I should say about what I thought I saw, and the only conclusion I can come to is this, that the thing won't bear recollection. As men live, I have lived soberly and honestly, in the fear of God, all my days, and all I can do is believe that I suffered from some monstrous delusion, from some phantasmagoria of the bewildered senses. You know we went home together in silence, not a word passed between us as to what I fancied I saw; had we not better agree to keep silence on the subject? When I took my walk in the peaceful morning sunshine, I thought all the earth seemed full of praise, and passing by that wall I noticed there were no more signs recorded, and I blotted out those that remained. The mystery is over, and we can live quietly again. I think some poison has been working for the last few weeks; I have trod on the verge of madness, but I am sane now."

Mr. Vaughan had spoken earnestly, and bent forward in his chair and glanced at Dyson with something of entreaty.

"My dear Vaughan," said the other, after a pause, "what's the use of this? It is much too late to take that tone; we have gone too deep. Besides you know as well as I that there is no delusion in the case; I wish there were with all my heart. No, in justice to myself I must tell you the whole story, so far as I know it."

"Very good," said Vaughan with a sigh, "if you must, you must."

"Then," said Dyson, "we will begin with the end if you please. I found this brooch you have just identified in the place we have called the Bowl. There was a heap of grey ashes, as if a fire had been burning, indeed, the embers were still hot, and this brooch was lying on the ground, just outside the range of the flame. It must have dropped accidentally from the dress of the person who was wearing it. No, don't interrupt me; we can pass now to the beginning, as we have had the end. Let us go back to that day you came to see me in my rooms in London. So far as I can remember, soon after you came in you mentioned, in a somewhat casual manner, that an unfortunate and mysterious incident had occurred in your part of the country; a girl named Annie Trevor had gone to see a relative, and had disappeared. I confess freely that what you said did not greatly interest me; there are so many reasons which may make it extremely convenient for a man and more especially a woman to vanish from the circle of their relations and friends. I suppose, if we were to consult the police, one would find that in London somebody disappears mysteriously every other week, and the officers would, no doubt, shrug their shoulders, and tell you that by the law of averages it could not be otherwise. So I was very culpably careless to your story, and besides, there is another reason for my lack of interest; your tale was inexplicable. You could only suggest a blackguard sailor on the tramp, but I discarded the explanation immediately. For many reasons, but chiefly because the occasional criminal, the amateur in brutal crime, is always found out, especially if he selects the country as the scene of his operations. You will remember the case of that Garcia you mentioned; he strolled into a railway station the day after the murder, his trousers covered with blood, and the works of the Dutch clock, his loot, tied in a neat parcel. So rejecting this, your only suggestion, the whole tale became, as I say, inexplicable, and, therefore, profoundly uninteresting. Yes, therefore, it is a perfectly valid conclusion. Do you ever trouble your head about problems which you know to be insoluble? Did you ever bestow much thought on the old puzzle of Achilles and the Tortoise? Of course not, because you knew it was a hopeless quest, and so when you told me the story of a country girl who had disappeared I simply placed the whole thing down in the category of the insoluble, and thought no more about the matter. I was mistaken, so it has turned out; but if you remember, you immediately passed on to an affair which interested you more intensely, because personally. I need not go over the very singular narrative of the flint signs; at first I thought it all trivial, probably some children's game, and if not that a hoax of some sort; but your shewing me the arrow-head awoke my acute interest. Here, I saw, there was something widely removed from the commonplace, and matter of real curiosity; and as soon as I came here I set to work to find the solution, repeating to myself again and again the signs you had described. First came the sign we have agreed to call the Army; a number of serried lines of flints, all pointing in the same way. Then the lines, like the spokes of a wheel, all converging towards the figure of a Bowl, then the triangle or Pyramid, and last of all the Half-moon. I confess that I exhausted conjecture in my efforts to unveil this mystery, and as you will understand it was a duplex or rather triplex problem. For I had not merely to ask myself: what do these figures mean? but also, who can possibly be responsible for the designing of them? And again, who can possibly possess such valuable things, and knowing their value thus throw them down by the wayside? This line of thought led me to suppose that the person or persons in question did not know the value of unique flint arrow-heads, and yet this did not lead me far, for a well-educated man might easily be ignorant on such a subject. Then came the complication of the eye on the wall, and you remember that we could not avoid the conclusion that in the two cases the same agency was at work. The peculiar position of these eyes on the wall made me enquire if there was such a thing as a dwarf anywhere in the neighbourhood, but I found that there was not, and I knew that the children who pass by every day had nothing to do with the matter. Yet I felt convinced that whoever drew the eyes must be from three-and-a-half to four feet high, since, as I pointed out at the time, anyone who draws on a perpendicular surface chooses by instinct a spot about level with his face. Then again, there was the question of the peculiar shape of the eyes; that marked Mongolian character of which the English countryman could have no conception, and for a final cause of confusion the obvious fact that the designer or designers must be able practically to see in the dark. As you remarked, a man who has been confined for many years in an extremely dark cell or dungeon might acquire that power; but since the days of Edmond Dantès, where would such a prison be found in Europe? A sailor, who had been immured for a considerable period in some horrible Chinese oubliette, seemed the individual I was in search of, and though it looked improbable, it was not absolutely impossible that a sailor or, let us say, a man employed on shipboard, should be a dwarf. But how to account for my imaginary sailor being in possession of prehistoric arrow-heads? And the possession granted, what was the meaning and object of these mysterious signs of flint, and the almond-shaped eyes? Your theory of a contemplated burglary I saw, nearly from the first, to be quite untenable, and I confess I was utterly at a loss for a working hypothesis. It was a mere accident which put me on the track; we passed poor old Trevor, and your mention of his name and of the disappearance of his daughter, recalled the story which I had forgotten, or which remained unheeded. Here, then, I said to myself, is another problem, uninteresting, it is true, by itself; but what if it prove to be in relation with all these enigmas which torture me? I shut myself in my room, and endeavoured to dismiss all prejudice from my mind, and I went over everything de novo, assuming for theory's sake that the disappearance of Annie Trevor had some connection with the flint signs and the eyes on the wall. This assumption did not lead me very far, and I was on the point of giving the whole problem up in despair, when a possible significance of the Bowl struck me. As you know there is a 'Devil's Punch-bowl' in Surrey, and I saw that the symbol might refer to some feature in the country. Putting the two extremes together, I determined to look for the Bowl near the path which the lost girl had taken, and you know how I found it. I interpreted the sign by what I knew, and read the first, the Army, thus: 'there is to be a gathering or assembly at the Bowl in a fortnight (that is the Half-moon) to see the Pyramid or to build the Pyramid.' The eyes, drawn one by one, day by day, evidently checked off the days, and I knew that there would be fourteen and no more. Thus far the way seemed pretty plain; I would not trouble myself to enquire as to the nature of the assembly, or as to who was to assemble in the loneliest and most dreaded place among these lonely hills. In Ireland or China or the west of America the question would have been easily answered; a muster of the disaffected, the meeting of a secret society, Vigilantes summoned to report: the thing would be simplicity itself; but in this quiet corner of England, inhabited by quiet folk, no such suppositions were possible for a moment. But I knew that I should have an opportunity of seeing and watching the assembly, and I did not care to perplex myself with hopeless research; and in place of reasoning a wild fancy entered into judgment: I remembered what people had said about Annie Trevor's disappearance, that she had been 'taken by the fairies.' I tell you, Vaughan, I am a sane man as you are, my brain is not, I trust, mere vacant space to let to any wild improbability, and I tried my best to thrust the fantasy away. And the hint came of the old name of fairies, 'the little people,' and the very probable belief that they represent a tradition of the prehistoric Turanian inhabitants of the country, who were cave dwellers: and then I realised with a shock that I was looking for a being under four feet in height, accustomed to live in darkness, possessing stone instruments, and familiar with the Mongolian cast of features! I say this, Vaughan, that I should be ashamed to hint at such visionary stuff to you, if it were not for that which you saw with your very eyes last night, and I say that I might doubt the evidence of my senses, if they were not confirmed by yours. But you and I cannot look each other in the face and pretend delusion; as you lay on the turf beside me I felt your flesh shrink and quiver, and I saw your eyes in the light of the flame. And so I tell you without any shame what was in my mind last night as we went through the wood and climbed the hill, and lay hidden beneath the rock.

"There was one thing that should have been most evident that puzzled me to the very last. I told you how I read the sign of the Pyramid; the assembly was to see a pyramid, and the true meaning of the symbol escaped me to the last moment. The old derivation from [greek], fire, though false, should have set me on the track, but it never occurred to me.

"I think I need say very little more. You know we were quite helpless, even if we had foreseen what was to come. Ah, the particular place where these signs were displayed? Yes, that is a curious question. But this house is, so far as I can judge, in a pretty central situation amongst the hills; and possibly, who can say yes or no, that queer, old limestone pillar by your garden wall was a place of meeting before the Celt set foot in Britain. But there is one thing I must add: I don't regret our inability to rescue the wretched girl. You saw the appearance of those things that gathered thick and writhed in the Bowl; you may be sure that what lay bound in the midst of them was no longer fit for earth."

"So?" said Vaughan.

"So she passed in the Pyramid of Fire," said Dyson, "and they passed again to the under-world, to the places beneath the hills."

ABOUT THE AUTHOR

Arthur Machen (1863 - 1947) was a Welsh writer, journalist and actor. He is best known for his supernatural, fantasy and horror fiction. He was a major influence on HP Lovecraft, who considered him a modern master who could create "cosmic horror raised to its most artistic pitch."

You might also like:

Best Ghost Stories and Horror Tales of Algernoon Blackwood

ISBN-13: 978-1480110670

ISBN-10: 1480110671

AT THE MOUNTAINS OF MADNESS

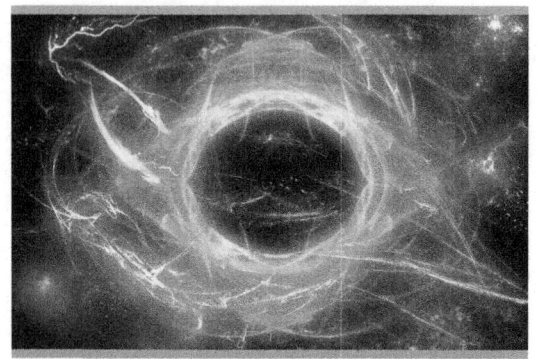

H. P. LOVECRAFT

At the Mountains of Madness

ISBN-13: 978-1480115927

ISBN-10: 1480115924

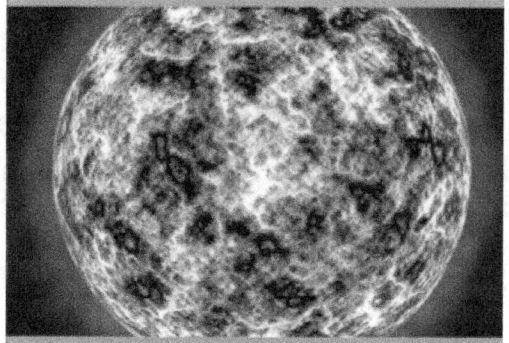

My Favorite Science Fiction Short Stories Anthology

A collection of science fiction works by various authors such as Isaac Asimov, Philip K. Dick, Murray Leinster, H. Beam Piper and other Sci-Fi masters.

ISBN-13: 978-1480115934

ISBN-10: 1480115932

JOHN CARTER

OF MARS SERIES
EDGAR RICE BURROUGHS

John Carter of Mars Series (5 in 1)
A Princess of Mars
The Gods of Mars
Warlord of Mars
Thuvia, Maid of Mars
The Chessmen of Mars
Glossary of names and vocabulary used in the Martian books.

ISBN-13: 978-1480104754

ISBN-10: 1480104752

Made in the USA
Middletown, DE
14 May 2020